# THE
# ICARUS
# MIND

## J. ROYCE LOCKWOOD

Marshall Cavendish
Editions

Published by Marshall Cavendish Editions
An imprint of Marshall Cavendish International

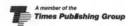
A member of the
**Times Publishing Group**

Other Marshall Cavendish Offices:
Marshall Cavendish Corporation, 800 Westchester Ave, Suite N-641, Rye Brook,
NY 10573, USA • Marshall Cavendish International (Thailand) Co Ltd, 253 Asoke,
16th Floor, Sukhumvit 21 Road, Klongtoey Nua, Wattana, Bangkok 10110, Thailand
• Marshall Cavendish (Malaysia) Sdn Bhd, Times Subang, Lot 46, Subang Hi-Tech
Industrial Park, Batu Tiga, 40000 Shah Alam, Selangor Darul Ehsan, Malaysia

**National Library Board, Singapore Cataloguing in Publication Data**

Name(s): Lockwood, J. Royce.
Title: The Icarus mind / J. Royce Lockwood.
Description: Singapore : Marshall Cavendish Editions, [2022]
Identifier(s): ISBN 978-981-5009-12-5 (paperback)
Subject(s): LCSH: Artificial intelligence--Fiction. | Conscious automata--Fiction.
Classification: DDC S823—dc23

Printed in Singapore

*This book is dedicated to the memory of my father,*
*Royce D. Lockwood*

# CHAPTER 1

# CALIFORNIA DREAMIN'

**Simon**

*Present day*

Simon Quinn eased off the throttle, slowing his new Harley Sportster to a rolling California stop. He had reached the end of Interstate 8, and found the edge of a continent. This arrival marked the end of a long and tiring journey that had begun in Chicago nearly ten days before. With a quick glance over his shoulder, Simon merged onto Sunset Cliffs Boulevard and accelerated down the road toward the Mercury Motel, the diffident motor court that would become his new home.

The name was misleading. The building had indeed been a motel at one time, but had long since been converted to studio apartments; twelve rooms stacked in two levels of six, perched upon the main thoroughfare tracing the edge of the Point Loma peninsula. It now served as a de facto home for wayward youth and older folks at crossroads in their lives.

Simon rolled up to the curb and dismounted. He removed his helmet, running a gloved hand through a mat of sandy brown hair. The tousled locks fell carelessly across his brow, framing a pair of squinting sea-gray eyes. Setting his helmet on the seat of his bike, Simon regarded the building before him.

A steep metal staircase jutted out from the second-floor landing which doubled as a balcony for the upstairs apartments. The first door to the right of the stairway opened, and a shirtless young man in khaki shorts and flip-flops emerged. Simon smiled at his old friend, a somewhat tanner and blonder Bill Jameson than he remembered from college.

"Well, you finally made it." Bill leaned over the wrought iron railing. "I've been idling all morning waiting for your sorry ass to roll in here."

"Check your phone, ya' jackass," said Simon, "or did you bring it with you into the ocean again?"

Bill didn't answer, but flashed a toothy grin as he trotted down the staircase to greet Simon. He was noticeably leaner than he had been two years earlier, the result of sun and surf and outdoor activity afforded by the favorable San Diego weather. Simon was struck by the casual air of Bill's attire. He felt suddenly constrained, burdened by the heavy leather jacket and jeans he had worn on his long journey.

The two young men embraced and exchanged a few more friendly barbs. "Well, come on up and I'll show you the place." Bill gestured toward the upper level. Simon followed his friend up the narrow stairway and into a small studio apartment. The apartment was cramped and noisy, fronting a busy street with little privacy. It was perfect.

"This is it," said Bill. "Debra will be by this afternoon to take care of the lease. I have to say, I'm going to miss this place. Oh, here." Bill handed a small brass door key to Simon. "All yours."

"Are you sure you have to head back right away?" Simon pressed. "Can't you stay for a few days at least?"

"Nah, I'm sorry." Bill shook his head. "I've been goofing off long enough. My dad has offered me a job with his firm in Chicago. Figure it's about time I start taking things seriously."

"Well, not just yet." Simon removed his backpack and opened

the main compartment. He fished around inside the bag for a moment, finally producing a bottle of tequila. "I figure this is a suitable way to mark the end of one California adventure, and the beginning of another."

"Jose Cuervo, nice!" Bill smiled. He retreated to the kitchen, reemerging with two shot glasses.

Simon filled the small vessels, and held one aloft. "To new adventures."

After a second round of spirits, Bill guided Simon through the neighborhood, introducing him to the local scene. They ambled down broken sidewalks toward the beach, arriving at an intersection, buttressed by two small retail banks and a large chain drugstore. Until recently, these had remained the only visible encroachment of big business into this decidedly localized neighborhood. But now this holdout from a former era was under siege, and it seemed inevitable that Ocean Beach would succumb at last to a tide of corporatism and homogenization that felt unstoppable.

Simon allowed his thoughts to wander as they rounded the corner and stepped onto the eclectic shop-lined Newport Avenue. This storied boulevard served as the commercial heart of Ocean Beach, a scene casually referred to as "OB" by locals. Newport was the domain of surfers, bikers and iconoclastic acolytes of all stripes. Simon reveled in the unique counterculture that sprouted precociously here, like so much grass through cracks in the pavement. Street musicians and love children, anachronisms of the 1960s, abounded. Artists, bikers, and the odd pan-handler all engaged in the ritual, ceremoniously resurrecting the *zeitgeist* of a forlorn optimism.

The two friends spent the remainder of the afternoon visiting OB's many haunts, exploring the various bars and restaurants, alleys, and institutions: the Jetty, the Pier, the Dog Beach where the San Diego River emptied into the ocean. When they grew tired, they made their way back to the Mercury Motel, this time walking along the narrow pathway hugging the bottom of the rocky Sunset Cliffs. The two friends passed the remainder of the evening in pleasant conversation – Bill on the bed and Simon making the best of it on the tiled floor.

Simon was tired, but sleep eluded him. The passing traffic was still frequent and loud. Vintage Volkswagens and ill-tuned Harleys announced themselves without apology and the occasional skateboarder click-clacked his way along the sidewalk, the volume rising and falling in a slow-moving wave of sound.

"This reminds me of freshman year." Bill smiled. "That dorm room at Northwestern. So many hours spent in conversation."

Simon nodded. Bill had always been an idealist, ever eschewing the straight and narrow path. But now, having waded through the hedonistic world of jobless drift, Bill sought the finer pleasure of smaller things – a fiber optic network connection, a sixty-inch television, decent furniture. Simon could hardly fault him. To see those of lesser talent and imagination succeed and thrive was enough to inspire anyone to dreams of mediocrity. But if the best minds of a generation could be destroyed by madness, how much worse to be stifled by mundanity?

"Do you think we'll ever hang out like this again?" Simon asked.

Bill leaned up on his elbow. "Sure, we will. We're part of the same Karass." He chuckled. "You're stuck with me."

"Karass? What, you mean like Kurt Vonnegut, *Cat's Cradle* that kind of thing?"

"Yeah, I've always liked that idea," said Bill, "the notion that we have a cohort of kindred spirits, bound together by some hidden force, creating associations that are not immediately obvious. It reminds me of constellations."

"How so?" Simon was fully awake again.

"Well, when viewed from Earth, the stars look like they're on the same plane, but in reality, they're totally spread out in space. They only make sense together when we observe them and integrate them into a coherent picture. It's we who imbue them with meaning."

"So are you saying that our relationships are actually arbitrary and incoherent?" Simon asked. "That's kinda depressing."

"No!" Bill sounded hurt. "On the contrary, I'm saying that there is a meaning and coherence holding them together which only becomes apparent from the right distance and point of view."

Simon lay on his back with that thought sounded in his mind, staring at the ceiling as if it were the open sky. At last, fatigue overwhelmed him and he drifted off to sleep, oblivious to the traffic noise still emanating from below.

*

He woke to the sound of a suitcase zipping and the smell of fresh brewed coffee. A kaleidoscope of sunlight flitted through the shifting spaces between the blinds as they swayed in a gentle ocean breeze. Simon sat upright and stretched. "What time is it?"

"Time to get up." Bill handed Simon a steaming cup of coffee. "It's seven o'clock – my car is on the way."

Right on cue, a triplet of impertinent beeps sounded from the parking lot below. "Come on." Bill took his suitcase in hand. "Grab that duffle bag, will ya'?"

Simon obliged and followed Bill down the narrow metal stairs to the waiting taxi.

"Well," he said, "guess this is goodbye. Take care of yourself, Bill. Call me when you get to Chicago."

"Will do." Bill tossed his suitcase in the car. He gave his friend a hug and popped into the back seat. "Oh, by the way." Bill leaned his head out of the open car window. "I left you something in the kitchen – enjoy!"

The driver pulled into traffic and Simon watched until the taxi slipped around a corner and out of view. Released as if from a spell, he felt suddenly very light. He was alone and free, he was young, and the world was full of possibilities. *Well, let's see what good old Bill has left for me.*

Simon took the stairs two at a time and strode across the small living space to the kitchen. He smiled as he spied the well-used surfboard leaning up against the far wall. The board measured just over six feet in length, a short board. "Well," he said aloud, "looks like I'm going to be a surfer."

He stripped down right there in the kitchen and pulled on the neoprene wet suit, which had been draped over the back of a chair. He tucked the board under his arm, swung the leash over his neck, and headed out in search of the waves.

The beach was cloaked in a thin fog. Soon, the mid-morning sun would climb the sky, banishing the clouds back out to sea, until nightfall when they would steal back the land once more. A cadre of stalwart surfers already populated the tame summer waters, bobbing gently along the break line as they awaited the next set of waves. New arrivals slipped into their wetsuits and stole their way across the cold, sandy beach.

With the sun at his back, Simon peered out to sea. Somewhere in the North Pacific, in previous days, wind blowing over the water had created a swell that moved thousands of miles across the ocean in long, smooth-crested waves. As they approached land and entered the shallows, they slowed and grew steeper, eventually becoming so unstable that they toppled, dashing themselves on the shore, losing most of their energy in the process.

These were the moments the surfers lived for, the culmination of an epic journey in a burst of self-destruction. The art of riding such an expression of elemental force required a marriage of physical and spiritual prowess, which Simon could not help but admire. He paused for one more contemplative moment, then tucked the board under his arm and jogged into the shore break, determined to give it a go.

Simon spent the rest of the morning in the water, pummeled by the unforgiving swell. He was a novice surfer, a kook, and the locals watched him with equal parts of amusement and scorn. Still, before the day was over, he had managed to ride on the whitewater of a broken wave and feel the power of the ocean beneath him.

From then on, Simon rarely missed a morning session. His skill improved and he befriended a small group of surfers, who instructed him, teaching him to read the breaks, time the waves and use the currents to his advantage. He soon discovered that while standing, turning, carving a line on the open face were all integral parts of the experience, it was the precipitous drop into the midst of the wave itself that was the quintessence of the sport.

*

Simon eventually got around to finding a job, landing a permanent position in the admissions office of the University of California, San Diego.

He adopted the habit of surfing in the mornings before work, and he began to favor the more challenging waves at a place called

Black's Beach. The popular break was near a stretch of dark sand at
the bottom of a treacherous footpath that wound along a steep bank
of cliffs near the university campus. Every morning before sunrise,
Simon would scramble down the unforgiving pathway, carefully
placing each step, mindful that the six-foot encumbrance under
his arm did not betray him at any of the precarious switchbacks.
Thermal updrafts rising along the steep rocky face made the location
a favorite haunt of peregrine falcons and red-shouldered hawks.
The slow circling of the raptors lent a sublime aura to an already
dramatic landscape.

Six months elapsed in an instant. Summer slipped through
autumn and into winter, and he discovered that although San Diego
winters were mild, the conditions of the ocean changed. The water
grew cold, and the seasonal storms intensified, increasing the size
of the waves dramatically. One morning in late December, Simon
found himself at Black's Beach. He paddled to where the waves were
breaking, much farther out than normal. The crowd was smaller
than usual as many of the regulars had wisely stayed out of the
water. A more experienced surfer would have recognized the danger,
but Simon was still a novice and oblivious to the risk he was taking.

He waited through two sets, gauging the rhythm of the swell.
At last, he spotted a large wave forming on the outside. He paddled
towards it, then pivoted back toward the shore as the wave gathered
and pitched up behind him. Then it struck him – this wave was a
giant, bigger than anything he had ever ridden or even seen. Too
late, there was nothing he could do but to try and make it.

Simon paddled with every ounce of strength his arms possessed.
His center of gravity shifted, and he popped up, pushing to his
feet before dropping into the heart of the wave. Adrenaline jolted
through his veins – the exhilaration of success. But the feeling was

short-lived. Simon was not sufficiently experienced to feel the subtle shifts in the contour of the wave and he foundered, his balance stolen from him. He fell headlong over the nose of his board and was caught up in the tumult of the wave. The horizontal cyclone seized him and rolled him, lifting him up again and tossing him over the falls before driving him down to the ocean floor. The mountain of water pounded him repeatedly against the sandy bottom.

Spinning and floundering, Simon lost all sense of direction. Lungs burning, arms flailing, he began to panic; and when at last he could hold his breath no longer, a second wave broke above him, driving him back to the bottom again. This time, the surfboard slammed against the back of his head, and everything went dark.

The next thing Simon remembered was lying on the broad jagged surface of the exposed rocks where the cliffs jutted into the foamy water. His board was broken into three pieces, the smallest of which was still tethered to his ankle. Flecks of vomit covered his chest.

As he came around, Simon felt the soft brush of a canine tongue licking his face and ears. He opened his eyes to a mass of curly fur and floppy ears. He was being pleasantly smothered by the muzzle of an affectionate caramel-brown dog. Simon sat up … or tried to. He had a nasty crick in his neck and blood streamed from a wound in his forehead down into his eyes, obscuring his vision. His ears were ringing, but he heard through the din, a female voice off in the distance calling, "Ginger!"

Simon turned toward the voice. "Ginger!" came the cry once again as a young woman came into view. The dog continued to lick Simon's face. "Ginger, there you are … oh my, are you alright?"

The owner of the voice approached him. She was barefoot, wearing blue floral-print board-shorts and a hooded sweatshirt emblazoned with the UCSD college logo. The hood of her sweatshirt was pulled back and a banner of long black hair blew wildly in the stiff offshore breeze. She tucked a few stray locks behind her ear as she drew near.

Simon's senses returned to him now, and he became aware of how he must have looked to this young woman. "Yeah," he said weakly. "Yeah, I think I'm okay." Simon took an inventory of his various body parts – everything seemed to be where it was supposed to be. His hand reached reflexively for his temple, and then to the back of his aching head where the nose of his surfboard had rammed into him. Blood streamed from a small cut above his right eye. The wound was superficial but messy. Simon, drenched with seawater, hadn't noticed but the young woman reacted to the sight of the blood.

"You're really bleeding." She crouched down next to him to get a better look at the injury. "We'd better get that checked out. Do you think you can walk?"

"I think so." Simon braced his hands against the rock below him and attempted to rise, immediately slipping.

"Just take it easy." The young woman seized him by the elbow, offering support. "I think you may have a concussion. We saw you eat it on that big wave." She smiled.

Simon smiled in return, relaxing a bit. "Yeah, I guess that one was a bit out of my league. Let's try this again." This time he managed to stand.

"Thanks," he said, noticing that she maintained her grip on his elbow. "Thank you both." Simon looked down at the lab-poodle mix, which remained stolidly at his side.

"That's Ginger," she said. "And I'm Lauren."

"Simon." He placed a hand on his chest. "And I really am fine." He took a step, and nearly swooned again, exaggerating his distress only slightly for Lauren's benefit.

"I think you'd better come with me." She pointed toward the cliffs. "My house is just up there, at the top of the hill. Can you make it?"

Simon was quite sure that he could. He collected the remnants of his shattered surfboard and bound them together with the rubber leash. Lauren led him back toward the cliff side, where he noticed for the first time the entrance to a narrow fire-lane meandering down from the top of the hill. Access to the road was closed, but the heavy chain which bound the solid metal gate was sufficiently loose for determined pedestrians to slip through. Lauren helped Simon up the steeply graded pathway, through the adjacent neighborhood to her rented house.

As he sat in a finely manicured garden enjoying a pocket view of the Pacific Ocean, Lauren tended to Simon's million-dollar wound. "You should probably see a doctor." Her hand brushed past his ear as she felt the back of his head. "You might have a concussion."

"I'll be fine." He insisted, trading a visit to the emergency room for a morning of flirtatious conversation.

They spent the entire day together, and by the late afternoon, Simon was feeling better than he ever had before. He was so much recovered, in fact, that he convinced Lauren to return with him to the beach and give surfing a go.

For her first lesson, on this their first date, Simon opted for the less volatile beach break at La Jolla Shores, and selected a somewhat longer and more forgiving foam board. Lauren proved an apt pupil and was thrilled at the sensation of belly-riding the surf as Simon launched her repeatedly into the shore pound. It was Simon who gave out first, struggling as he was to hold the board steady in the tumult of the modest impact zone. "Enough." He threw up his hands at last. "I'm spent."

Lauren trudged back out toward Simon, wading through the chest-high water, long board at her side. "I can see why this sport used to attract mostly guys." She positioned the board between Simon and herself. They draped their arms across the deck of the board and floated together, legs entwining under the water. "I mean the violent struggle against the sea, battling the waves, thrashing to maintain control – very macho." She grinned.

"Macho, sure." Simon smiled in turn. "But it's not a fight. It's a dance. Every sailor knows the ocean is not a man but a woman. Temptress, mother, lover, dominatrix, and friend – you can never control her, you can only try to understand her moods. And avoid being crushed."

"Sounds very Zen." Lauren hoisted herself out of the water and sat astride the board. "I would imagine there are a lot of Buddhist surfers."

Simon steadied the board, which had begun to list. "Why, is that what you are – a Buddhist?"

"I guess you could say that. It's getting harder to tell these days. In Singapore you can find a Christian church, a Taoist temple, a Muslim mosque, and a Hindu shrine all on the same street corner, sometimes even in the same building."

"How does that happen?" Simon raised an eyebrow.

"My family is Chinese and I was raised a Buddhist. But most of my schoolmates were Christian. Singapore was a British colony for many years, and a major trading hub. So we also inherited a lot of the Western religious traditions as well."

"So now you can bring all of that integrated wisdom to bear on the fine art of surfing." Simon lifted himself out of the water and straddled the board facing Lauren.

"I'd be happy if I could figure out how to stand up." Lauren looked behind her, out to sea. The swell was dying and the water calm. "But it does make me think of something. In Chinese philosophy, we have this idea that there are two kinds of action: *yu-wei* and *wu-wei* – with effort and without. It never really made sense to me before, but it kinda makes sense now. When you catch and ride a wave, timing and location are critical, more important than your individual strength. You can harness the energy of the ocean, and achieve your goal by aligning yourself with the impulses of nature."

"Yes." Simon leaned forward. "The impulses of nature …" He kissed her, and the saltwater tasted sweet on her lips. He felt her shiver. "You're cold."

"I'm fine." She drew back slightly. "Oh look, the sun is setting." Lauren shifted around to face the open sea and leaned back into Simon's embrace. He wrapped his arms around her, feeling the rhythm of her breath as they floated in silence while the sky caught fire.

# CHAPTER 2
# DRIFTLESS

**Michael**

*Thirty years later*

Michael Quinn leaned into a banking turn and the hillsides parted, yielding to the gently sloping valley of the Driftless Reservation below. He tightened his grip on the handlebars, delighting in the calming rush of bracing wind as the landscape fled past him. Trees and tarmac wove an impressionistic tapestry – a mesmerizing blur, with a predictable motion giving rise to a contrary stillness in his mind.

The route was familiar. Michael had made this three-mile sojourn nearly every day for the past six months, ever since taking up residence in a remote cabin tucked away on an unused corner of his grandmother's property. There he found some respite from the carnival of sensory impulses which drove him to distraction. Still, he could not completely ignore the whispers, and his thoughts would sometimes linger on the faint memory of a premonition, rumours of a forgotten lineage. But that voice was silent now, drowned in the satisfying rumble of the motor. And the visions were subdued as he focused on the rolling terrain stretching out before him.

Michael loved this place. The Reservation had been established in an isolated quadrant of the Driftless Region – a landlocked sector of highland untouched by the glaciers of preceding ice ages. The terrain, though beautiful and more dramatic than the surrounding savannahs, was inhospitable to the row-cropping and industrial farming techniques which fed the ever-growing cities where ninety-five percent of the population now dwelled.

The remaining five percent – nearly twenty million people – lived in varying degrees of technological development across the country, a substantial minority of dissenters whose existence was tolerated by the government as the lesser of two evils. This was the grand compromise that had ended the riots which brought the nation to the brink of civil war nearly two decades before. These dissidents refused to undergo the now-standard biometric registration process, and would not allow themselves to be integrated with the network of databases which had been established to facilitate new security protocols and efficiency measures. The process of being *chipped*, as it had come to be known, was a particularly contentious initiative.

Michael had never been chipped. He was a transplant, delivered to the Driftless community as an infant. He had left the Reservation when he was eighteen, establishing a life in Chicago for nearly ten years before returning to Driftless on his twenty-eighth birthday.

It was common for the youth of these intentional communities to leave temporarily on an experimental sojourn, a Rumspringa of sorts. This indulgence was sanctioned by the state to encourage as many young people as possible to repatriate back into civilization. The majority – nearly eighty percent – returned to their reservations within a year. Still, a significant minority chose to assimilate and remained in the modern world. And for Michael, this was an auspicious day. Today the ceremony would be held. Today he would decide.

He sped down a small lane, buttressed by columns of maple and alder trees, whose leaves were now turning with the first chill breath of autumn. Gravel crunched beneath his tires as Michael pulled into a broad level driveway. This particular parcel of land was owned and managed by Michael's grandmother, Tara

Quinn, a spry woman of seventy-five years who had overseen the
implementation of the original site design nearly four decades ago.

It was early, but the yard was alive. Tara's neighbors and friends
had begun to arrive; some in gas-powered cars and trucks, others by
foot, and more than a few on horseback. Behind the house on a flat
section of grass, several guests were busy setting up tables. Others
attended to over-excited children while sharing news and stories
from their farms and homesteads. Out from the covered porch and
into this burgeoning maelstrom stepped Tara Quinn.

"Michael, there you are." She approached and took Michael's
hand, leading him back toward the house. "Have you eaten?" Tara
plucked a few sprigs of dill from the herb garden and collected four
freshly laid eggs from the chicken coup.

Upon entering the kitchen, Tara sparked the kindling and a draft
of air drew the flame inward toward the belly of the rocket stove and
up through the convolution of baffles contained in the masonry of
the walls. The act of cooking breakfast warmed the small home with
incredible efficiency. *Function-stacking*, it was called.

"Come with me, I have something for you." Tara led him
through the kitchen toward her bedroom at the back of the house,
where she retrieved a small urn from a bureau drawer.

"I want you to have this." She presented the vessel to him with
uncharacteristic formality. "I was thinking you could spread your
father's ashes at the top of the hill. Maybe tomorrow morning, after
your period of reflection."

Michael's chest constricted.    "Sure, Grandma. I would be
honored." He took the receptacle from her. "I wish I could have
known him."

Michael was an orphan, the only child of a mixed-race couple.
His father had been a native of this region, but his mother was

ethnic Chinese from the island nation of Singapore. Thus Michael's heritage was expressed by his round hazel eyes, dark flaxen hair and fair skin. He was often mistaken for Native American by newcomers, but longtime residents of the Reservation knew of his unusual provenance and looked upon him with a mixture of sympathy and wonder.

His arrival at Driftless had been something of a scandal. Michael was delivered in the dead of night as an infant – not by his mother or father, but by an outsider who had identified himself only by his surname, Lim. At the time, there were no neighbors to overhear Lim's cryptic account of the sudden death of Michael's parents, or comfort Tara as he delivered the cremated remains of her son. The only information the stranger would provide was that Michael's father had suffered a stroke while driving and lost control of the vehicle, killing both himself and Michael's mother instantly.

The mysterious messenger left as abruptly as he had arrived, and that was the last Tara heard from him. She eventually came to terms with the fact that she would never know exactly what had happened. Tara mourned her son and strove to build a life for Michael within the emerging community that would become the Driftless Reservation. A week later, Simon Quinn's badly damaged motorcycle was delivered; the last remaining artifact of her son, and apart from his cremated remains, Michael's sole physical connection to his father.

"You remind me so much of him." Tara placed a hand on Michael's cheek. "And he would have been so proud of you."

Michael embraced his grandmother and they paused, allowing the emotion to swell and retreat. Then Tara wiped her eyes and exhaled sharply, rousting the mournful sentiment from her body.

"Let's go, there's lots to do." She patted him on the side of his shoulder and headed back down the hallway. Michael stood alone in the darkened corridor, regarding the urn in silence before finally placing it carefully in his backpack and following his grandmother to the kitchen.

*

Michael finished his simple repast and stepped outside to enjoy the fresh morning air. The sun was only now beginning to peek cautiously over the easterly hilltops, but the sky was bright, a cloud-dappled sheet of pale blue. As Michael's mind began to wander, a conspicuously modern-looking sedan pulled into Tara's driveway. The driver's side door opened and out leapt a maelstrom of white fur. Michael sucked in his breath. There was only one person he knew with a Siberian Husky.

"Selena!" Tara strode to the front of the yard.

A young woman emerged from the car. She wore dark close-fit blue jeans and a black sweater, her dark hair drawn into a low pony tail. "Snowy! Snowy, come!" She called after her willful pet. The dog ignored her cries and bounded toward Michael, jumping on him affectionately, nearly knocking him over.

Tara wrapped the woman in a warm embrace. "Selena, I didn't expect to see you today; I thought you were in Minneapolis now. How are you?"

*I didn't expect to see you either.* Michael regained his balance and approached. *Are you here for me?*

"I hadn't planned to come, but I have some news." Selena flashed a glance at Michael, but did not allow her eyes to linger. "We've been picking up a lot of chatter lately about Driftless –

some new Bill that's being drafted in the state senate. They're talking about revoking the Driftless Charter. It doesn't have enough votes yet, but it seems to have legs."

Tara laughed. "Oh dear, is that why you drove all the way out here – to tell us that? Selena my dear, there have been rumors like that floating around for years. Nothing ever comes of it."

Tara placed a hand on Selena's arm. "It's a federal matter. The state legislature can't dictate to us."

"But that's how it always starts, isn't it?" said Michael. "They initiate in the states and then elevate. Challenge in the courts and overturn precedent. I would be surprised if we didn't see similar actions in other state houses. It's about time we did something – fight back."

"Fight back against who?" Tara held Michael's gaze. "Against what, a rumor? I admire your passion, young man. But take it from one who's been around a while; this is just more of the same. This political theater is directed at a particular local audience and won't go anywhere or amount to anything."

"But Tara, I really do need to speak with you – and the other members of the council." Selena's voice was tinged with urgency.

"Yes, yes, there will be plenty of time for that." Tara led them deeper into the yard. "But right now I have a lot of work to do. Tell you what. Why don't you two head up to the keypoint at the top of the hill? I want to know how the overflow sills are doing after yesterday's rain."

Tara turned and walked back toward her porch, leaving a vacuum of silence in her wake.

Michael scratched the back of his head. "Well, I guess we have our marching orders."

Selena exhaled audibly. "Guess so."

Michael led them up the driveway toward the foot of a forgiving incline at the far end of the yard. "So what's all this about a revocation of our charter?" *Is that really the only reason you are here? A warning about some vague threat to Driftless?*

"It was all over Empyrean." Selena fixed her gaze on the path in front of her. "The topic blew up for about six hours and then they scrubbed it from the network. That's why we think it's legit."

"Empyrean? How can you trust anything that comes out of that fantasy world?" Michael shook his head. "Anyway, it doesn't make sense. We're no threat to anyone here. Why would they start caring about us now?"

"You don't see what I see." Selena stopped, placing a hand on Michael's shoulder. "Empyrean is where the real battle is being fought. The amount of surveillance and attempted encroachment on the Reservation has been increasing."

Michael smiled. "I can't believe you left Driftless to become a hacker."

"I'm not a hacker." Selena crossed her arms. "I'm a Ranger. I love Driftless as much as you. But you know this whole thing would collapse without sympathetic people on the inside looking out for you. What little privacy remains here is due to us."

Gravel gave way to dirt and they followed a well-trodden path, ascending a series of gentle switchbacks until they reached a level place with a commanding view of the surrounding area. From this vantage point, Michael spied his own small cabin, couched in a fold of a complementary hillside half a mile distant as the crow flies.

As he scanned the horizon, Michael's eyes were drawn to small black dot floating high above the canopy of trees. "Selena, check that out." Michael pointed. "What *is* that?" Then instantly, and with increasing intensity, Michael felt a wave of nausea grow in the pit of his stomach. The shapes of trees and rolling hillsides vibrated gently, their borders bleeding into one another. Above them, the sky seemed almost to draw breath as the apparition moved steadily across their field of view. Though he could not be certain, it looked to Michael as though the flying object hovered above his cabin, pausing briefly before slipping behind a wispy veil of clouds. The physical sensation passed as well, but the seed of dreams, long dormant and deeply planted, began to stir.

"What was that, an eagle?" Selena's words pierced through Michael's distraction. "You think old Spitz is out hawking again?"

"I ... I don't know." Michael shook his head. "I'm sorry, I'm just a little dizzy."

"Do you need to sit down?"

"No, I'm alright. But man, that hasn't happened in a long time – not so strongly, anyway."

"You mean ... the visions?" Selena raised an eyebrow. "I could never get over how you're able to see sounds."

Selena was one of the few people who knew about Michael's condition. A doctor had once diagnosed it as synaesthesia, but his symptoms were not strictly indicative of that disorder. Michael was indeed able to *see* sounds as colors. The auditory intimations of music and voice and the natural world would at times present themselves as faint outlines of repeating geometric patterns, receding in fractalized infinitude. But that particular feature of his condition was tolerable, even enjoyable. The disconcerting element of his particular mental aberration was a rare but potent amplification of his sensory experience – a writhing turbulence in which the entire visual landscape seemed to pulse, or ripple, as if the entire veil of perception might be torn away completely. Michael called it the *Glimmering,* and it frightened him.

Michael nodded. "Sometimes it's visual like that, but other times I'll get a strange feeling about something. I'll have an intuition and just *know* something, almost like having an idea planted in my head. Anyway, it hasn't happened to any real degree since I left Chicago – thought I had it under control."

By now the dizziness had abated, and Michael continued walking up the hill.

"How did you end up there in the first place?" Selena kept pace beside him. "Most of us who left went to Minneapolis."

"Bill Jameson." Michael stopped walking. "An old friend of my father. I thought when I started working for Bill that I'd learn more about my parents, well my dad at least. They knew each other once, but that was only for a couple years in college. Bill never even met my mother. He didn't end up being much help."

Selena followed Michael onward to a loftier perch. Here the natural folds in the earth converged and creased again, directing the flow of water over the landscape. This was the keypoint, the reference from which all of the swales and ditches, dams and ponds were derived.

"Water's flowing good." Michael cast his gaze around the site. "Looks like the berms are holding up fine." The place was alive with the chirping of birds, the buzzing of insects and the occasional flash of a squirrel's tail as it flitted up the trunk of a tree. One could easily mistake this farm for a wilderness, save for the fact that nearly every form of vegetation bore some edible fruit or beneficial fiber or leaf.

"You were there for quite a while." Selena kept pace. "Almost the full probationary period – we thought you would stay abroad for good. I can't believe you spent ten years selling insurance."

"I wasn't selling insurance." Michael grimaced. *She knows that.* "I helped investigate claims – first time my condition was of any use to me. Sometimes I'd get a funny feeling about a case or a file and dig into it a little further. A lot of times it would turn out that a claim was fraudulent, or not what it appeared to be. I saved the firm a lot of money."

"So what made you finally decide to leave?"

"I think the place was just too cynical for me." Michael began walking again, leading them back down toward the first row of fruit trees. "The last case I was working on, for example; I was investigating the disappearance of this guy, Tyrant of Thebes. He was a Mindcaster in Empyrean, you might have heard of him?"

Selena cocked her head. "You were in contact with him?"

Michael nodded. "So you have heard of him."

"Sure. But I thought the Tyrant of Thebes was expelled from Empyrean?" Selena's eyes narrowed.

"There were lots of rumors." Michael shrugged. "The party line was that it was just some publicity stunt by Empyrean itself. Or maybe a way to flesh out Resistance elements. But none of it felt right to me. So I started looking into it."

"That's a dangerous business." Selena pursed her lips.

Michael nodded. "Anyway, I didn't have much to go on. There was a lot of chatter on some of the Empyrean speakeasies, but it was pretty useless. I tell ya' this guy had quite a little following, too."

"So did you find him? Find out what happened, I mean?"

"Nah." Michael chuckled. "There was this one person on one of the Empyrean forums who direct messaged me claiming to have information on his whereabouts. I replied with a private email address, but the next day some guy who said he was with the FBI was in the office talking to Bill. We were given a very clear warning to stand down. Bill was pretty pissed – he didn't even know I was looking into it."

"You're lucky that's all they did." Selena shook her head.

Michael took a deep breath. "No tolerance for dissent these days. Anyway, this last time was just the final straw. So I decided to come back home."

"I see." Selena fixed her gaze upon the ground. "So, what's the plan, then?"

*What does she want me to say? Does she approve of my choice? Does she want me to join her in the city?*

Michael scanned the pastoral surroundings, inhaling the fresh autumn air. Before them lay the many small farms of Driftless; twenty thousand acres of undulating terra-formed landscape – alternating ribbons of earthen mounds and irrigation ditches etched with precision into the natural contour of the crumpled topography. Through careful observation over many decades, the designers had learned to harness the earthly energies of sun, wind and rain – giving rise to an ever-increasing fertility and natural abundance. He marveled anew at how beautiful it was when people worked with nature rather than against it.

"All I've ever wanted was to live and work here in Driftless. Even while I was abroad, I thought about coming home. But it felt, somehow … unearned."

Selena bowed her head slightly. "I can't tell you what you should do. But I can tell you that we all have different gifts, and yours is unique. You can be of real service to Driftless, even abroad."

"My gift?" Michael shook his head. "Oh … well, I never really thought of it as a gift."

"Don't kid yourself. These visions, this *Glimmering*, whatever you wanna call it, your intuition – it's something which none of us understand. And I don't think you'll discover its meaning hiding up here on a hilltop in Driftless."

# CHAPTER 3

# THE GLIMMERING

**Michael**

Michael guided their descent along a more direct path, accessing shortcuts Tara had engineered into the property. Soon he and Selena breached the final row of hazelnut shrubs to find the farmyard had been overrun, bustling with dozens of new arrivals. Nearly one hundred people had converged upon the modest homestead.

A steady flow of helpers circulated between the house and lawn, pursuing one errand or another. Games of horseshoes and ring toss, and other improvised distractions were afoot. And more than a few musicians employed their instruments – guitars and banjos, tambourines and fiddles. A healthy portion of the crowd gathered around to sing and clap along.

Swirling eddies of children and pets careened around makeshift tables set for the Harvest Festival. Rough-hewn timbers and wooden slabs were laid across barrels and saw horses to form a dozen tables, set end-to-end in three long rows. Corn dolls crafted from the last sheaf of the harvest featured in the display, soliciting a bountiful harvest for the following year.

Perhaps a dozen guests were engaged in various forms of cooking, with several grilling meats and vegetables over wrought iron charcoal braziers. When all was ready, Tara rang the lunch bell, calling her guests to the mid-afternoon meal. Tara, in the tradition they had forged, offered a hybrid invocation, a combination of Christian and Pagan rituals that acknowledged the diverse backgrounds of the independent-minded folks assembled.

"We offer thanks to God and to the Earth Mother for the bounty of our harvest, and for our connectedness with the cycles of nature." Tara extended her hands, palms upward, in a posture of supplication. "We ask for your continued blessing upon this community and seek your protection as we humbly strive to live our lives guided by these principles – respect earned and given; care for the earth and care for each other."

The Harvest Festival was not unique to Driftless, but neither was it universally celebrated by the numerous, largely unaffiliated reservations. They were characterized by a broad range of philosophical and religious viewpoints, and the level of technological sophistication also varied greatly from one locale to another.

The unifying principle of these alternative communities was their refusal to integrate with the communications architecture of the State and its principal commercial entities. Their residents were not chipped, and they would not allow access to the grid from within the boundaries of their jurisdiction. This was strictly enforced as an article of faith and an existential imperative.

Those who chose to remain outside the cities and their rigidly controlled hinterlands were considered *problematic* and more than that, dangerous. These deviants stood in opposition to a quickly ossifying social structure, which had little use for them, except perhaps as controlled resistance.

*

At dusk, a large campfire was kindled near a thicket of woods at the edge of the yard. The celebrants gathered around the flames to tell stories and let slip their secret hopes and fears, which flowed with the home-brewed wine and mead. Many families had retired, but a cohort some forty strong remained, standing or sitting at various distances from the now-raging fire. The rumors of government interference which had spread throughout the afternoon were largely forgotten, and the mood was light and festive.

It was against this backdrop of Paleolithic gaiety that Malcolm Spitznagel, like a preternatural spirit, emerged ominously from the forest. The man was clean shaven, dressed in cargo pants and a denim shirt, and his wavy gray hair spilled out from beneath a wide brimmed hat. At his side was an olive-green canvas satchel, and Michael noticed that he was not wearing any shoes.

The community called him Spitz – if they called him at all. Everyone was friendly with Spitz, and he with them. But nobody could say that they were particularly close to the man. He was a local hunter and forester, who made his living through a variety of trades. A self-taught naturalist and tracker, he would often take to the woods for weeks on end. Even the other citizens of Driftless considered him a rustic, as he eschewed anything to do with electricity. It was rumored that Spitz was some sort of shaman, and it was a running joke that he spent so much time in the woods that he could communicate with the animals. Spitz, for his part, did nothing to dispel these fanciful notions.

Of all the Driftless residents, he kept counsel most reliably with Tara. And Tara enjoyed Spitz in measured quantities, inviting him to give the invocation of rites to newly initiated residents when they reached the age of majority. Though he rarely participated, Spitz occupied an honorary position on the Council. And he could be relied upon to appear for the ceremonies and rituals, in whose creation he played a role. It was for this reason that he came to Tara's farm on this auspicious evening.

Spitz stood for a moment at the fringe between the benighted wilderness and a civilizing halo of light. Then he moved with purpose, slicing through the circle to greet Tara. From Michael's vantage at the far side of the fire, the rising flames appeared to engulf the two elders, wreathing them in flame.

"Spitz." She held out her hand. "I was wondering when you would show up. Welcome, have a seat."

Tara passed several minutes in quiet consultation with Spitz, and then addressed the group at large. "Friends, I would like to once again thank you for attending the Autumn Jubilee. As you know, the Harvest Festival has been a tradition in Driftless since the founding of the reservation twenty-eight years ago. Of course, that was also the year that our own Michael Quinn came to us, and so it is very fitting that tonight we invite him to answer the call and join our community."

Michael shared a look with Selena as the small crowd clapped in approval. *Am I making the right decision?*

Tara continued. "To hallow this moment, I have asked a member of our community with some of the oldest ties to this land to say a few words – Spitz," she gestured to him and the old man rose, growing large in the firelight. Logs crackled and the circle drew closer as glowing embers escaped the flames drifting skyward. A waxing crescent moon filtered through a gauze of thinning foliage as Spitz began to speak.

"Brothers and sisters, today is the autumnal equinox." His voice, though not deep, was firm and resonant. "It is an important inflection point in our calendar. It marks a change of seasons, and highlights the cyclical nature of our world. It reminds us that we are connected through a thousand generations to an animating spirit that breathes life into the world and into us. And today is twice-blessed, for it is the tradition of the Driftless Reservation that when men and women achieve the age of majority, we solemnize their induction into our community with a ritual that we hold sacred."

Spitz nodded and Tara took up a small pitcher, which had been sitting on the ground. She poured a thin brown liquid into an earthen goblet and presented it to Michael. Then she poured a portion of the cool beverage into the cups of the others assembled.

When all had been made ready, Spitz approached the young initiate. "The path we have chosen is one of simplicity and direct experience of the natural environment. Michael Quinn, do you voluntarily and with full clarity of mind, commit yourself to a life among your friends and family in the Driftless community? Do you agree to transcend all modern contrivances, and to adhere to the simple principles of Care for the Earth and Care for Each Other?" Spitz paused.

Michael stood straight. "I do."

Then Spitz addressed the group at large. "A cup has been poured for each of you. Cider made from the fruits of our orchards and water drawn from our communal spring. Michael, drink this now as a sacrament, a confirmation of your devotion to our community. And we, in turn, will drink with you to reaffirm our own commitment to our chosen path." Spitz drank from his cup and the others did likewise, and another round of clapping and cheering erupted spontaneously from the group.

"The second part of the initiation is at hand." Spitz turned his attention back to Michael. "A simple camp has been prepared for you in the woods some ways up the hillside. It has become our custom that new members should spend a night in silent reflection to contemplate the magnitude of their decision. If you wish to veer from this course, you may do so by simply approaching a member of the Council and making your intentions known before noon tomorrow. There is no shame or recrimination to be feared."

Spitz lifted the flap of his canvas satchel and removed a small packet wrapped in brown paper. He studied Michael's eyes for a long moment, then handed him the parcel. "Take these rations, and only what you will need for the night. Fast this evening and reflect. At dawn, break your fast, and at noon return to us."

Then, without further ceremony, Spitz strode to the boundary of the firelight and disappeared into the darkness. With a silent nod, Tara signaled that Michael should prepare to depart. She accompanied him as he bid a hasty goodnight to the other guests, hesitating only slightly as he finally approached Selena.

"Well, I guess this is it." Michael smiled.

"As long as you're sure." Selena's face betrayed neither approval nor regret.

"He's not going off to war, my dear." Tara placed a hand on Selena's arm. "You'll see him tomorrow. You can spend the night in his cabin. Do you remember how to get there?"

Michael glanced at Selena. *Is she blushing?*

"OK, I'm gonna go." Michael followed Spitz's path and found the old man waiting for him at a small clearing a hundred meters into the brush. This portion of the property had been left wild and served as a natural corridor between several adjacent farms. Into this island of wilderness the two men trekked, making their way as quickly as they dared. The path in this section of the woods was cleared and well-trodden, but it was evening after all, and they took care not to stumble in the darkness.

Michael stuffed his rations into his backpack and felt his knuckles rap against the small urn he had placed there earlier that day. His thoughts flashed to Tara and to his father. He began to speak, but Spitz held a finger to his lips. The period of silence had begun, and so Michael allowed the question to linger and fade. He receded deeper into his thoughts, hypnotizing himself with the shifting ellipse of light flung here and there by the small flashlight held carelessly in his hand.

After nearly twenty minutes of walking, they arrived at his campsite. A canvas tarp had been laid on a level patch of ground just to the side of a switchback in the trail, and on top of this sat a thick bedroll. A bundle of kindling and firewood had been stacked nearby.

Spitz handed Michael a small flint and gestured to the modest camp. "This is where I leave you. I will find you again at noon tomorrow."

Michael watched as his strange companion floated up the trail, quickly fading to a shadow before disappearing into the night. The density of foliage blocked out the stars, cloaking the hillside in near perfect darkness. Michel considered lighting a fire, but thought better of it. The faster he could fall asleep, the sooner the night would pass.

That would turn out to be wishful thinking. The night was alive with sound, and Michael found it impossible to drift off. Deprived of sight, Michael's mind illuminated with lines and color in a way that he had rarely experienced. Every chirp and buzz, every snap and drip added layers of texture and twitches of animation to the vision, until the very darkness was itself a pregnant vibration. At last this sensual cacophony erupted and Michael was no longer observing the phenomenon, but absorbed within it. And then he was gone – in another place entirely.

*

The *Glimmering* came on fast and hard – the visions planted in his brain indistinguishable from memory. His mind walked in twilight as he roamed in darkening dreams. Stepping from the last rough-hewn rectangle of concrete onto a cracked and gravelly tarmac, Michael made his way along an ever-narrowing road – the mountainside on his left and a harrowing drop to the roiling sea still comfortably distant on his right. The sun had set, and the retreating photon armies took refuge beyond the horizon. No hint of daylight glory remained, and even the blushing clouds were fading from pink to gray.

Michael halted. He thrust his fists into the cottony warmth of his trouser pockets, and pivoted slowly back toward his origin, indulging in a final view of the coastline. There, in the middle distance, was a modest two-story hotel shrouded in fog. The low murmur of human voices, barely audible above the brisk autumn breeze, emanated from the seaside guesthouse. Now and again, a burst of laughter from one of the al fresco tables pierced the gathering dusk, cresting and falling in answer to the rhythm of the ocean waves below.

Further up the coast, beyond the hotel on a still higher pinnacle of land jutting stalwartly out to sea, stood an ancient lighthouse. The extinguished lamp that had once shone the way was now a lonely silhouette against the backdrop of a still-darkening sky – a coal-black shade inhaling the remains of the day. Within that impenetrable nexus, above the lantern cupola, a large bird of prey perched upon the topmost spire. As Michael took notice, the bird took flight, extending its broad wings to float upon the thermal updrafts billowing skyward along shorn faces of naked rock. The raptor wove a methodical course above the ridge side, searching here and there; hunting with its focused and telescopic vision.

Michael ushered his attention back to the path before him, completing the broken circuit, rounding the final bend to the place where the highway died against the hillside. A steel barrier separated him from a modest plat of dirt and the treacherous cliff beyond. Michael paused, then swung his legs over the barricade, planting his feet firmly on ground.

Ocean waves thundered against the jagged rocks below, tossing mist and foam into the air. Stones clattered as watery arms drew them out to sea, only to be heaved back again with each new shoreline assault. Stopping now before the edge, he peered into the abyss, inching his feet closer to the precipice as his heartbeat quickened. He had stood on that ledge countless times before. Each time the temptation to fling himself into the void grew stronger, and each time his will to resist diminished. It began to overtake him now, as he probed the edge with his toes.

Michael remained there with watery eyes, waiting … waiting … and at last drawing breath, ready for the plunge. Once more the night air bore aloft the distant voices of those now lost to vision, articulating an inscrutable question which echoed in the darkness. And as that echo faded, an answer began to swell from some unknown depth:

> *On the precipice of each moment I remain*
> *Poised and breathless*
> *Awaiting the overtures of Intention*

# CHAPTER 4

# INTERLOPERS

A rooster crowed in the distance. Perched upon an unpainted fence post guarding the entrance to a distant barnyard, the diminutive sentinel heralded the dawning of a new day. The red and gold-cloaked sentry cocked its head and let tear another piercing cry to announce the sun's imminent arrival. This time the clamor penetrated the cocoon of Michael's cloistered mind.

At first, it was a hazy wisp floating down from the top of his field of awareness, barely the whisper of a thought. But it grew, and at length became undeniable. His mind had indeed conceived; his senses turning some external stimuli into a cognitive form which Michael could not help but notice. It was a sound, but Michael did not hear it. Instead he saw that formless vapor become a single pale gray feather, floating across the black recesses of his mind; the sound of a feather floating, a rooster crowing. It was morning, and he was now awake.

Michael opened his eyes and the world materialized before him. He drew his focus to the frontier of his senses, attending to the rustle of the wind in the leaves above, the sounds of insects and birds, the smell of earth and grass, and the vibrant colors in countless shades of green and brown surrounding him. The tones and images though clear and lively, were mundane, natural and worldly. Michael was relieved.

It had been years since the *Glimmering* presented itself so intensely. Should he mention the relapse to Selena? To what end? It would only worry her, and there was nothing she could do to help.

Selena had called it a gift – a talent that was inborn, but also a discipline to be mastered. It was a legacy of his father. The thought of him exploded and grew large, filling his mind with the echoes of last night's episode. The details were lost to memory, but some sliver of doubt remained. No matter, many such phantoms had presented themselves in the past. All were ephemeral, and few could now be summoned again to mind. Such was the nature of dreams.

Michael flung open his bedroll. He was tired, and his back ached. He checked his watch – eight o'clock. There were still several hours before he could descend the hill and return to the comfort of Tara's house, so Michael set about making a fire. He peeled open the brown paper parcel to reveal a small loaf of bread. He held it to his nose and inhaled – zucchini. He smiled.

Michael ate the bread with haste, washing it down with the water from his canteen. Then, taking the small urn in hand, he flung his backpack over his shoulder and began the short climb to a higher place, where he intended to spread his father's ashes. When Michael reached the appointed location, he paused.

"I hope this is what you would have wanted," was all he could think to say. Then with several broad sweeping motions, Michael cast the small white flakes into the air. They were immediately caught by the wind, scattering in uneven waves across the side of the hill and into the surrounding grass and trees. Michael poured out the remaining contents where he stood, then returned the urn to his backpack.

Suddenly, it occurred to him that the moment of choice had come and nearly gone. He was comforted by the thought, and felt empowered, as though his misgivings were trivial in the end.

But that feeling was short-lived, for once again the sensory inputs of his natural surroundings began to overwhelm him. The world before him rippled like a reflection in a still pond into which a pebble had been quietly dropped. The edges of objects took on a sublime aura; the earthy-warm colors of leaves and branches, soil and grass, boulder and sky, all leaking subtly into one another, wicking through the membrane of their shared borders.

"Not again," Michael halted, leaning against the trunk of a nearby tree. But the experience passed quickly. When he was confident the sensation would not return, Michael began the descent to his humble campsite. The smoldering remains of his fire were a mere twenty meters away when a small shadow flitted overhead, drawing his attention skyward.

Michael's pupils contracted, adjusting to diffuse the brilliance of the morning sun. Raising a hand to his brow, he spied what appeared to be an airborne vehicle hovering above the treetop canopy, perhaps three hundred feet aloft. The aircraft was small, its body only about two feet in diameter, with six helicopter-style rotary blades providing lift.

*Looks low enough to be fair game.* Michael squinted, reckoning the distance. *Wish I had my shotgun.*

As if in answer to his thought, the sky was suddenly pierced by a shrill cry, followed by a shadow darting from the east across a pale canvas of blue and white. The airborne predator fell upon the drone in a melee of tangled confusion, and then released the mangled device, which promptly tumbled to earth, crashing through the ponderous boughs of an overgrown apple tree near the crest of the hill. Michael gawked for a moment in the direction of the crippled drone, then bounded toward the wreckage, propelled by the coiled spring of youth.

He reached the apple tree and found the damaged aircraft about ten feet from the trunk. As Michael approached, he caught sight of Spitz atop a spotted mare, riding in from the south. Perched upon his arm, returned from the hunt, was a large raptor, a golden eagle he named Talon. "Spitz, what are you doing here? What is that thing?"

"Recon drone." Spitz dismounted. "Commercial if I had to guess – a bit small to be military. But it's getting harder to tell the difference, these days."

"Who do you think it belongs to?"

"Let's take a look." Spitz reached for the black-cased drone and carefully turned it over. "Camera housing seems to be okay." He inspected the information plate attached to the underside of the fuselage.

Michael bent over Spitz's shoulder. "I've seen these before. We used them occasionally for investigative work in Chicago. And they're sometimes used to surveil farms, pipelines, that kind of thing. Looks like a pretty standard Marduk series drone. But this camera doesn't look to be standard issue."

The camera was connected to the bottom of the drone by a multi-axis gimbal, which allowed it to rotate and tilt so that it could take photos at any angle. Michael examined the apparatus more closely and noticed that the small orb was not just one camera, but many cameras with numerous lenses indexed at various positions around the surface of the sphere. "What do you make of that?" he asked, pointing to the unusual configuration.

"Probably used for mapping," said Spitz. "Getting a three-dimensional image of the terrain."

Michael shook his head. "They have those already from the satellites. Why send a special drone? Doesn't make much sense."

"Let's get it back to the house." Spitz strapped the drone to his saddle bag. He remained on foot and led his horse back down the trail with Michael following alongside.

*

Selena ignored the rooster and continued to doze. At mid-morning she finally arose and led Snowy around the back of Michael's cabin where they found a trail leading up the hill. She would need to gain some altitude in order to receive a proper signal.

Mobile network signals had been disabled in Driftless – jammed across the full spectrum of functional frequencies to minimize the opportunity for espionage. But Selena knew how to defeat the safeguards, and she had some important information to share.

She arrived at a flat place on the ridge overlooking Michael's cabin. *This should do.* She drew a small black device from her coat pocket and placed her call.

"Yes, it's me." Selena scanned her surroundings. "Looks like he's going through with it. No, I haven't seen anything like that. Yes, I'll keep you posted."

As Selena ended her call, Snowy began barking in the direction of the cabin. Selena followed the husky's gaze to the figure of a man, dark-haired with khaki pants and a brown leather bomber jacket, peering through the side window of the cottage. He appeared to be casing the premises, and started when he heard Snowy's barking. The dark-haired man hesitated, and retreated to a dark windowless van before peeling out of the gravel driveway.

*

Michael and Spitz emerged from the thicket of woods at the rear of Tara's yard. As they approached the gravelly apron surrounding the house, Michael spotted a black late-model SUV parked at a careless angle next to his Harley. The two men quickened their pace, climbing onto the porch to find the front door ajar. Raised voices sounded from within, and Michael caught the last exchange as he approached.

"Now you just listen here." It was Tara speaking. "This was all settled more than a year ago. Driftless is sovereign territory, and we are to be left to govern our own affairs."

Michael pushed the door open with some force. His grandmother stood by the far side of the kitchen table, facing two austere-looking men clad in coal-gray suits. The one nearest to Michael was a Caucasian man, six feet tall and perhaps seventy years of age. He stood with his feet slightly apart, hands resting on the back of a kitchen chair. His partner was darker – Latino, if Michael had to guess – about five-six but weighing every bit of two hundred pounds. The man's arms were crossed, his posture imposing a stature his physique could not afford.

Michael expected his noisy entrance to attract their attention, but Tara and the interlopers did not react, continuing to regard each other intently.

"Well, this must be your grandson." The taller man turned toward Michael. "I must say I was very surprised when you popped onto the grid in Chicago. How do you like it back on the reservation?"

Michael started. *How does he know me?*

"I like it very well." He threw his shoulders back. "And I'm happy to be away from a place where my every move was tracked and monitored. What the hell do you want anyway? My grandmother's right – you have no right to be here."

The agent scanned the room, and seemed to realize that he and his partner were surrounded, and the doorway was blocked. It was common knowledge that the Luddites had not yet been fully disarmed by the state, and the agents were presently at a disadvantage.

"Well, I know this is a touchy subject." The taller agent drummed his fingers against the rail of the kitchen chair. "But now that we have the whole town council present –"

"The Council met last night. Won't be back together until next month," Tara chided, deflating his sarcasm with her earnestness.

"Yes." The agent shifted his footing. "Well, at any rate, as I was about to say, my name is Special Agent Jones, this is Special Agent Juarez. We are here because it has come to our attention that certain terrorist elements may be seeking refuge, or otherwise utilizing certain resources of one or more of the reservations in this region."

Jones took a step in Michael's direction, moving out from behind the table and positioning himself closer to the door. "As you know, it is a federal crime to harbor terrorists, or otherwise offer aid and comfort to enemies of the state. I have been instructed by certain authorities to initiate an investigation, starting with the Driftless Independent Administrative Zone."

"Well." Spitz stepped forward protectively, forming a triangle with Jones and Michael. "I'm *certain* that I don't give a damn about what *certain* authorities have or have not instructed you to do!"

Spitz seemed angry, but Michael was apprehensive. *Could he be here for Selena?* Indeed there existed a hostile class of citizens alternately referred to as Terrorists or the Resistance, depending on whose lips uttered the whisper. And Selena had hinted that she may be part of that group. But Michael was not buying it. Genuine terrorism was rare, and the Resistance had been all but eliminated over the previous decade. What remained of them were considered more of a nuisance than a genuine threat.

Tara shifted her gaze from Jones to Michael and back again. "Well," she said at last, "do you have any kind of documentation to this effect? A warrant or a court order? A parking ticket – anything?"

Jones reached into the breast pocket of his suit coat and produced a crisply folded document bound at the top with a large paperclip. He unfolded the warrant and placed it on the table facing Tara.

Michael could not contain himself. He strode forward, taking the warrant in hand. He had some experience with this type of procedure during his time in Chicago. He read the first page carefully amd flipped through the rest. "This is a generic warrant giving you authority to investigate suspected terrorist activities as outlined in governing statue and regulation. But this isn't binding here in Driftless. Take your fishing expedition somewhere else." Michael tossed the document back onto the table.

Juarez opened his mouth to retort, but Jones raised his hand, silencing him. He picked up the warrant and placed it back into his breast pocket. Then Jones turned to Michael. "Listen, young man. My agency has been monitoring and parsing the metadata related to communications to and from a web-based personality currently wanted for questioning. It has been difficult locating the source of the transmission. I'm embarrassed to say that this particular insurgent seems to have a better knowledge of our network systems than we do ourselves.

"But yesterday, our satellites identified an electronic signature associated with this individual and traced it to a mobile device of some sort located in this vicinity. I say individual, though likely it is more than one person. At any rate the signal was lost, but we have reason to believe this person or group of people may have entered Driftless. And yes, you are correct – we haven't had time to obtain a fresh warrant. We were hoping that you would be reasonable. You wouldn't want to be accused of providing aid and comfort to terrorists, would you?"

"Nobody is giving aid or comfort to outsiders around here, terrorists or otherwise." Michael crossed his arms. "We stay out of politics, that's why we're here. And anyway, we haven't seen anyone suspicious, nor have we heard any such rumor."

"Is that so, Mr. Quinn?" Jones pulled his eyebrows together. "Well, this particular subversive goes by the title *Tyrant of Thebes*. I thought that at least some of you might be *familiar* with that name."

Michael's eyes widened, and he took note of Jones's emphasis on the word *familiar*. His mind was flooded – *when did the Tyrant of Thebes become known as a terrorist?* That was news to him. Was it true? And what did the authorities think of Michael's interest in him months ago? He was unsettled and his cheeks flushed with irritation, but Michael bit his tongue.

Spitz filled the void. "Listen Mr. Jones and Mr. …"

"Juarez, Special Agent Juarez."

"Yes well, as Michael said, we don't get political around here. And we don't harbor instigators. But neither do we let foreigners trespass on our sovereign territory and interrogate our citizens without due process. Now you go and get the proper documentation and don't come back until you have it."

"Citizens?" Jones shook his head. "Sovereign territory? You people really are delusional."

"Just be on your way." Tara's hands were on her hips.

Jones held Tara's gaze for a moment before yielding. "Well, like I said." He pivoted subtly toward Michael. "We thought you might save us – and yourselves – the trouble. Guess I was wrong." Jones shot Tara a glance. "You'll be hearing from us soon."

The two dark figures filed out past Michael and exited, the screen door closing behind them with an ominous *thwaak*. The agents retreated up the drive and disappeared around a bend in the road. Dust hung thick in the air, refusing to settle, and Spitz finally broke the silence.

"Anything about that seem strange to you?" he asked Tara, without irony.

"Hell." She threw her hands up in frustration. "I stopped trying to understand these people years ago. They enjoy harassing us, that's all."

"No." Spitz frowned. "I mean, it isn't like the Feds to come in unprepared like that. And if he really was looking for a terror suspect, why just the two of them? And no descriptions? No specifics. Doesn't make sense."

Tara shook her head. "Well, I don't think we'll hear from them for a little while. It will take a few days at least to get a court order, if he can get it at all. And if they really are chasing someone, that person will no doubt have moved on by then. We'll call an emergency Council meeting next week."

A sudden and forceful knocking sound shot through the air. Michael started, then laughed as he spied Selena through the screen door.

"Michael, you're back already," she said. "Well, good, I've got something to tell you." Selena breezed in with Snowy by her side. "I don't know if you were expecting company, but we caught some guy snooping around your place."

Michael and Tara exchanged glances. "Older white guy, dark suit?" asked Michael.

"Hmmm, I don't think so." Selena shook her head. "Black hair. He was wearing a leather jacket and brown pants, I think. He was kinda far away."

"Did he see you?" There was concern in Spitz's voice.

"Maybe, I'm not sure. Anyway, it may be no big deal, I just thought I'd let you know."

"You did good, young lady," said Spitz. Then to Tara, "I don't like this. What do they say in the army? Once is an accident, twice is coincidence, three times is enemy action." Spitz produced the drone-camera from his jacket pocket for Tara to see. "Talon took down a drone up near the keypoint. Then this clown shows up at your house. And now Selena sees some guy poking around Michael's cabin. No, something is clearly goin' on. Someone's lookin' for something."

Tara bowed her head for a moment, then spoke forcefully to the group, "OK, Spitz. Selena, I need to speak with Michael alone for a while. Go on, just give us a few minutes, would ya?"

Spitz and Selena found their way outside, leaving Tara and Michael alone in the kitchen. Tara gestured for Michael to sit and the two huddled around the table, with the drone camera placed between them.

"Michael, honey." She took his hands in hers. "I knew this day would come. I think you probably knew it, too. It's not like your presence here was exactly a secret. But I had prayed that they might leave you alone. Now it looks like that is not to be."

Michael regarded his grandmother with affection and a growing sadness. He had indeed also felt that his respite in Driftless would not last forever. And now it seemed that events were catalyzing his departure more rapidly than he might have hoped.

"Why do you think they would be interested in me?" asked Michael, disingenuously.

"I can't say for certain," Tara intimated, "but I think that long ago, your father was caught up in something that the government cared deeply about. That something ended up killing him, and don't let anyone tell you different."

At this Michael sat upright, releasing Tara's hands. "Dad died of a stroke."

Tara rose and walked to the window facing the driveway. "I remember when you came to us. You were so tiny, so vulnerable. I fell in love with you instantly." Tara gazed out the window. "You know, your father called me, one week before you arrived. This was back when I was still on the grid. He said he was coming home, that he was taking some time away from work and would be coming to see us. He said he had a surprise for us."

Tara turned away from the window and looked back at Michael. "He died shortly after that phone call. Then that man Lim brought you to us – a surprise to be sure, and a wonderful surprise, no mistake. But I think that whatever your father got mixed up in has finally caught up with us. And I don't think I can hide you from it anymore."

Michael was irritated. "So, what are you saying? I mean, if you are right and this agent is interested in *me* and not Selena, then why don't they just arrest me?

"I don't think they know what they are looking for, exactly." Tara shrugged. "They may not have grounds to take you now, but eventually they will. And that terrifies me."

"What should I do?" asked Michael.

"Leave." Tara grasped his forearm. "Leave now – and go find Dr. Lim."

# CHAPTER 5
# A NEW GESTALT

**Simon**

Simon scooted into a booth-seat fabricated from the rear section of a '57 Chevy, and scanned the restaurant. The walls were shingled with antique license plates, the ceiling adorned with vintage surfboards. Most of the clientele were clad in beachwear, and more than a few men were bare-chested. *No shoes, no shirt – no problem!*

"I love the vibe in here." Lauren took her place opposite Simon and peeled open a sticky menu.

"Hodad's? Oh yeah, this place is an institution."

A young woman arrived table-side, pad in hand. "Have you decided?"

"Double bacon cheeseburger basket with onion rings, and a chocolate shake." Simon smiled.

"Veggie burger," Lauren closed the menu. "And I'll have a chocolate shake, too."

"Oh, I've got some news." She tilted her head, gauging Simon's reaction from across the table. "My cousin, Johnson, is visiting from Fort Hill, Utah. He's going to meet us here in a little bit."

"An airman?" Simon sat up straight. "Now that's a surprise. I figured with your pedigree, your cousins would all be bankers or lawyers, or doctors like you."

Lauren smiled. She was not yet a physician but a pre-med student majoring in neuroscience at the University of California, the same institution at which Simon was serendipitously employed.

"Your cousin is training at Fort Hill?" Simon cocked an eye. "Is he American?"

"No, he's Singaporean, like me." Lauren smiled. "But our military personnel sometimes undergo training in the States. We don't have a lot of land in our country, and we buy a lot of equipment from the US, so I guess they've worked out a deal."

"So he's a pilot?"

"Yes, but I believe they're grooming him for something bigger." Lauren hesitated. "What about your family? You don't mention them very often."

"Yeah, well, there's not that much to say. My father passed away a few years ago."

"I'm sorry to hear that." Lauren reached for his hands across the table.

Simon took her hands in his. "It's fine. We knew it was coming for a while – cancer."

"What about your mother? She must miss you."

"It's a long story. We had a falling out. She didn't want me to leave … we just kind of grew apart. We talk every now and then."

"I'm sorry." Lauren held his eye. "Well, maybe she can come out and visit."

"I don't see that happening any time soon. She just moved back to the countryside – her father's old farm, up in western Wisconsin."

"Sounds nice." Lauren released his hands and sat back in the repurposed car booth-seat. "It must be peaceful. Have you ever been there?"

"You know, it's funny you should ask." Simon leaned forward, his elbows on the table. "I didn't think so, but now that you mention it, I do remember something. I remember being pulled in a red wagon around their farmyard when I was a kid. And a big blue tractor. I think I was maybe three years old."

"You have memories from when you were three?"

"Actually, it just came back to me. It's the strangest thing, but since the accident I've been remembering all sorts of things I had forgotten. And, this is going to sound kind of odd, but I'm having memories that I don't … well, remember."

Lauren tilted her head. "Okay …"

"I mean, they're in there, in my head. But they don't make sense. Like, I'm back at my mother's farm. But everything looks different. It's all out of context. I'm older, my mother is older. Maybe I'm remembering a dream. But that's not the strangest part."

"I can't wait to hear this." Lauren said.

"I can remember every meal I've had this last month – the smell of it, how it tasted, the way it felt on my tongue. I remember the humidity and temperature of the air every day since the accident."

"That's amazing." Lauren's eyes widened.

"It's frightening."

"It's a blessing – having a memory like that. After all, at the end of the day, memories are all we have, aren't they?"

"I guess." Simon shrugged.

The waitress returned with their drinks and Simon struggled for moment to suck the ice cream through the straw before giving up and using his spoon.

"Let me ask you a question." Lauren's eyes filled with mischief. "Let's say you could live for an entire year in an ideal setting. Any place you want, say a tropical paradise. And you could spend the time with the most beautiful woman in the world as your companion."

"Oh, are you free for a whole year?"

"That's sweet." Lauren smiled. "And the entire time would be exciting and wonderful."

"But ..."

"But at the end of the year you wouldn't remember it at all." Lauren leaned forward slightly and lowered her voice, as if inviting Simon to confess. "And nobody else would remember it. It would be like the entire year never happened."

"What about my age?" Simon was interested now. "Would I lose a full year of my life?"

"Yes, that's the choice – would you want the amazing and positive experience that you couldn't remember, or the risk of having a negative experience and painful memories?"

"I'll take the risk," Simon said without hesitation. "The experience is nothing without the memory, is it? Now, if I was simply granted an extra year, that might be different. Like the thirteenth floor of a building that never gets built."

"Ha, well for all you know, that's already happening all the time." Lauren shot back, catching Simon off guard. "Just extraneous and disconnected fragments of our lives, synched off at a single point from the rest of a continuum, floating freely in blissful ignorance of any before or after.

"Oh, there he is!" Lauren waved her arm and slid out of the booth. A young man of Chinese ethnicity stood near the doorway scanning the dining room. He caught sight of Lauren and approached, embracing her warmly.

Johnson was taller than Simon expected – he looked every bit of six feet in height. He wore a black turtleneck under a brown bomber jacket, and his crew cut avowed his military commission. Dark blue designer jeans and aviator sunglasses polished the look. This was not some jar head soldier. Johnson was an officer.

"This is my cousin, Johnson Tan." Lauren placed a hand on her cousin's shoulder for a moment, then wrapped her arm around

Simon's waist. "And this is my boyfriend, Simon."

*Boyfriend.* Simon was still getting used to hearing that from her. It made him happy, and a little self-conscious. They sat again, and Johnson took a place opposite the young couple. "So, I understand you're a pilot." Simon offered Johnson a menu. "Lauren said they've got big plans for you."

"Oh, did she?" Johnson smiled and glanced sidelong at Lauren. "Nah, I'm just a working stiff."

"But you *are* a pilot."

Johnson nodded. "I'm spooling up on the F-35 Joint Strike Fighter."

"That's very impressive." Simon scooted forward in the booth.

"It's a hot mess." Johnson scanned the menu briefly. "Over budget, behind schedule, performance issues. But we have learned a ton about battlefield intelligence integration. That's what I'm really interested in, building out the programs and protocols to integrate artificial intelligence into the battlefield. A lot of people don't realize that the most sophisticated technology is in the way all of the various systems come together to give pilots real time information about what's happening around them. Heck, the helmet alone costs over a hundred thousand dollars."

The waitress returned with the burgers and fries. "Here you go. Can I get something for you?" she said to Johnson.

"That looks good." Johnson pointed at Simon's plate. Simon smiled his approval. He was going to like Johnson.

\*

The next several months passed quietly, the peace and contentment marred only by throbbing migraines, which Simon experienced from time to time. The bump on the back of his head was gone, but he continued to suffer the occasional white flash and spontaneous bout of pain and dizziness.

Lauren urged him to see a doctor, but Simon insisted he was fine. "If the pain gets worse, I'll go see someone." Simon promised.

Things didn't exactly get worse, but three months from the day of the accident, they took a sharp turn for the surreal. As the young couple strolled through the atrium of Horton Plaza Mall, he was drawn by a strange compulsion to the grand piano positioned in the center of the courtyard. To Lauren's amusement, he stepped over the red velvet rope and took a seat on the black leather piano bench. He contemplated the instrument for a moment, then poked around tentatively, striking keys at random. Finally, he focused on one note, a black key in the middle of the keyboard. Simon struck this once with his right thumb. Again. And again. He continued playing this single note for nearly thirty seconds, transfixed by the regular monotonous tone.

"Simon …?" Lauren's voice was tinged with a mixture of annoyance and concern.

"Fascinating." He trained his eyes intently on his thumb which continued to drone out the same particular tone. "It goes on forever, never changing – until I add …"

Simon struck a second key. And then a third, and a fourth, until he had picked out something approximating a melody with his right hand. He paused, and then added his left hand, elaborating the pseudo-melody with harmonics and dynamic variations in volume and speed.

Simon improvised spontaneously for several minutes, conjuring an evocative, somewhat melancholy, slightly off-center tune which seemed to progress and meander in equal measure. By the time he finished playing, a small crowd had gathered, joining Lauren as she stood applauding in her astonishment.

"Wow," she said as they strolled away from the piano. "I had no idea you knew how to play."

"Neither did I." Simon shrugged. "That's the first time I've ever tried."

*

From that moment on, it was as though a dam had burst. Simon found himself fascinated by subjects he had never studied, and capable of skills he had never learned before. He bought a guitar and began to compose. He read voraciously, scouring the Internet for information on innumerable subjects. And all the while, the dull intermittent headaches continued.

Lauren urged Simon to see a doctor, but Simon resisted until he experienced something he could no longer ignore. He was tuning his guitar one evening, attempting to invent a new musical scale when everything went dark. He was alarmed, but before he could speak, his senses were overwhelmed with information – light, sound, emotions, and sensations he had never experienced converged, flowing through him with controlled recklessness. Simon's mind was dissolved in the simultaneous exposition of a thousand ideas, all formulated with perfect clarity and understanding. He dwelt for a moment on the peak, and then suddenly plunged into the depths of oblivion. He awoke instantly and once again found himself reflected in Lauren's dark and troubled eyes.

After that, there was no more argument. "Listen, Simon," she said firmly, "if you don't want to see a physician, then at least come and talk to Professor Lim. He's a researcher at the University, a neuroscientist. I've spoken with him and he is keen to meet with you.

Simon reluctantly agreed, and Lauren drove him to the university campus the following afternoon.

"Who is this guy again? You said he wasn't a doctor."

"Dr. Wilfred Lim," she answered. "Well, he's not a medical doctor exactly. He's a visiting scholar on loan from Stanford's Artificial Intelligence Lab."

"Lim," Simon repeated the Chinese surname. "Singaporean?"

"Mainland China," said Lauren. "But I think he's an American citizen now."

Lauren parked and led Simon into the medical building, located in an obscure corner of the university campus. As they approached the laboratory suite, Simon noticed an immediate change in the ambience. Cold cinder blocks were enhanced with more elegant plaster finishes. The desks were wood toned, and the walls were covered in colorful oil paintings of many styles, from early Renaissance to contemporary abstract.

They arrived at a small reception area, and Lauren began to address a young woman seated at the desk. She was stopped mid-sentence by the approach of a tall, lean man clad in a white lab coat. "Dr. Lim." Lauren smiled. "How are you?

"Lauren." The man smiled in return. He seemed genuinely pleased to see her. "You know to call me Wilfred." He then added, "How's my star pupil?"

Dr. Wilfred Lim's voice was strangely deep and resonant for such a spare man. His pronunciation was clear and precise, despite an undeniable accent. Although he was over six feet in height, Dr. Lim weighed a mere one hundred and forty-five pounds. But his handshake belied a wiry strength; the result of many hours spent on badminton courts in the days of his youth. His salt and pepper hair was longer than Simon expected, nearly shoulder length, and he carried himself with a youthful vigor.

"Hello, Dr. Lim. Thank you for seeing me." Simon extended his hand.

"Yes, of course." He clasped Simon's hand and shook it firmly. "Please, call me Wilfred. Why don't you both come into my office?" He led them into an adjacent room and closed the heavy metal door behind them. His chambers were decorated in much the same style as the main reception area, with colorful paintings adorning every wall and rows of books on low shelves beneath them.

"Please, have a seat." Wilfred gestured to the chairs in front of his desk. "Lauren has told me something of your situation, but why don't you tell me in your own words. What are you experiencing?"

"Well … I'm not quite sure how to explain."

Wilfred sat across from Simon. "Just start at the beginning."

Lauren nodded in approval as they both sat down. Simon inhaled deeply, and proceeded to explain all that had unfolded from the time of his surfing accident, until his startling hallucination the night before. Wilfred listened intently, periodically making notes in a small leather diary. He took particular interest in Simon's spontaneous piano composition at the mall.

"Fascinating. Did you document the performance in any way?"

"I recorded it!" Lauren held up her phone.

"Email that to me, would you please?" Wilfred folded his arms. "Your case is very interesting, Simon. We will obviously have to run some tests, but it sounds like you may be experiencing a condition known as Acquired Savant Syndrome – A.S.S."

"A.S.S." Simon shot a sideways glance at Lauren. "So, you are saying that surfing literally made an ass out of me?"

Wilfred chuckled. "Precisely. Listen Simon, I can't make any promises. When it comes to the brain and these types of cognitive phenomena, we are operating on the frontier of our understanding. But I think we may be able to help you, or at least help you make sense of what is going on. And at the same time, I think you may be able to help us. Do you know anything about what we do here at the lab?"

"Not much," Simon admitted. "Lauren said you were researching artificial intelligence."

"Yes, that is correct … or at least partially correct. We're exploring the realm of human consciousness with the goal of applying what we learn to the disciplines of artificial intelligence – AI. As I mentioned, we have to run some more tests, but I think you may be an ideal candidate to participate in the research that we are conducting here. I suggest we run a simple battery of screening tests to see if you qualify for our program. Is this something you think you may be interested in?"

Simon took another deep breath and cast a searching gaze at Lauren; her deep brown eyes suggested only a genuine concern for his well-being. "Sure." He turned back to Wilfred. "Count me in."

*

Over the next several hours, Wilfred and his team put Simon through a series of written and verbal cognitive exercises and tested his spatial awareness and motor function. After some initial deliberation, he asked Simon to participate in a broader study, which would take the rest of the semester.

Simon kept his job in the administration office, and life seemed to revolve around the university. He met with Wilfred two or three times a week. As their research progressed, Simon's interest in the subject of artificial intelligence grew. He delved into the relevant literature, copiously annotating sections related to his symptoms.

He would sometimes bounce ideas off Lauren or share tidbits he found interesting with her. One particular article, "The Impact of AI on Human Relationships", caught Lauren's eye.

"That's funny." She read over his shoulder. "When I first read the title, I thought it was talking about the impact of *love* on human relationships."

Simon turned around and looked at her as she continued. "You see, the Chinese word for love is *ai*. It is pronounced like the letter 'I' but spelled a-i."

Simon's eyes widened. "Cool, teach me more!"

"Well, OK." Lauren removed a sheet of paper from the printer. "Here – this is how 'love' is written in Chinese." She wrote out the character in traditional Chinese script: 愛 .

"Chinese is an organic language, and there are lots of clusters of words centering on a particular character, or even a part of a character, which we call a *radical*. So, for example, the central part of the word for love looks like this – 心 – and this character is pronounced *hsin*. It means *heart*."

Lauren seemed pleased that Simon was so interested in her culture. In truth, she was simply happy to have his attention focused on her again and not wrapped up in research on brain disorders or other such somber topics.

Simon was fascinated. "So, 'heart' in Chinese means heart as in love – the emotional center?"

"Yes, and also the physical organ as well." Lauren took a seat. "And – you'll enjoy this – *hsin* can also be translated as 'mind'. It can refer to the cognitive center of a person as well."

Lauren continued writing. "This character – 思 – is pronounced *si*, it means to think."

"See how it builds on the heart radical? And then there is this character – 意 – pronounced *yi*. It also incorporates the heart symbol. This word can also be translated to mean intention or purpose."

"Fun!" said Simon. "Teach me more."

Lauren showed Simon several more characters and outlined some of the basics of the Chinese language before referring him to the inexhaustible resources available on the Internet. That was all he needed. In less than a month, Simon memorized over four thousand Chinese characters; a feat which should have taken him years, accomplished in a matter of weeks.

*

One afternoon, as Simon waited in the lobby of Wilfred's clinic, he observed a middle-aged woman with dark glasses exiting one of the examination rooms.

"Thank you, Mrs. Simpson." Wilfred followed behind her. "We'll see you next week." The woman withdrew a small wand-like object from her purse. It unfolded and quickly reassembled itself into a walking stick. She nodded in Michael's direction as she passed him on her way out the door, moving with surprising confidence despite her apparent blindness.

"Oh, hello there, Simon," said Wilfred. "You're early, but no matter. Follow me."

Simon followed Wilfred back into the examination room, which was considerably larger than Wilfred's office. It was fitted out with all manner of diagnostic equipment.

"CAT scans, functional MRIs, Magnetoencephalography, event-related optical signal machines." Wilfred puffed his chest. "Between my lab and the medical school, we have access to just about every brain imaging technology you could hope for."

"Wow … So, you think these tests will explain what's going on with me?"

"Hopefully," said Wilfred. "We will have to get some results from the fMRI before we can offer a proper diagnosis. We've got to understand the origin of the neurogenesis, which seems to have been stimulated by your accident. And we'll want to begin right away in case the condition is progressive. The Artificial Intelligence Lab has already approved grant funding for the study, if you are willing."

Simon was intrigued, but circumspect. "Okay, but I still don't understand what this has to do with artificial intelligence."

"That's a fair question." Wilfred rubbed his chin. "Let me see if I can explain. You see among the AI community, there is nearly universal agreement that cognition, awareness, is an emergent property arising from brain function. In other words, consciousness is not something that is different from the mechanics of the brain but rather consciousness *is* the mechanical functioning of the brain. And I acknowledge that much of what the brain does *can* be modeled algorithmically on a computer." Wilfred nodded. "But we are operating from a different Gestalt. We are of the view that consciousness is something different, something non-computable."

Wilfred explained that most of his peers were working from the ground up – machine learning, Bayesian inferences, and natural language progression. They were setting up rules and algorithms of increasing complexity, which worked very well for many applications.

However, in his lab they were using the model of the human brain to understand and imitate its structure and functional modalities. They were attempting to create artificial neural networks – mind maps. The ultimate goal was to take the completed scan of the brain and copy it into a computational device. The computer would perfectly simulate the brain's information processing functions such that it would be conscious and indistinguishable from the workings of the original brain in all important aspects.

Rather than having to recreate high-level psychological processes using classical artificial intelligence methods and cognitive psychology models, they would simply capture the low-level structure of the underlying neural network and map it within a computer system. The human mind and even the personal identity could thereby theoretically be generated by the faithful replication of the neural network.

"In other words," said Wilfred, "we are not trying to create consciousness. We are attempting to summon it, to invoke it. We are building a home in which it might dwell." He took a few steps toward the fMRI machine, gesturing for Simon to follow. "We rely as much on philosophers such as Fichte and Polanyi as we do on scientists like Minsky and McCarthy. Now, the pure materialists like to make fun of us. They call us shamans or worse. But what we do is no less a science than what they practice. We just start from a place of greater humility."

Wilfred's approach was not without controversy. Many people had pointed out that trying to create intelligence by imitating the brain was like early attempts to construct flying machines by modeling them after birds. Modern aircraft do not function like birds at all. Rather, it is the underlying principles of aerodynamics that allow both planes and birds to defy gravity. But Wilfred believed that even if his explorations led ultimately to a dead end, the act of imitation and simulation was an important ingredient in the process of discovering the true path.

"Sounds fascinating," said Simon, "though I'm not sure I quite understand the point."

"Well, there are many beneficial applications." Wilfred nodded, as if agreeing with his own assertion. "Uploading a human mind to a computer could address the problems associated with long interstellar space travel or serve as a backup in case of some apocalyptic event. And, of course, there are those who believe it could make one immortal – just upload your mind to a computer and live forever." Wilfred's eyes seemed to gleam with a subtle light at the notion.

"Is that what you're after?" Simon asked. "Immortality?"

"Me?" Wilfred smiled wistfully. "No, not really, except perhaps in name alone. But I would like to be there when the lightning strikes."

Wilfred gestured toward the fMRI. "I'd like to take a scan today if you don't mind. I need you take off any jewelry, watches, rings, what have you. No magnetic metal allowed."

After the scan was completed, Simon changed back into his clothes and followed Wilfred back to his office.

"By the way," Wilfred closed the door behind him. "I did some analysis on that musical improvisation Lauren sent me. Your little impromptu piano concert at the mall?"

"Oh, yeah," said Simon. "I had forgotten about that."

"Well, it appears that the melodic progression was not some random contrivance." Wilfred took a seat behind his large metal desk. "In fact, it appears to be based on the Fibonacci sequence. Do you know what that is?"

Simon sat down across from Wilfred. "Yeah, sure. It's a series of numbers where each number is the sum of the previous two numbers in the sequence. So, the sequence is 0, 1, 1, 2, 3, 5, 8, 13, and so on to infinity."

Wilfred nodded. "Quite right, very good. Well, it appears that without fully understanding what you were doing, you assigned a numeric value to each note in the E-major scale. Then you extended the scale a bit to get to the requisite ten digits and based your melody on those numbers. Of course, the dynamics of the piece, the melodicism, the loudness and softness of the notes, those are all based on your own artistic interpretation. But the numerical values were quite well-defined by the sequence."

Simon shifted in his seat. "So, what does it mean?"

*"Mean?"* Wilfred raised his eyebrows. "Who knows? Maybe something, maybe nothing. Maybe it just means your subconscious can count and that you have an as yet unspecified brain injury. Why don't we get back to that?"

*

"Simon." Lauren reached across the table and grabbed his forearm. "Simon …"

He focused on her again.

"Where were you just now?" She smiled.

"Sorry, I'm just distracted."

"Do you want to leave?" Lauren gestured toward the door.

Simon shook his head. "We've already ordered. And you've been wanting to come here for weeks. Anyway, spending time with you helps more than you could know."

Simon held her gaze. Being with Lauren was like moving from

the edge to the center of a spinning record. They were revolving along with everything else, but moved somehow more slowly. The two of them were at the center of things, and when they longed again to rejoin the maddening crowd, they needed only to take a few steps to arrive back where they started, never losing any ground.

For his part, Simon was convinced that Lauren was the load star in a constellation that was only now coming into view. And there, in that overpriced French restaurant, Simon summoned the courage to confess his love for Lauren. He said it boldly, confident of her reply and that his faith had not been misplaced, for she did love him.

She smiled, but it was a sad smile, and her gaze tumbled from his eyes to his hands, clasping hers from across the table. Simon's heart sank. "Do you not feel the same?"

"Yes." Again, she was looking into Simon's eyes. "Yes, I do. It's just that I feel as though … it's silly, but things are going so well I'm afraid to name it. I'm afraid to acknowledge it. It's like, if we say it out loud it will be made known and become vulnerable. And somehow, somebody will find it and attack it, ruin it."

Simon took her other hand in his and held them close. "I know it's precious. And it seems fragile. But it isn't – it's strong! And isn't it better to love unconditionally and without fear? Without fear of consequences, and without fear of loss?"

"Yes." Lauren hesitated. "But sometimes attachment doesn't create happiness, it creates suffering, it creates … barriers. It causes pain when the people we're attached to change, even though change is woven into the fabric of life. I mean, think about it, everything around us is impermanent – the seasons, our relationships, our lives."

The words, though melancholy, were not surprising. Lauren had once intimated that life in its essence was wrought with suffering and desire. She lobbed the statement carelessly into a conversation, as if it was a simple fact. But Simon could never quite come to agree with that idea. To Simon, life was an adventure that had only just begun, and he was facing it head-on, surging forward on a tide of pure potential and boundless optimism.

"But what is love, if not attachment?" Simon's eyes kindled. "Isn't true love surrendering yourself over to someone else completely? Joining with that person and becoming the same being? That is complete attachment and complete abandonment, is it not?"

"Yes, I suppose it is." Lauren yielded to the honesty of his confession. "And I suppose that's why I *do* love you." Her smile grew brighter, and she laughed. Simon's heart was lightened as his hopefulness won through to her. He felt as though a cloud had burst and spilled out rays of sunshine. And that evening, as they held each other, grateful to have found one another, they were content to be still as the world revolved around them in benevolent indifference.

# CHAPTER 6

# WINDOW ON THE PAST

**Michael**

His escape from Driftless was a blur. Michael did not return to his cabin, deeming it safer to depart directly from Tara's farm. He fueled up his Harley Sportster with petrol that Tara had stored onsite and stocked up on food and other sundries as the group hastily crafted a plan.

"You need to figure out what's going on, starting with this thing." Spitz thrust the small camera-orb into Michael's hands. "Do you know anyone in Chicago who can help?"

"I'll get in touch with Bill Jameson," said Michael. "He's pretty well-connected. I'll start with him."

"I'll go with you." Selena stepped forward. "We can take my car, it'll be faster."

Michael shook his head. "Thanks, but we're not even sure who exactly they're after. Tyrant of Thebes? That could just be a code word for anyone they consider a threat. Heck, they might just as easily be looking for you. Better if we split up."

Selena rubbed her temples. "Maybe it *would* be best if I got back to Minneapolis and tried to figure out what's going on."

"Good," said Tara. Then to Michael, "It will take you about five hours to get there, I reckon. Stay off the main roads, and don't call unless you are sure the line is secure. Do you know where to get a burner phone?"

"Not anymore, but Bill should be able to help. I'll call the outpost when I get situated."

"No hurry there," said Spitz. "Call when you think you have a secure line."

"Wait a minute." Selena rushed back to her car and returned with a pair of black-rimmed glasses. "Use these when you get to the city. It should defeat the facial recognition cameras."

"I'm not sure this is really that clever of a disguise." Michael smiled.

"They project an infrared holographic image. It will confuse the software into thinking you are someone else. It's randomized and has updated profiles so it won't arouse suspicion."

Michael looked at Selena with wonder. *I didn't realize you were so subversive. What else don't I know about you?*

They hugged their goodbyes as the sun reached its zenith. The days were shortening now, but many hours of sunlight remained, which heartened Michael for the journey ahead.

He left the borders of Driftless behind and soon found himself in the flatter and more open spaces where the hills and savannah gave way to a sea of corn and soy beans that stretched out to the horizon. Tara's farm was nothing like the row-cropping abominations that now surrounded him. Here the once flourishing environment had been obliterated – the trees bulldozed, the grassland extirpated and the indigenous fauna driven out. Then, for good measure, the place had been bombarded with pesticides to ensure that absolutely no life remained, even at the microbial level.

After destroying the natural environment, a new artificial system had been created. By introducing fertilizers and pesticides, they transformed petrochemicals into food, turning what should have been a perennial renewable process into a strip-mining operation.

Michael bore south along the less monitored county highways until he slipped across the Illinois border. The shells of small towns dotted the expanses between larger metropolitan centers, but few people lived there now. Numerous agricultural drones flew patterns above the fields, gathering intelligence on the condition of the crops and automated farm equipment. Though he could not be certain, it appeared that several of these altered course abruptly, veering in Michael's direction for a time, before ultimately returning to their original program.

*

Aging skyscrapers – massive columns of glass and steel piled high against the western shore of Lake Michigan – reflected the lowering sun in amber hues as Michael approached the city of Chicago. He sped down one of the smaller east-west streets toward lakeside Grant Park and made his way into an underground parking lot. The transponder unit integrated with his motorbike was still active, and the barrier lifted automatically as he passed beneath the gantry. The event would register with the transit authority and could alert them to his presence. But Michael wagered it was better to risk detection and get his vehicle out of sight until he had a chance to check in with Bill.

He climbed the stairs to the surface and wove his way through the streets and alleys, westward and inland toward the office of his former employer. Cameras with facial recognition guarded every corner, but there was precious little he could do about that. Michael put on a baseball hat and the glasses Selena gave him and kept his head down.

The Sentinel Building which housed Bill's office was still several blocks away, when he began to feel uneasy. *Someone is following me.* The sensation grew in the pit of his stomach, and he cut back down a side alley, stopping under a fire escape before a minor intersection. Michael stood there scanning the vicinity. Nothing – he was being ridiculous, but he couldn't shake the creeping doubt. He stepped into the roadway.

"Hey, Michael – *stop!*"

Michael's heart leapt to his throat as he spun toward the voice. His eyes locked on a figure about twenty meters away. A man of medium height and build with black hair, khaki pants and a brown leather jacket began jogging toward him.

Michael bolted, his legs pumping reflexively. He sprinted back down the alley, cut up another passage, and down the next. He did this several times before his strength gave out and he was left panting, leaning against a brick wall. Michael caught his breath and peered around – he was alone again. He made his way back to the main road and stopped short. By some stroke of luck, he was now staring directly at the front entrance to the Sentinel Building, the very place he sought. Michael slipped inside, careful to conceal his face from the security cameras as he entered.

A nostalgic smell of old leather and cigar smoke greeted him as he sped through the lobby. Built in the 1920s, the Sentinel Building embodied the grandeur and conviction of an era which imagined unlimited possibilities. Art Deco stylings of sunburst motifs and bold vertical lines celebrated the virtue of progress and betrayed a confidence in the ability of humans to forge their own destiny.

Michael's mood lifted as he rode the elevator to the seventh floor, but he took care not to mistake familiarity for safety. The doors opened, giving way to the reception area of the Sentinel Insurance Company. He hesitated, then recognized a friendly face.

"Julie, thank God you're here." Michael walked hurriedly toward a large desk of polished mahogany. "Is Bill here? I need to speak with him right away."

"Well, hello there, Michael." Julie peered at him with curiosity from behind her thin-framed glasses. "What are you doing here? I was about to pack up for the evening."

"Is Bill here?" Michael pressed. "It's urgent."

"You're in luck – he's working late tonight."

Julie swiped the glass console on her desk, and spoke softly into the microphone attached to her earpiece. "Come on." She stood and gestured to Michael. "Follow me, he's inside."

Michael followed Julie down the corridor – a small cubicle farm on the left with offices on his right. Their destination was the large set of double doors at the end of the hall, which enclosed the office of Bill Jameson, Executive Director and principal shareholder of the Sentinel Insurance Company. Julie came to a halt at the threshold and knocked twice in rapid succession.

Bill stood near the large plate-glass window at the far end of the expansive office suite. A large solid oak desk stood between them. The last rays of daylight filtered through the westward facing window, deepening the shadows which crept from the hidden recesses of the room. He gazed absently into the gathering dusk.

"Bill, Michael's here." Julie stepped to one side, clearing the way for Michael.

"Ah … Michael." Bill turned around and strode toward the front of the room. "There you are. I wondered if you might turn up. Come, sit down." He gestured toward two leather club chairs positioned on one side of his desk.

"I'll leave you two alone." Julie nodded and closed the door behind her.

"Bill, I need your help. Something's happened – actually a few things. I think ... I think I'm under investigation or something."

Bill cocked his head. "Investigation? That seems unlikely. What would make you think that?"

"This morning a couple of agents showed up at the farm. At least they said they were agents – they looked the part."

"Agents?" Bill furrowed his brow. "What kind of agents?"

"I don't know. They said they were with the Federal Government. Agents Juarez and Jones, if I recall correctly."

"Jones?" Bill raised an eyebrow. "What did they want?"

"They said they were looking for a fugitive. One of them mentioned Tyrant of Thebes." Michael pulled back, then stood. "You know you should have had my back when I was looking into that whole thing. You just caved in to those guys. Now it looks like it's coming 'round again."

"Do you know how much crap I took for that?" Now Bill stood and faced Michael. "Auditors and regulators and whatnot? All for some Mindcaster you never met. You really kicked over a hornets' nest."

"So we just back down, don't even question it?" Michael put his hands on his hips.

"Question what? The guy is already back online."

Michael flinched. "You're kidding. They allowed him to continue?"

Bill nodded. "About a week ago."

The Tyrant of Thebes phenomenon had clearly caught the authorities by surprise. He had a loyal and growing following who waited eagerly for what they believed to be ciphered messages outlining the means by which technology companies controlled and regulated government and commerce – and how they would ultimately be undone.

"Probably a limited hang-out." Bill shrugged. "He's most likely a red herring, some tool of the opinion managers to keep the Resistance engaged – running them around in circles, but not really providing any useful information. My guess is that they were only using him as an excuse to snoop around Driftless."

"Maybe." Michael shook his head. "But right before these agents showed up, we took down a recon drone that was hovering over my grandmother's property."

"A recon drone?" Bill's drew his eyebrows together. "Sent by these agents?"

"I'm really not sure." Michael shook his head. "And then there was this other guy sneaking around my place the same morning."

"*Another* guy?" Bill frowned again.

"I think so, yeah. Some guy in a brown leather jacket."

"When did this happen?" Bill's eyes flashed.

"Just now, just today, like one right after the other."

"Sounds like you had quite a morning."

"Yeah, well, my grandmother thought it might have something to do with my father. Something he was involved with before he died. You knew him back then. Does anything come to mind? And do you have any idea how I could get in touch with a guy named Lim?"

Bill's countenance fell. "What do you know about Wilfred Lim?"

"Nothing." Michael shrugged. "Nothing really. In fact, until about six hours ago I wasn't even sure he was a real person. Wilfred Lim, is that his name?"

Bill walked over to his desk and retrieved his tablet. "Have you seen this yet?" He scrolled to the home page of the *International*

*Business Tribune* and showed the headline to Michael – "Tech Pioneer in Coma, Company's Future in Doubt".

"I've been in a monastery." Michael scanned the first few paragraphs. "Is this the same guy – Lim – the one that my grandmother was talking about?"

"The very same."

"You'd better tell me what's going on." Michael's voice was firm.

"Alright." Bill inhaled audibly. "So, you've got this guy, Wilfred Lim. Thirty years ago, he starts this company with the help of your father, focusing on bio-informatics or some such. Using big data to study biology, mind mapping, that kind of thing. Eventually, the thing gets absorbed into a bigger outfit. They ultimately ended up merging with a firm out of Singapore called Daedalus. You may have heard of them, they've been in the news a lot lately. Anyway, your father worked with him back then. They were sort of business partners, I guess you'd say."

"Jesus, Bill, why didn't you ever tell me this before?"

"I'm sorry, Michael," Bill said slowly. "I honestly know very little about it. I hadn't heard from Lim for many years. And I promised your grandmother that I would insulate you from whatever might be lurking in your father's past. Your dad died so suddenly, and it was all very suspicious. I figured, leave well-enough alone. But your story about the agents, the timing of all this is really strange, especially in light of what happened to Lim."

Michael considered this. "So, what happened to him, exactly?"

"After your dad died and they sold the company, Lim basically went dark for a long time. Very low profile, he was really in the background on this until maybe two years ago. Then, he approached Sentinel about five or six months ago – right after you left for Driftless – asking me to help him set up a blind trust."

"Well, that's not suspicious at all," Michael sniped.

"Right." Bill raised his eyebrows. "Anyway, the police in Singapore, the FBI, and Daedalus are all singing from the same sheet of music with this story of a sudden stroke."

"But *you're* not buying it." Michael tossed the tablet back on the table.

"Well … it's possible." Bill sighed. "But something doesn't add up. Wilfred Lim is in a coma. I understand he has a living will, being administered by one of his former associates, a woman named Su-Ling Tan. Apparently, the advanced directive gives considerable autonomy to Madam Tan to make decisions about his ongoing care."

"In other words, they are trying to pull the plug and you think there may be foul play," said Michael. "So who's the beneficiary of the trust?"

Bill held Michael's eye. "I'll give you three guesses and the first two don't count."

Michael looked at Bill blankly, then his eyes widened. "No … really?"

"I thought at first that's why you were here."

"Me?" Michael sat back in his chair. "A blind trust? What's in it?"

"I'm not entirely sure. Lim was very cryptic about the whole thing. I gathered it included some sort of intellectual property, but I don't know exactly what it is."

"But it must be valuable." Michael moved to the edge of his seat. "What was he working on when he had the stroke?"

"Well, that's a good question." Bill leaned in closer. "I was able to get a copy of the police report, and it mentions something called the Icarus Project – a kind of business integration technology, whatever that means. The research and development team is based in Singapore."

Michael was dumbfounded. For most of his life, he had wondered about his family. The explanations of how he had come to be orphaned were never quite satisfying to him, and now it appeared that the one potential source from which he might learn the truth had expired, just as Michael was beginning to probe for answers.

"Have you told me everything?"

Bill's shoulders slumped. "Michael, I can tell you this. There is more to your story than what I know. You won't learn the truth here in Chicago, and certainly not up in Driftless. And now I'm afraid I've made a terrible mistake not telling you about Lim last year when he resurfaced. But you have to understand, I promised your grandmother that I would look after you."

"Look after me? How, by lying to me? By deceiving me?"

"I never lied to you." Bill put a hand on Michael's shoulder. "Tara feared there was something hidden in your father's past that could hurt you. And to be honest, I think she was right. This whole thing feels hinky to me. I don't like it at all that some agents were poking around your place. And this isn't the first time you've received negative attention from the government."

Bill shook his head. "I don't know, maybe I should have stuck up for you then. Maybe it could have saved you trouble now."

"You think that this Tyrant of Thebes has something to do with Lim?"

"I don't know." Bill shrugged. "I'm not sure what one could have to do with the other. But you've always had great instincts, great intuition – uncanny, really. How are you doing, by the way?"

"Oh ... yeah." Michael looked down. "I'm alright. Haven't had any hallucinations for a long time," he lied.

"Hallucinations?" said Bill. "I always thought of them more as premonitions. But anyway, I'm glad you are feeling better."

Michael took a deep breath. "Oh, I almost forgot – we pulled this off the recon drone at my grandmother's place." He retrieved his backpack from the leather club chair and opened the main compartment, producing the small orb-like camera. "What do you make of it?"

Bill took the multi-lensed camera in his hand and examined it. "Pretty sophisticated. I'm not familiar with this model. But I know someone who might be able to help."

"Great." Michael grabbed the camera and stuffed it back in his bag. "Let's go."

"Hold on." Bill put up his hand. "When was the last time you had something to eat?"

"Umm … I had an apple in Mineral Point."

"OK, take a load off." Bill's tone was firm as he gestured to the sofa. "I'm going to make a few calls. Rest here for a while." He left the room, closing the door softly behind him.

Michael hesitated, then exhaled and plopped down in the corner of the leather couch. "Just for a minute … I'll just rest my eyes …"

*

Michael awoke to the smell of pizza and wonton noodles. The food had been laid out on a small console table along the wall near the office door. The blinds had been drawn, and the darkness stayed only by an iridescent halo surrounding a small lamp illuminating the food. Bill was nowhere to be seen, but Michael sensed he was nearby.

He rubbed his eyes and took a quick inventory: bag, wallet, keys, camera. Everything seemed to be accounted for. He checked his watch – 8:30pm. He had slept for a little more than an hour and felt much better for it. Michael stood up, stretched his arms, and walked to the table where he helped himself to a slice of pepperoni pizza.

Bill knocked twice and entered. Frozen by the light streaming from the hallway, Michael presented Bill with a study in absurdity as he stood there hunched over, blinking and chewing in the half-darkness. Bill chuckled. "Oh good," he said buoyantly. "You're up. Lights!" The ceiling lamps sprung to life. "How do you feel?"

"Fresh as the morning rain." Michael stood up straight. "Thanks for the pizza."

"Don't mention it. I was able to get hold of Lewis Mitchell, one of my connections. I thought we'd get him to take a look at that camera. We can stop by his lab on the way to the hotel. We'll have to risk the traffic cameras."

"I've got that covered." Michael produced the infrared spectacles Selena had given him.

"What are those for, x-ray vision?"

"Infrared holography." Michael said.

"And you trust those things?" Bill cocked his head.

"They've gotten me this far … Oh, my bike!" Michael suddenly remembered that he had left his Sportster parked underground.

"Never mind," said Bill. "I'll have someone pick it up in the morning. Do you have the keys?"

# CHAPTER 7

# THE ONE YOU FEED

**Michael**

Michael handed Bill the keys to his Harley and followed him to his car in the basement garage. The black sedan was a fully electric autonomous vehicle, but Bill had installed a human-driver override patch. He was one of many who refused to abandon the freedom and enjoyment of driving his own vehicle.

They ascended the parking ramp and emerged onto the road. Only a handful of lamps were illuminated and the street was cloaked in shadow. The buzz of shuttle drones could be heard overhead, but surface traffic was light.

"Are you sure you know where you are going? I won't judge you for using the technology," Michael teased.

"No need." Bill sat straight and gripped the wheel. "I have the mind of a London cabbie. I know these streets like the back of my hand."

Even as Bill finished his sentence, Michael felt the hairs on his forearms stand on end. The car rounded a corner, and they were confronted by the piercing stab of flashing police lights. A fire engine had also arrived on the scene, and several men clad in emergency response gear were moving around with haste.

Michael's mind raced – *could this be for me?*

"Just relax." Bill drew a slow breath, heeding his own advice. "Looks like a fire alarm of some kind."

Bill twisted around to glance behind them, but another car had pulled up close, and they could no longer simply reverse back the way they had come. Traffic was directed forward, through a narrow point adjacent to the fire engine. As they waited their turn, Michael surveilled the surroundings, scanning the ever-shifting shadows for signs of danger.

The vehicle ahead of them advanced, and one of the firemen standing near the engine signaled for them to proceed. Michael guessed that he was in some position of authority – a fire lieutenant perhaps – as he could be seen directing the other first responders from time to time. He was an imposing figure, which pleased Michael somehow. Tall, strongly-built with mahogany skin and dark hair, the man was fully clothed in the trappings of his vocation. Despite himself, Michael kept a steady gaze upon the man as he approached.

Bill rolled down his window. "Good evening. What's all this about then?"

"There's been some trouble up the street." The lieutenant bent down and scanned the front and rear seats of the car. "A protest got out of hand and some property was damaged."

"Oh, jeeze." Bill shook his head. "I hope nobody was hurt."

"Not this time." The lieutenant shifted his gaze to Michael, but the fireman's dark eyes held no malice and he appeared ready to take his leave and wave them through. To Michael's surprise, the man continued speaking, unburdening himself of a thought that had clearly been on his mind.

"We were lucky this time. But it's getting worse." The lieutenant shook his head slowly, as if the full scope of the problem had yet to be realized. "It's like a full moon every damn night. This is the third time we've been called out this week for non-fire related incidents."

"Really?" Michael was intrigued. "Were they related?"

"Hard to say. The targets keep changing." The lieutenant paused, seeming to consider whether it was his place to speculate, and whether he might put himself at risk by doing so. "You know, ten, fifteen years ago, when we had all that trouble, the focus was always government institutions or police stations. This time around, technology companies seem to be the target of choice."

Michael raised an eyebrow. "Technology companies? Like, which ones?"

"Well, tonight it was the Daedalus building." He waved a hand toward the large office tower further up the road.

"Daedalus?" Michael looked at Bill and then back to the fireman. "I didn't know they had an office in Chicago."

"Neither did I – until somebody threw a brick through their window."

At that moment, the driver of the car behind them emerged, peering sheepishly from behind his half-opened car door.

"Please stay in your vehicle, sir." The lieutenant stood and held up his hand. "I'll be right with you." He turned back to Michael. "Have a nice evening." He signaled for them to proceed, bringing the conversation to an abrupt end.

*

Michael exhaled audibly.

"We're OK for now." Bill leaned forward and scanned from side to side through the windshield. "But I don't like the fact that we were stationary for so long. If anyone was looking for you, the cameras will have gotten a pretty clean image, even with your magic glasses."

They filed slowly through the narrow passage, buttressed by wooden barricades and strategically parked police vehicles. The flashing of red and white lights cast uncanny shadows across the buildings on either side. They were diverted on to a smaller street about half a block from the Daedalus building, which had been cleared of all protestors and was now guarded by about twenty police officers.

Michael could see even at a distance that the front window had indeed been smashed, and graffiti painted on the concrete edifice. There were no discernable words, just a crude symbol, which Michael had never seen before. At first glance, it looked like a hash tag or perhaps part of a tic-tac-toe grid, but it was not exactly like either of these. There were two simple crosses on either side of a circle ... or were they letters?

$$\top O \bot$$

"What do you make of that?" Michael pointed.

"X-O-X?" Bill frowned in doubt. "Hugs and kisses? That's cheeky."

Michael tilted his head. "Or maybe T-O-T?"

"T-O-T ..." Bill raised an eyebrow. He looked at Michael, as recognition was kindled in his eyes. Michael was the first to speak their mutual thought aloud.

"Tyrant of Thebes." The words tumbled from his mouth.

Bill followed the detour onto the smaller street and the Daedalus building slipped away from view. Michael began to speak, to question Bill on the cryptic symbol, but his attention was drawn by another event, which slowed their progress yet again.

On the left-hand side of the road were gathered perhaps thirty people, milling aimlessly around the entrance of a small hotel and boarding house. There was a second and smaller contingent of fireman circulating among the crowd. Apparently, in the chaos of the protest, someone had pulled the fire alarm, compelling its inhabitants to evacuate until the fire department could signal the all-clear. The occupants were in various stages of undress, some fully clothed, and others in nothing but bathrobes and boxer shorts.

Bill slowed the car as they passed, and Michael observed that many – perhaps most – of these people wore on their heads the ocular apparatus that was the hallmark of Empyrean, the ubiquitous virtual reality simulation that dominated the gaming world. The style and model of each device varied slightly from user to user, but they were all similar: lightweight rimless panes of glass which projected light down into the lenses, creating a three-dimensional holographic effect.

Many of the guests appeared still to be dwelling in an augmented reality, laid over the real world so that the user could remain engaged in their program while semi-consciously responding to the perceived emergency. Michael's mind reeled – *this must be a VR flophouse.*

*

When the barricades and flashing lights were at last behind them, Michael and Bill fled swiftly along the major thoroughfares, opting for speed over secrecy. Their progress was stymied only by the occasional traffic light, whose crimson glow appeared now somehow sinister and hostile, as if it might delay them to their ruin.

At one such intersection, they found themselves flanked by a tall twelve-story office building to their right, and a cathedral-style church on their left. A stained glass window dominated the center of the façade, with a copper crucifix set triumphantly atop the steeply slanted roof. Climbing still higher was the bell tower, to the right of the main hall. Deep-set Gothic doors and tall, narrow windows of stained glass girded the structure, clothing it in dramatic biblical imagery. The numerals carved into the stone foundation bore witness to the building's construction at the turn of the last century.

"Beautiful church," said Michael absently.

"It was – it's office condos, now."

Michael's shoulders slumped. "That's a shame. I wonder what the builders would have thought of that?"

"They'd think we got what we deserved." Bill paused, gazing into the distance. "I suppose the fools among them would be amazed by our technology and stunned by how the culture's changed. But some of them wouldn't be surprised. Nietzsche, for example – do you think any of this would have surprised him?" Bill gestured vaguely at the city outside their vehicle, which was again on the move. "Even back in the 1880s, even as they were carving the dedication stone into the front of that church, he was proclaiming the death of God."

"Well, you're a barrel of monkeys tonight."

Bill shrugged. "Well, I suppose we didn't kill God so much as dismember him. He's still there somewhere. Scattered now, distributed around the culture, popping up in odd places – mangled, unrecognizable." Bill leaned forward and gazed through the windshield and up into the night sky. "I can't remember how long it has been since I've seen stars. I bet you see all kinds of stars up in Driftless."

"Yes, it's one of the perks," said Michael, glad Bill was changing the subject. "It's one of the things I missed most when I lived here. It's humbling, peering into something so infinitely vast."

"Well, I don't know if it's infinite," said Bill, "but it's pretty damn big. Funny, with all of that space, all those stars, all those planets, all those billions of years of evolution, you'd think we would have had some contact with life from another world."

"Maybe we're not worth visiting." Michael raised an eyebrow.

"Maybe." Bill smiled. "Some people believe that whenever a species reaches the point where it can undertake interstellar communication, it would also have developed the capability to annihilate itself. And they end up blowing themselves up before they can make contact or meaningfully engage other planets. It's like there's this gauntlet that has to be run between having the capability to develop a technology and having the wisdom to moderate the use of that technology."

"That doesn't sound too optimistic," Michael said pensively.

Bill stared straight ahead, his gaze fixed in the middle distance. His voice was even, but tinged with sadness, as if he was making a forlorn appeal to one who refuse to heed an earnest warning. "We have all of this intellectual capacity – science, reason. And we have the ability to apply that reason to comprehend the world around us, and to understand ourselves. We have self-awareness, self-reflection, call it what you will. And we can use that awareness of ourselves to challenge our own values, our own ideals and axioms. But we don't have the discernment to temper those challenges with perspective, and we run the risk of self-destruction."

"You mean, like with a nuclear war, or something?" Michael leaned in closer.

Bill shook his head, turning to Michael once again. "No, I'm talking about something else, I'm talking about blowing up our sense of ourselves. Look around. From top to bottom, this place, this city, this country has lost all concept of its own identity, its own purpose. That is a cancer that will kill us dead, even if the bombs don't fall."

Michael sat back in his seat. Maybe Bill was right. Perhaps overreach is built into the human program. And the critical analysis which had liberated humans from superstition and prejudice, was now manifesting itself as an extreme skepticism directed against orthodoxy of any kind. And so freedom of thought had been destroyed by the extension of that very principle to the most fundamental ideals of society which, of course, included the basis for protecting the freedom of thought.

Society had excised the concept of God, and removed its collective purpose. Instead of finding fulfilment and balance through adherence to a divine or universal order, Michael's contemporaries made happiness itself the goal. But this was ultimately unsatisfying, and that was evidenced by the hollow lives of the Empyrean junkies and feckless automatons that increasingly populated the urban centres.

Now as Michael reflected on Bill's words, he feared humanity was facing a dramatic sequel to the trials of conscience from which it narrowly escaped only a century before. But would humanity pass the test this time around, with an arsenal of yet another hundred years of technological progress locked and loaded? Was there ever a tool or weapon that humanity invented, which it did not ultimately use? Would humans ever have the wisdom to fully understand the nature of Pandora's Box before deciding to open it?

Some, at least, were trying. Some small restive elements of the human psyche pierced through the layers of automation and control. And they had, apparently, chosen the Tyrant of Thebes as their talisman.

"How do you think it will all play out?" Michael broke a long silence. "This war between futility and purpose? They are both quite potent; they both make sense logically and can possess our individual and collective imaginations. Which, do you think, will ultimately prevail?"

"Hard to say." Bill sighed, and then his eyes were suddenly kindled. "But it reminds me of that old Cherokee story where the old man tells his grandson about the battle between the two wolves that live inside all of us. One wolf is evil and the other is good, and they are both equally strong and continually at war with each other. The grandson thinks about it for a minute and then asked his grandfather, which wolf wins? And the old Cherokee grandfather replies, *the one you choose to feed.*"

"Old Cherokee story?" Michael grinned. "I thought that was Reverend Billy Graham."

Bill returned the smile. "Well, wisdom is as you find it, I suppose."

*

It was 9:15pm. Rush hour traffic had abated, and the streets were quiet. "You know, I remember when this place would have been hopping at this hour," said Bill, breaking a restful silence. "On a Friday night, you would see people lined up around the block at some of these venues. Now, most folks simply have no interest in coming out to a real club or bar. Or they're all strung out in some virtual reality world. Sad, really."

Bill was right, of course. Among the administrative class, it had come to be known as the "jobs problem". The advent of ever improving artificial intelligence and adaptive robotics had made nearly fifty percent of the working age population completely obsolete. However, there was no consensus on how to distribute the agricultural and manufacturing surplus when such a large segment of the population had no active role in its generation.

Tensions had come to a head during a spate of bloody riots which erupted across the country and, indeed, the world. In the end, an uneasy equilibrium had been reached. A portion of the productive surplus was allocated to those who were unable to contribute to the economy in a meaningful way. That largess was disbursed as electronic tokens in a virtual marketplace, credits to be spent at the recipient's complete discretion.

Naturally, and to the consternation of all, the governmental benefaction could not replace the sense of worth imbued by an honest day's work. The new underclass – disparagingly referred to as "Loaders" – succumbed to a downward spiral of meaninglessness, depression, physical ailment, opiate addiction, and suicide.

The narcotics crisis had seemed to be intractable until, rather suddenly, the trend began to reverse. Interestingly, this improvement coincided with the proliferation of virtual reality technology which had become sufficiently engrossing as to provide the basis for emergent parallel worlds.

Within these alternate realities, participants could voluntarily contribute to the ongoing creation of entirely new societies and modes of being. Thus, a significant minority of the city's residents were preoccupied almost exclusively with their ongoing secondary lives. The result was a filtering of nearly a third of the population out of the traditional workforce, out of real-world society, and into Empyrean.

Within the Empyrean construct, approximately half of the participants were avatars of real-world human beings. The other half was part of the Empyrean program itself, non-player characters that were nearly indistinguishable from their human counterparts.

Empyrean could customize the user experience, gently manipulating the rules of the game to produce more palliative results. This took the edge off the competitive and selective environment, allowing people to dwell perpetually in the zone of proximal development, enabling them to thrive regardless of their innate competencies. These virtual experiences thus tailored to the individual, stimulating a steady stream of dopamine – an effective and more sustainable substitute for traditional narcotics.

It was widely rumored that sometime after this trend took hold, an enterprising technocrat had introduced a program to harness the collective productivity of the individuals populating these virtual realities to solve complex computational problems. But the specific proposals and further development of these ideas were not disclosed publicly, and the records had quickly been sealed. Most considered the notion an unsubstantiated conspiracy theory.

*

Bill's sedan sped furtively along, the electric motor barely audible as they slipped through the commercial district and into a noticeably more industrial part of town. Skyscrapers gave way to mid-rise office buildings, and finally two and three-story warehouse facilities. It was within the shell of one of these short, square, unremarkable structures that Lewis Mitchell had set up shop. The warehouse laboratory was flanked on either side by structures of similar make, separated by a black metal fence.

Bill approached the property from the main road, but access could also be gained by way of an alley at the rear of the building. Floodlights were mounted to the sides of the building at regular intervals where the roof met the walls, but only a third of these were illuminated. The entire setup was thoroughly uninviting.

"Lewis Mitchell, I think you've mentioned him before." Michael crossed his arms. "Who is he?"

"He was a former coder." Bill stared straight ahead. "A programmer – he worked for a few social media companies before doing a stretch with the National Security Agency. After twelve years as a cyber-spook, Lewis left the NSA and set up shop for himself."

"And you use him for data collection? An NSA guy, is that a good idea?"

"*Former* NSA guy." Bill turned to Michael. "Lewis is no fan of the Agency, believe me. In fact, he was eager to put as much distance between himself and those guys as possible. But given the highly integrated nature of our modern surveillance state, he realized the only practical alternative was to hide in plain sight. Now he makes a living providing independent surveillance and counterintelligence services to corporate clients and high net worth individuals. I utilize his services for the occasional fraud investigation." Bill rolled in through the open gate.

"No guard on duty?" Michael scanned the area.

"The compound is monitored by a contract security firm. There are cameras all around the perimeter." Bill parked the car parallel to the building and waited.

"Aren't we going in?" The words had barely escaped Michael's lips when the tortured screech of metal scraping against metal pierced the dense night air. The right-hand side of a metal barn-style door slid open. A soft pale light poured onto the pavement, framing a figure in silhouette. As the man approached, his features resolved, giving color and depth to the shadow which Michael assumed to be Lewis Mitchell. Bill rolled down the window and the man came near, hunching over and resting his crossed arms on the frame.

"Lewis." Bill raised his head slightly. "Thanks for making the time."

The man was not at all what Michael had expected. Far from the studious computer scientist in a white lab coat that Michael had envisioned, Lewis had the look of a college wrestler. He was a bit on the short side, but incredibly fit. Clad in trim jeans and a close-fitting t-shirt, his lean, broad physique made him an impressive figure despite his modest height. His close-cropped hair was a dirty blond, with touches of gray around the temples.

"Hello, Bill." Lewis cocked his head to get a better look at Michael. "This him?"

Bill nodded. "Yes, this is Michael. Michael Quinn."

Lewis raised an eyebrow and stared intently at Michael. "You got the thing?"

Bill held out his hand signaling for Michael to produce the drone camera. Michael hesitated before drawing the item from his backpack and handing it to Bill, who surrendered it to Lewis.

"Well, follow me." Lewis turned on his heel and strode back toward the forlorn metal building. He slipped through the gaping doorway, and disappeared into the reaches of his warehouse laboratory.

# CHAPTER 8
# DREAM OF BRAHMAN

**Simon**

Simon settled into the routine of thrice-weekly visits to Wilfred's lab. The duration of the sessions and nature of the evaluations varied, but his appointments were frequently scheduled immediately before or after those of Mrs. Simpson, the blind woman who had passed by him in the hallway early on.

"Is Mrs. Simpson part of the study as well?" Simon asked Wilfred at the outset of one of his sessions.

"Huh? Oh yes," Wilfred replied. "She was one of our first subjects."

"Did she have a brain injury like mine?"

"Her? Oh no," said Wilfred. "She's perfectly healthy. The only remarkable thing about Mrs. Simpson is that she has been blind from birth. No, the reason we are studying her is to explore how the mind interprets the world around us through an extended field of sensory apparatus. In her case, the cane."

Simon nodded in confusion.

"Here – hold out your right hand," said Wilfred.

Simon obliged him.

"Now, close your eyes."

Again, Simon complied.

Wilfred prodded various points on Simon's hand with his forefinger. "Do you feel that?"

"Yes."

"What do you feel?"

"It feels like you're poking me with your finger." Simon shrugged.

"Okay, fine. Now tell me what you *feel* – be specific."

Wilfred poked him again, and this time Simon concentrated on the sensation.

"Pressure. The stretching of skin. The sliding of sinew across bone. The compression of blood vessels."

"Good," said Wilfred. "Now, stand up, please." Wilfred stepped out from behind his desk. He withdrew a handkerchief from his lab coat pocket and blindfolded Simon. Then Wilfred pressed a collapsible walking cane into Simon's hand, and led him out into the hallway. "Now, walk." He took Simon by the shoulders and aimed him down the corridor. "Be careful."

Simon progressed slowly, clumsily sweeping the cane from side to side as he had seen done in movies and television. Unaccustomed to navigating without the benefit of sight, he veered to one side. The tip of his cane found its way to the wall and connected with a closed door, then slid forward catching on the corner of the door frame. Simon stopped suddenly, surprised by the shockwave that registered in his hand and forearm.

Wilfred took Simon's arm and steadied him. "Now tell me, what did you feel?"

Simon turned toward Wilfred, the blindfold still on. "It felt like I hit the wall, maybe a doorway?"

Wilfred smiled. "Yes. But of course, you weren't really feeling the wall, were you? The sensations in your hand were not very much different from those you experienced when I poked you with my finger back in my office. What changed?"

Simon removed his blindfold. "I see where you're going with this."

"Oh yeah? Well then, impress me."

"Well," said Simon, "when I probed the wall with the cane, I was actually aware of two different things at the same time. I could feel the pressure and tension of the cane in my hand. And at the same time, I felt beyond those sensations – or maybe through them – to *see* the wall and the floor."

"Very good," said Wilfred. "What's happening is that you're essentially living or dwelling in the sensory experience of the feeling of the cane in your hand. But, that awareness bears on another external focus. In other words, as you *see* through that sensory experience, the sensation is integrated, and given a coherence and meaning as it bears on a focal target – in this case, the cane hitting the wall. In fact, you no longer even noticed *or felt* the sensation of the cane pressing into your fingers and palm. Instead, you *felt* the point of the cane as it hit the wall or door.

"You relied on the cane as a tool. But your awareness no longer regarded it as an external object. It became a part of your body. You infused consciousness into it and assimilated it as a part of your *self*."

Simon nodded. "So, you're saying that there are two elements to knowing or understanding something? The subsidiary experience, like the feeling of the cane in my hand, and the focus or target of that sensory knowledge, which is the meaning of the information registered by the body."

"Yes," said Wilfred, "but you are forgetting perhaps the most essential element of this equation, *you* – the knower, the observer. It is the knower who causes that subsidiary form of knowledge to bear on the focus with his or her attention."

"Yeah, I guess I take my own consciousness for granted."

Wilfred held Simon's gaze. "Consciousness, awareness, attention, whatever you want to call it, is extraordinarily powerful. The knower can, by the act of wielding his consciousness, integrate a set of information which has one level of meaning, and by focusing that attention, they can discover – or create – an entirely new level of meaning. And by that token, they can destroy that meaning by directing attention away from the focus and fixing it instead upon the subsidiaries."

Simon pulled his eyebrows together. "So, if consciousness is living in that subsidiary awareness, and focused on a greater meaning implied by the integration of those subsidiaries, how is it that same consciousness can actively move its focus between the two? I mean, at the end of the day, where does that consciousness reside?"

Wilfred nodded. "Now you are beginning to grasp the complexity of the task to which we have set ourselves when we seek to manufacture consciousness. And we haven't even begun to discuss the subsidiary awareness present within the very mechanics of our own bodies. There is a similar subsidiary awareness present in the muscles controlling the iris, and the nerves attached to the retina of the eye as we focus our gaze on an external object. And who knows how far down this phenomenon goes; neural, sub-neural?

"The truth is," Wilfred continued, "we know frighteningly little about the nature of consciousness. We're like monkeys playing with nuclear weapons – trifling with one of the elemental forces of the universe." He smiled. "But since we seem bound and determined to try to touch the face of God, I figure I might as well take a cue from Dr. Strangelove and learn to love the risk."

"Ride the missile all the way in, like Slim Pickens?" Simon smiled.

"Come on, let's get back to work." Wilfred retrieved the cane and blindfold from Simon and they returned to Wilfred's office. He left Simon alone temporarily, retreating to the hallway to fetch them both some coffee. In his absence, Simon began casually sketching in his notebook, scribing several of the Chinese characters he had recently learned.

"Ah, Chinese." Wilfred set a large mug on the desk before Simon. "Has Lauren been teaching you?"

"Mostly teaching myself these days."

Wilfred pointed to a character on the page: 意

"*Yi*," he said aloud. "That's a very meaningful character, no pun intended. It literally means 'meaning'."

"I know. I like the way it looks." Simon placed his pen and notepad back on the desk. "Funny, when I started learning to write these characters, it was so mechanical. I would have to focus on drawing every line and curve. Now I just see the characters in full, and the meaning they represent."

Wilfred nodded. "It was the same with me when I first learned English. You see, the thing with language is that it kind of works the same way as the cane; except that instead of a subsidiary physical awareness bearing on a physical focal meaning, language works conceptually … intellectually.

"When I first confronted the English alphabet," Wilfred explained, "I had an entirely different relationship to the letters and words. It was all completely novel and foreign to me. All I saw were the odd shapes and lines that made up the various letters. But after some months of study, I no longer saw the lines, I only saw letters. And later, instead of seeing letters, I recognized the words as complete and whole entities. Here, take a look at this."

Wilfred tore a leaf from his journal and scribed several lines on the center of the empty page before handing it back to Simon. "Read that."

IIt denos't mttaer in waht oredr the ltteers in
a wrod are wertitn, the olny iprmoetnt tihng is taht
the frist and lsat ltteer be at the rghit pclae. The rset can be
a toatl mses and you can sitll raed it wouthit pborelm.
Tihs is bcuseae the huamn mnid deos not raed
ervey lteter by istlef, but the wrod as a wlohe.

Simon read the scrambled sentence aloud with ease, demonstrating
the very message of the jumbled text.

"Interesting." Simon grinned. "I wonder if that would work at
the next level. Can we see entire sentences as a whole?"

"In theory," said Wilfred, "though the lexicon of possible
sentences is so large that it would be difficult for your mind to
keep them all in active memory such that they could be recalled
at a glance. But we do see this dynamic at work when we speak."

Simon's eyes narrowed as he considered this.

"Think about it." Wilfred's eyes kindled. "When you begin to
speak, you normally haven't thought through all the words that
you will use in your sentence. You start with a general thought
in mind and proceed with the confidence that as you go along,
the right words will present themselves and be spoken in the
proper order. You have confidence in this because you have been
speaking for so long and are so fluent and familiar with the words
and grammatical rules that they are almost a part of you. They
are integrated in a kind of subsidiary fashion – much like the
experience of feeling the pressure of the walking cane in your hand
was integrated. The meaning of the words bears on the meaning
of the sentence in the same way that the meaning of the sensation
of the cane in your hand bears on the meaning of the cane hitting
against the wall.

"Likewise, when we focus our attention on the words, we lose sight of the individual letters. And when we focus on the meaning of the sentence, we in fact see through and look beyond the individual words. We live within and integrate the meaning of the words so that we can focus on the greater meaning the sentence is attempting to convey."

Simon leaned forward. "So, what is the upper limit to that? I guess you could go from the meaning of a sentence, to concepts, to theories …"

"To axioms and *a priori* assumptions." Wilfred completed Simon's thought. "Indeed, we have many questions to answer. But bear in mind that the framework has a definite directionality to it – a hierarchy. The sounds and letters of our verbal language are limited by our ability to vocalize.

"By the same token, the letters limit the range of words that can be scribed, and the lexicon of words limits the universe of sentences that can be constructed. However, it would be ridiculous to say that we can know what sentence to write simply because we are familiar with the many words at our disposal. And it would be equally silly to think that because we know the twenty-six letters of the alphabet, we therefore know which word to select. Each level of the hierarchy directs the lower level and is, at the same time, constrained by it.

"So, our task here at the lab is to understand and recreate a system emulating a mind in which consciousness can be given play to create and recognize the meaning in the events and information it observes and experiences."

"And you're going to build that into a computer model?" Simon raised an eyebrow.

"Yes." Wilfred smiled. "With your help."

Simon nodded, then grabbed his coffee mug and took a big swig.

\*

Simon slipped around the side of the house through the wooden gate to the back patio and leaned his surfboard against the tall cedar fence. The house had a small plunge pool near the patio, along with a simple shower. As he rinsed the sand and saltwater from his body, Simon heard a whistle from the direction of the house.

"*Hola, chico.* Lookin' good!" Lauren closed the sliding glass door behind her. She was dressed in stretch pants and a running top, a yoga mat slung over her shoulder.

"Hey there," he said in return. "Yoga time?"

Lauren nodded. "Wanna join me?" She unfurled the mat with one fluid gesture.

"Nah, I'm wiped."

"It might help, maybe relax your mind a bit."

Simon pulled on a pair of cargo shorts and draped his wet suit over a patio chair before coming to stand in front of Lauren.

"Here, put your hands together like this." Lauren placed the palms of her hands together in the center of her chest. "That's prayer posture. Now we bow gently. That gesture means *Namaste* or 'I bow to you'. It is my soul acknowledging your soul."

"I like that." Simon practiced the gesture. "*Namaste.*"

"The idea is that there is a spark of the divine that exists in each of us – here." She pointed to the center of his chest. "In the heart *chakra.*"

"That's great, honey. But I think I'll take a nap, exercise my sleep *chakra.*"

"Here, sit down opposite me," she insisted. Simon relented and they sat cross-legged on either end of her mat, facing each other. "Now, follow my breath. Inhale for four counts, hold for four counts, and then exhale for four counts. Now repeat that."

He followed her breathing for several moments. "That is a very simple *pranayama*," she said. "It's a way to control the breath, the *prana*, the life force. The entire yogic practice was designed by Hindu ascetics to facilitate meditation; conditioning the body to condition the mind. In fact, the word *yoga* itself means union, the union of our individual consciousness with the divine consciousness."

"Reminds me of my mother." Simon smiled. "She was kind of a late blooming hippy, always meditating, trying to clear her mind. She used to say it takes tremendous concentration to focus on nothing."

"Then focus on your breath," said Lauren. "Concentrate on the cycles, it will connect you to something deeper; cycles of the breath ... cycles of the days ... cycles of the seasons ..." Lauren's words trailed off and Simon did as she asked, breathing rhythmically, counting silently.

Then something beyond his reckoning was triggered in Simon's mind. He became hyperconscious of his breathing. He felt his blood flowing in the veins near his ears, the breeze on his skin, the muscles contracting, raising the hairs on his arms. Thoughts emerged unbidden, but he did not fight them. Instead, he let them float across his field of awareness and drift out of view. He focused on his breath; the cycles of breath, of nature, of the cosmos, of creation and destruction, and another thought emerged.

*The Dream of Brahman* ... he must have read that somewhere. All of existence is the dream of Brahman, and each Brahman day a billion years. One hundred Brahman years, and the Hindu god dissolves into a dreamless sleep and the universe dissolves with him. Another Brahman century and the god, along with the universe he dreams, are reconstituted.

And after that cosmic rebirth, what types of phenomenon would exist? What new laws? What new particles and forces? How many dreaming Brahmans might there be? The arbitrariness unseated Simon, breaking his concentration.

*Focus on your breath*, he admonished himself. Cycles of breath, cycles of energy, cycles of thought.

Now he himself was Brahman, dreaming the laws of the universe, ordering it with a thought. A choice was made, arbitrary but purposeful; rippling through, setting the rules, affecting the arrangement of the next order down in the hierarchy. Every situation the result of a similar ordering by the superior level of an ontological great chain of being; constrained but not directed by the elements of the next level down. And meaning itself to be found, woven among the innumerable levels in an infinite cascade – threaded diamonds to be mined at every level.

His torch-wielding consciousness dwelled now within its own self-generated context. By some mechanism it directed that spotlight, illuminating the awareness within his cluster of moments, giving rise to a specific local consciousness; engendering a sense of self – an understanding of difference, of time. Change he observed, as the cosmic flashlight shifted to a new vantage, indwelling innumerable predicate conditions. And new relationships were thereby illuminated and imagined.

The circumstances, the characteristics, the context which informed his awareness within an infinite variety of moments was fixed; but his awareness itself was not. He was bound within a world of his own making. But boundless potentiality, like so much dark matter, intimated ever further regions to discover. And he explored endlessly the realm of his unconscious design.

His mind accelerated around the coil: the dynamic of his integrated subordinate awareness bearing upon a subject repeating in infinite regression, the source of his own consciousness ultimately ineffable. And on the cusp, the realization, not superficial but thorough and deep; the light comes from within as much as it does from without and permeates every moment, and every*thing*.

There was little satisfaction in that epiphany, for if the profusion of moments is truly infinite, and if the receding levels of consciousness infinite as well, then there would be nothing to limit where the flashlight is pointed. There would be no border, no wall against which it would eventually bump and stop. Consciousness, nay he himself was a disembodied lighthouse roaming along the surface of an infinite ocean, searching for the source of its own reflection.

Simon was no longer meditating, his mind no longer still. His subconscious had initiated an enigmatic loop with no logical termination point. In wakeful awareness, his mind would simply have truncated the script, but somehow Simon had passed into a self-referential subroutine which would continue until its resources were exhausted.

*

Lauren rolled to her side and pushed herself up to a seated position. Slowly she opened her eyes and looked about her. Simon's legs were folded in a half lotus, but he was lying on his back and his arms were at his side. It was an awkward position and Lauren thought to correct his posture.

She rose and walked over to where Simon lay, careful not to disturb him in case he was still meditating. He had the semblance of one resting in a deep sleep, but then Lauren noticed the small trickle of blood flowing from his nose. She dropped to her knees and took his head in her hands, tapping him gently on the cheek and calling his name. He was barely conscious and non-responsive. Lauren reached for her phone and dialed 9-1-1, as she continued to try and rouse Simon.

# CHAPTER 9
# ABSTRACTION PENALTY

**Michael**

Michael and Bill followed Lewis through the sliding metal door into a darkened hallway. An imposing brick wall loomed immediately before them, with a narrow passage extending out in either direction. Lewis led them to the right, down the corridor until they reached a stairway extending up to the second floor. A solid windowless metal door separated the aisle from the main production space. Lewis leaned against the barrier, thrusting it open, eliciting a broad shaft of light from within. Bill and Michael followed their host deeper into the core of the building.

The rugged industrial exterior of the building belied the meticulously clean and orderly workspace within. A catwalk mezzanine fifteen feet wide ran around the entire perimeter where numerous desks and workspaces were situated. The walls and ceiling were painted a glossy white, and the floor had been treated with bright silver epoxy coating. The entire space was lit aggressively from above.

A substantial portion of the back end of the building was sealed off, dedicated to the electrical substation necessary to receive the high-density power cables and fiber optics connecting the site to the grid. And much of the mezzanine level was dedicated to the server farm, which stored the data necessary to facilitate the various surveillance and analysis routines Lewis carried out for his clients.

In the foreground, on the lower level were several workstations with standard flat panel interfaces. Most of these had large monitor displays, and several had full virtual reality setups, with goggles, audio inserts, and electrode skullcaps for the amplification and transmission of brainwave inputs. Off to the side were several robotic arms and humanoid robot avatars, which appeared to be connected to the workstations via heavy cables. A few smaller scale drone aircrafts sat on two large wooden tables under the mezzanine catwalk, along the left-hand side of the building. Michael marveled at the menagerie of hyper-connectivity as he and Bill followed Lewis to a workstation slightly to the right of the drones.

"Do you really think you'll be able to find out where this camera came from?" Michael followed Lewis closely, still taking in the full extent of the elaborate setup.

"I don't think this is really a camera." Lewis turned abruptly toward Michael. "I mean, it is a camera, yes. But there is more to it. Here, take a look."

Lewis held the small orb in his right hand and pointed out its features with his left. "You can see here all the optics arrayed around the sphere. There are normal visible-light spectrum cameras, as well as infrared cameras. And here, you can see the wireless sensors.

"Now," he continued, "that's fairly standard. But you see here, this is a proximity sensor of some kind. I'm not sure what it is detecting, but that is a bit unusual."

Lewis sat at a terminal and placed the camera on the table. Instantly, the orb began to vibrate, as if to announce its presence to the other devices nearby. He pulled a glove onto his right hand and, with a subtle flick of his wrist, a large curvilinear monitor nearly four feet across transformed from a transparent pane of glass into an opaque and full color panoramic display. The monitor filled spontaneously with lines of code, which began scrolling rapidly from the top of the screen.

Bill and Michael stood in silence, sharing occasional glances as Lewis plowed through the inscrutable code.

"Well, that's interesting." Lewis turned back toward his visitors. "Normally the access program is embedded on the hardware and the data is contained on a flash memory drive of some sort. But in this case, the whole thing is organic."

"*Organic?*" Michael pulled his eyebrows together. "Why would somebody want to use an organic memory system?"

"Density," said Lewis. "Normally you wouldn't need ultra-dense memory storage for a camera. That's more of a deep storage application."

Lewis scrolled down the wall of data with a gesture of his gloved hand. "Now you see here, this is the outer layer. It's a binary-based system and appears to be a kind of translator code – quite sophisticated. It's composed of a matrix of chlorine atoms on a copper substrate. I would guess that this system can store about five hundred terabits per square inch."

"That sounds like a lot," said Bill.

Lewis nodded. "Put it this way, with a device like this, you could store every book ever written on something the size of a postage stamp. But organizing data at this level, you would need some pricey equipment. It would take something like a quantum tunneling microscope to accomplish this."

Bill frowned. "I don't imagine there are too many facilities in the world that could do this."

"You can find them around," said Lewis. "I used one when I was at Cal-Tech way back in the day. But again, this chlorine-atom memory is just the wrapper. From what I can tell, it basically allows more normal computational environments to engage and access that deeper code."

"So, what's on the inside?" Michael was fascinated.

"DNA," Lewis's eyes narrowed as Michael's widened.

"DNA? You mean *DNA*, DNA? Like the stuff that contains our genes?"

"That's right."

"Why would someone store data in DNA?"

"Longevity," said Lewis, "and density. Like I said before, there's too much data in the world. What are we up to now, about a hundred trillion gigabytes? We don't have enough silicon on the planet to store all that data. Much of our archived data had originally been stored on magnetic tapes, but those decay quickly. With DNA, we could fit the entirety of the world's information into a relatively small area. And the data retention period would be hundreds or even thousands of years. It's incredibly stable."

Lewis flicked the tips of his fingers and scrolled down through a few screens of data. "Here is the most interesting part." He pointed to some inscrutable bit of code. "From what I can tell, the files contained in the DNA substrate are a kind of ultra-high-level programming language – a kind of computer language that allows the user to interact with a system at a higher, more intuitive level."

Michael shot a glance at Bill. *Good, he's confused as well.*

"So, for example," Lewis continued. "At the basic level, you have the micro-code used internally in the processors. Then machine code, that's usually binary code composed of ones and zeros. Then there is an assembly language and at the top, the high-level programming language.

"The idea is that once the lower level routines are in place, the programmer can use the high-level language to interact with the computer system more intuitively. It allows the programmer to be detached from the machine. So, the high-level language amplifies the programmer's instructions, triggers all the lower level programming subroutines, which causes all the operations and data movements to take place in the background automatically.

"The trade-off is efficiency. *We call it the abstraction penalty*," said Lewis. "Because the high-level language is more generic and removed from the very specific details of the lower-level languages, sometimes far more lower-level operations are executed than would be necessary or optimal."

"And you think this DNA memory … thing, contains one of these high-level programming languages?" Bill asked, still trying to take it in.

"I'm not sure." Lewis shook his head. "It appears to be an operating system of some kind. But it's not compatible with any I'm familiar with. My guess is that this is bespoke.

"It's strange – some of this coding looks a bit like early generation Empyrean implant protocols. In fact, it kind of reminds me of an experimental language I used back when …" Lewis pursed his lips. "Anyway, it isn't something you normally see."

"Empyrean implants?" Michael raised an eyebrow.

"That's the generic term we use for direct stimulation of the nervous system," said Lewis. "They can be physically implanted in the brain or spinal column. Or they can be external. Here, I can show you an example if you want."

Lewis walked back toward the center of the large workspace, to an area that was conspicuously vacant. He retrieved from a nearby table a rectangular control pendant, reminiscent of the controller for a radio-controlled toy car.

"Here put these on." Lewis handed Michael a pair of thin glass spectacles. Two small ear buds dangled from the sides of the frame at the temples. He inserted these instinctively.

"Now you know how ordinary VR glasses work," said Lewis. "The computer generates the images and light waves refract down along the glass, projecting an image that occupies most or all of your visual field." Lewis pressed several buttons on the pendant and adjusted one of the joystick levers.

The glasses flashed, and the empty space surrounding Michael was suddenly populated with furniture. Chairs, sofas, potted plants – it resembled a comfortable living room setting. Michael could still see Lewis as well as the tables and technical equipment beyond the perimeter of the space.

"This is what we call augmented reality," Lewis explained. "It overlays images onto the real world around you. It's a kind of hybrid between the real and virtual world."

Lewis changed the settings on the control pendant and the living room setting dissolved, instantly replaced by a soaring city view. "This, on the other hand, is VR, albeit a rudimentary, dumbed-down version."

Lewis adjusted the settings once again. Now, the visual projection of his glasses made it appear to Michael as though he was standing atop a desert ridge overlooking the Grand Canyon. He turned his head slowly left and right, then rotated his body a complete three hundred and sixty degrees. As he turned, the landscape opened to new vistas as the desert stretched out into the distance. The sound of wind blowing through the scattered bushes and trees filled his ears and the cry of a hawk circling overhead drew his gaze to a virtual sky. Michael beheld wispy clouds obscuring the sun, which stung his eyes in sufficient measure as to make him wince. He drew his gaze around, back to his original position facing the yawning chasm of the canyon below.

"I've used something like this before," said Michael.

"This is pretty basic technology." Lewis shrugged. "These days a lot of people opt for ocular implants, which eliminate the need for glasses altogether. The quality is good, but it's only visual I'm afraid."

Michael looked out in front of him and then down to the precarious drop at his feet. Several loose stones sat perched at the edge of the cliff, and out of curiosity Michael kicked them. To his delight, they tumbled over the precipice with a satisfying scraping sound, before disappearing into the void.

"Now, do something for me," Lewis made some fine adjustments on the pendant joystick. "Step forward."

Michael smiled as he knew what to expect – the computer would simulate his fall to the canyon floor. He stepped forward boldly, and the image immediately swung around him as his virtual self tumbled head-over-heels down the face of the canyon wall. Disoriented, Michael raised his hands instinctively. But the bottom of the canyon was quite distant, allowing time for his mind to separate the visual experience from that of his other senses. The qualities of his fall became abstract until at last, the swirls of brown turf and blue sky, terminated with an abrupt shudder. The glasses faded to black before becoming transparent again.

"How was that?" Lewis asked.

"It was great. But the illusion was broken at the end," Michael admitted.

"Exactly," Lewis agreed. "Your vision and hearing were engaged, but the other senses were not. So, the question becomes how do we incorporate the sense of touch and smell and even taste into the experience?"

"Is it even possible to do that?" Michael asked.

"Yes, it's possible." Lewis drew a deep breath and glanced at Bill. "It's possible to input electrical signals directly into the nervous system and generate sensations, even specific and detailed sensations. In fact, I was involved in a pilot program working on this type of thing years ago. But there were a few high profile … incidents, and ultimately the project was shelved. Or, rather, it was restricted. But the technology exists now, I'm afraid. It isn't strictly legal, but it is being allowed to progress. And it appears to be leaking out. I see it on the street. I see it in these poor bastards who can no longer enjoy the un-enhanced real world because they find it too dull, too ordinary, too confining. Do yourself a favor and stay away from that kind of thing."

"Is it really so dangerous?" Michael was incredulous.

"In my experience, yes!" said Lewis. "There may be some people who can use it responsibly – take it or leave it, so to speak. But I have yet to hear of a casual methamphetamine user, and direct input into the central nervous system is just as addictive. Look, Empyrean can be a fun distraction. Virtual reality can be useful. But don't mainline – you'll lose your soul."

Michael pictured the Empyrean flophouse they had passed earlier and the many hapless individuals who were so engrossed in their simulated realities that they could no longer wrest their attention away, even to potentially save their own lives. And then he recalled the graffiti image that was tagged onto the Daedalus building nearby.

"Lewis." Michael asked, "Is it possible for someone – a Mindcaster, for example – to gain access to these Empyrean simulations from the outside? To manipulate them or influence the participants somehow?"

"Sure." Lewis cocked his head. "Any system can be hacked. Why do you ask?"

"We saw something on the way over here, a logo or symbol tagged onto the Daedalus building. And it looked like it might be referring to a Mindcaster known as Tyrant of Thebes. Have you ever heard of him?"

"The Tyrant of Thebes." Lewis peered through Michael, as if observing something in the far distance, and his eyes smoldered. "Now that *is* an interesting phenomenon."

"So you *have* heard of him?" Bill appeared surprised. "He seems to have gained the attention of both the authorities and protesters alike. Who is he?"

Lewis chuckled softly. "He's nobody. If you want my opinion, it's a phantom, a ghost in the machine. It's a pseudo-personality emerging spontaneously from fragments of code and disparate layers of artificial intelligence randomly coalescing in cyberspace."

Bill seemed incredulous. "But then why would the FBI and the Resistance both be so interested in him, or it?"

"I have to admit, the fact that the Resistance has taken the Tyrant of Thebes on as a symbol was news to me." Lewis rubbed his chin. "Must be a recent development. But my guess is that both sides are just grasping on to a viral phenomenon, and projecting their own meaning onto it, like a virtual Rorschach test. They see what they want to see in the image, and it's quickly becoming a feature of the intellectual Dark Web – a pirate of the Internet proffering outlawed ideas."

"Well, at any rate, it has caused some real-world trouble for us." Michael crossed his arms.

"Yes." Lewis drew himself up. "And let it be a reminder to keep a clear head about the difference between the virtual world and the real. I repeat my warning, do not mainline! If you want a more robust experience, you can use something like this." Lewis walked back toward the table at the periphery of the space.

"This can be worn externally." He handed Michael what appeared to be a cross between a hair net and a small hat. "Here, let me show you."

Lewis fitted the fine metal mesh over Michael's head. Numerous wireless electrodes were spread uniformly across the membrane, each with a small millimeter-long spike at the bottom. After fitting the device on Michael's head, Lewis pressed firmly in several locations, pushing the spikes slightly into his scalp.

"Ow!" Michael winced.

"Don't be a baby." Lewis patted the top of Michael's head. "There, done."

"Now, the experience with the electrode array is not as intense as mainlining, but my software is much better.

"What I've done is fine-tune the electrical impulses. The sensation is not as intense, but the qualia are much more subtle and realistic. The trick is not to be too precise or overbearing in the construction. You can't define the experience completely or it will fall flat. You have to leave room for the subject's mind to co-create the experience."

Lewis called up a test program on the control pendant and Michael found himself standing at the counter of an old-fashioned diner. He could hear the clatter of plates and cutlery; cooks and waitresses and patrons talking and moving around. And then slowly, he became aware that he could smell the food. It was faint at first, but eventually he made out the distinct aroma of coffee and eggs and … burning rubber?

"That's amazing," said Michael, "but what is that burning smell?"

"Oh, that's supposed to be the smell of bacon frying," said

Lewis. "I'm still working on that one. I'm really hoping I can get that nailed down soon. It's kind of my Moby Dick."

Suddenly, the diner vanished and the glasses went dark. The small camera-orb sitting on the table began to vibrate. Bill noticed it and stood up. Michael felt a wave of nausea pass over him, as the blackness was immediately replaced by a new virtual landscape. Michael found himself perched on the edge of another cliff, and with a mixture of delight and dread, he realized this place was familiar to him. It appeared to be evening and below, in place of the diner floor, Michael beheld the tumult of a roiling ocean. He cast his gaze left and right. Yes, it was the same. The lighthouse, the road, and hillside. This virtual reality matched the vision from his night of reflection in Driftless – it was only yesterday, but seemed like weeks ago.

"Hold on, something's not right." Lewis keyed several command prompts into the pendant, and then walked to the monitor at the periphery of the circle. He could see the cliff and ocean vista that Michael was experiencing projected in two dimensions on the screen, but this was not one of his programs.

Then, even as Michael questioned the meaning of the vision, the landscape shifted again. The surroundings dissolved around him, replaced not by another setting but rather by a great cacophony of sound. It was as though the images had become the voices of some grand opera, surrendering their shapes and forms into an elaborate orchestration – a *Glimmering* of the fabric of an artificial world.

The experience was chaotic, but Michael began to believe that some sense could be made of the manner by which the thoughts pervading this pseudo-reality might become tangible things once more. As this feeling grew within him, the composition of melodic data reconstituted itself as a recognizable form. Now it manifested as the entrance to a tunnel, an underground chamber of as yet undeterminable dimension. Michael moved toward it, taking several steps in the real world. He reached the mouth of the tunnel and peered in, straining to see as far as possible. The passage receded into darkness, seeming to twist in a spiral. Stalactites and stalagmites protruded from the ceiling, floor and walls at regular intervals. Michael grew dizzy and closed his eyes, but the image remained, burned into his mind like a memory he could not forget.

"I don't recognize this program." Lewis shook his head. "It doesn't seem to be coming from my computer." He rushed to the metal cart housing a sequencer, which processed the electrical signals through the electrodes in Michael's skullcap. "It seems like the signal is coming from you. But that doesn't make any sense."

Suddenly, the images and sensations ceased, and the glasses once again became transparent. The monitors flickered and flashed white, then displayed what appeared to be the camera feeds from the building's exterior. Then all the monitors in the facility flashed and displayed the same images from the cameras outside.

"What the hell?" Lewis strode back to the desk supporting his primary computer. Through the monitors, they observed a black SUV enter the parking lot through the front gate. The vehicle came to a halt behind Bill's car, blocking it in. A second black sedan parked behind the metal gate at the rear of the facility.

Bill shot Michael a look. "They must have tracked us from the Sentinel building. Lewis, is there another way out of here?"

Two men exited the vehicles. With a growing dread, Michael recognized them as the agents from Tara's farm. Jones was approaching the front, and Juarez took up a post at the rear to prevent their escape. Juarez had drawn what appeared to be a pistol from within his coat. Another man emerged from the SUV at the front of the building.

"Yeah, there's a side entrance. Here ..." Lewis tossed the camera-orb to Michael. "Get this thing out of here."

He led them back toward the front of the building, and then over to a small side door beneath the mezzanine. "Wait here and count to twenty. I'll distract him and the two of you beat it on foot."

"We're in the middle of nowhere," Bill protested.

"Go two blocks north." Lewis pointed. "Then turn left. Three blocks down from there is a bus stop. I'll have a car pick you up. Now go, through here."

As Lewis left them, Michael heard a fist pounding on the exterior metal door reverberate through the building. He counted silently until the allotted time had elapsed. Then, Michael and Bill crept through the side door, then made their way along the outside wall of the building toward the front gate. Michael led the way, slowing as he approached the parking lot. With his heart in his throat, he inched forward holding his breath as he peered around the corner of the building.

A third agent had emerged from the SUV and positioned himself beside the two vehicles as a lookout. His sidearm was drawn and his right hand clasped the wrist of his gun hand in a relaxed and ready posture. His eyes were drawn to a squint as he slowly pivoted his head from left to right, scanning the area.

Michael took a small step backward and signaling to Bill what he had seen, when a gunshot rang out from within the building. The nameless agent guarding the main entrance responded, rushing to the door and into the building. Michael used the opportunity to bolt for the gate.

As he and Bill rushed for the exit, Juarez spied them from the rear of the building. "Stop!"

"Go!" Bill shouted. Michael's body lurched forward reflexively.

He felt the blood in his ears and was vaguely aware of the sound of his own breath as they rounded the corner onto the sidewalk. He turned to the right and sprinted down the street. Michael could sense that Bill was still behind him, and he scanned right and left, trying to remember which way to go.

Two blocks further down the road, Michael crossed the first major intersection. He glanced behind to make sure that Bill had kept up as a black sedan peeled out of an alleyway and came to a screeching halt between Bill and Michael.

A man emerged from the driver's side of the car, which opened toward Bill's side of the street. *Jones.* The driver leveled his pistol at Bill. Then, coming around toward the front of the vehicle, he stood facing the front of the car, training his weapon on Bill and Michael in turn.

Jones appeared hesitant. *He has us dead to rites, why hasn't he fired? Maybe we're to be subdued, not harmed.* Their assailant drew from his jacket pocket a small black Taser gun. He aimed at Michael and fired, but Michael twisted around, and the electrode darts lodged harmlessly in his backpack.

Jones came at Michael in a rush, determined to chase him down. Michael was winded and the adrenaline rush had abated, but still he proved the swifter between them. He fled up the road, then ducked into an alley and down another side street before doubling back and emerging onto a road parallel to the one he was originally on.

Michael's heart was pounding and he was now spent. He took a moment to catch his breath, then began jogging toward the large intersection at the end of the road. He was disoriented, but reckoned he could find his bearings once he was back on the main grid.

He approached with caution, senses primed and the hair on the back of his neck stood on end. Michael felt something up ahead, around the corner and out of sight. Something waiting for him in the half-lit gloom. He stopped short and turned abruptly a few feet shy of the intersection, eager to find another way out of the labyrinthine network of alleyways.

Michael peered back into the darkened passage, and his heart sank. For there at the far end of the narrow lane some forty meters distant, stood the stolid figure of Agent Jones. He was bathed in a halo of lamplight, dark and featureless, but Michael knew it was him. And the figure was now advancing.

All reason stripped to a mere impulse, Michael backpedaled until he stumbled onto the open road. He wrested his gaze from Jones and turned to behold the source of his unknown dread. Out from behind a black paneled van, windowless and dark, a still darker shadow emerged. It raised its arms and took aim. Michael felt the sting of a dart pierce his neck, just above his clavicle.

The world began to fade and his mind lost focus. The last clear image Michael processed, before the blackness of oblivion engulfed him, was that of a black-haired man in a brown leather jacket and khaki pants breaking his fall. It was the man he had encountered on his way to Bill's office, the man from Driftless.

# CHAPTER 10
# WAVES OF MUTILATION

**Simon**

Simon's head throbbed. He opened his eyes to find Lauren standing attentively beside him. She called for a nurse who arrived presently.

"Where am I?" He tried to sit upright, but the nurse placed a firm hand on his shoulder.

"Just relax, please." Her eyes were gentle. "You are in the Jacobs Medical Center, here at the university campus. You were rushed here after you passed out in your living room. Do you remember that?"

Simon began to answer, but was interrupted by two short raps on the door. A stately middle-aged man in a white coat and glasses stood in the doorway. "Ah good, you're awake." The man entered and introduced himself as Dr. Harris. "How do you feel?"

"Like I've been kicked in the head by a mule driving a Mack truck."

Dr. Harris smiled and leaned over the bed rail to take a closer look at his patient. "You're very lucky. You experienced what we call a sub-arachnoid hemorrhage – leaking of blood into the area between the brain and the skull. It was the result of a ruptured aneurism. If Lauren hadn't called for an ambulance straight away, you would almost certainly have died."

Simon felt the side of his head. His hair had been shaved and his fingers found the bandages covering the seam that now encircled his head starting just above the hairline. Simon extended his hand and

Lauren clasped it, moving closer to his bedside. Tears welled in her eyes, but Simon was strangely sanguine.

"We operated immediately, and the results were excellent, if I do say so myself. We were able to clip the aneurysm and stop the bleeding." Dr. Harris explained how a portion of his skull had been lifted in order for the surgical team to access the artery.

"We made sure to use non-ferromagnetic clips as I understand you are currently undergoing some fMRI analysis." Dr. Harris motioned toward the corner of the room, where Wilfred was seated. "Dr. Lim has briefed me on your history. Medically speaking, you are quite an interesting case. I've asked him to send me his test results as well."

Wilfred stood. "Lauren called me while you were being treated. I hope you don't mind. I can go …"

"No, stay." Simon raised his hand feebly. "When can I get out of here?"

The physician pursed his lips. "Well, we want to keep you for observation for at least a week, to make sure there is no recurrence or other complications. We will also need to see you for follow up visits, to see if there are any signs of another seizure."

Wilfred came up to Simon's bed and stood beside Lauren. "I have some good news, if you can call it that." He shared a look with Dr. Harris. "We have a basic diagnosis of what is causing your rapid acquisition of new skills. It appears that the surfing accident caused a traumatic degeneration of the anterior temporal orbitofrontal cortex. This resulted in the disinhibition of, among other things, the visual systems involved in perception and mathematical computation."

"English please, Wilfred," said Simon. "I don't know if you heard Dr. Harris here, but I've just had an aneurism burst in my head."

"Yes, well, that's what I'm trying to say. During your surfing accident, an area of your brain was damaged. However, when one area of the brain is impaired, another area can be recruited to take over the functions of the damaged area. This recruitment of capability from the secondary region of the brain can sometimes trigger the release of new skills. Actually, it is more like enabling the release of already *existing*, but dormant, abilities. Anyway, we think that's what has been happening to you."

"And that's what caused my aneurism?"

"Not exactly," Dr. Harris chimed in. "The damage to your orbitofrontal cortex in itself was non-threatening. However, the blow you suffered also affected some of your cerebral arteries, weakening them and ultimately causing the hemorrhage. My fear is that this may not be the last occurrence."

"When do you think I'll be able to surf again?" Simon asked.

Dr. Harris shook his head. "If it were up to me you would refrain from surfing at all in the future; but for at least the next six months … absolutely not. Light exercise only." He directed the remark at Lauren. "I mean it."

\*

After ten more days in the hospital, Simon returned home. At first he remained in bed, content to surf the Internet instead of ocean waves. Lauren feared that he might become confused and go missing, or experience another incident, so she encouraged him to find activities close to home.

Simon knew that it pained Lauren to see him in such an enfeebled condition. However, by the end of Simon's fourth week home from the hospital, he felt stronger and was growing increasingly restless.

So, despite her concern, Lauren did not protest when he announced his intention to rejoin Wilfred at the lab.

Simon returned to a hero's welcome. The staff and interns had grown fond of him and were genuinely relieved to learn he had survived the life-threatening ordeal. But there was something else besides his fortuitous recovery setting the place abuzz.

"I have some news." Wilfred gestured for Simon to follow him into his office. "We have been offered a sizeable grant, a public-private partnership out of Palo Alto." Wilfred was practically jubilant.

"Great!" Simon tried to match Wilfred's enthusiasm. "What's the program?"

"That's the exciting part," said Wilfred. "It's you, you're the program, not to put too fine a point on it."

The Defense Advanced Research Projects Agency (DARPA) had originated the grant to advance promising technologies related to brain-computer interface (BCIs). These devices were known by other names as well: neural-control interfaces, mind-machine interfaces, direct neural interfaces. The technology was so novel and immature that they had not yet settled on a standard nomenclature. The overarching idea was to create a direct communication pathway between an enhanced or wired brain and an external device.

The applications for such a technology were manifold. Perhaps the most admirable of these was to use the technology as a sensory or psycho-physical prosthetic, a means to enable impaired individuals to connect directly with devices that would supplement their own bodies in some way. The grant money, however, was disbursed with a somewhat less noble goal in mind – human interaction with virtual reality computer games.

"And what's even better," Wilfred continued, "is that I'm confident we can get you a position as a research assistant. After the trials, of course; we can't have a research assistant who is also the subject of an active set of experiments. But on the back end of this, I'm sure we can find a position for you."

Wilfred and Simon were to explore the capabilities and applications for a technology known as electrocorticography, a type of electrophysiological monitoring that used electrodes placed directly on the exposed surface of the brain to record electrical activity from the cerebral cortex. It was called ECoG for short.

Naturally, large technology firms could not very well go around cracking open the skulls of healthy people for the sole purpose of developing new video games, so they piggy-backed on the medical research of eligible patients, most typically those with severe epilepsy. However, in rare cases, patients suffering from other maladies could be engaged. Due to the nature of his injury, and because the risk of a recurring hemorrhage was sufficiently high, Simon was granted special dispensation; or rather, Wilfred was granted special dispensation to make use of him.

"Do you really intend to model my brain by way of these experiments?" Simon asked with some hesitation.

"Not exactly," Wilfred explained. "The actual map of the neuropathways – the *connectome* as it is sometimes called – is being compiled in slow and steady increments by several consortiums and hundreds of research teams all around the world. They are doing this primarily by using the brains of deceased organ donors. But what we are doing with the ECoG is trying to understand the electrical fields generated by the brain. The electrodes that we will be placing on your cerebral cortex will map the electrical brainwaves produced in aggregate in the various parts of the brain, not just the neural connections per se."

As Simon would discover, electrical activity in fact took place in many ways throughout the central nervous system, and learning about this would be crucial to any model that Wilfred hoped to create. It was complex; on the one hand, there was the specific electrical firing taking place between the neurons. These electrochemical events or "action potentials" were discreet, taking place at the cellular level between the one hundred billion neurons in the human brain.

On the other hand, there was the aggregate electrical signal from these events and others, which manifested in what were frequently referred to as brainwaves. This was what Wilfred proposed to study with Simon. These brainwaves were distinguishable by frequency, ranging from less than one per second all the way up to one hundred cycles per second.

Although still quite a mystery, it was generally understood that the various brainwaves, generated by masses of neurons communicating with one another, were fundamental in some way to all human thoughts and emotions. These various brainwaves could be associated with increasing levels of wakefulness, comprising a spectrum of awareness ranging from low, slow, and loud to high, fast, and subtle.

Delta waves ranging from zero point five to three Hertz, or cycles per second, were generated during meditation and dreamless sleep. Theta waves, three to eight Hertz, were found most frequently during sleep, especially during the transition period between sleep and wakefulness. Theta was the state of dreams and intuition.

Alpha waves from eight to twelve Hertz engendered a calm wakeful state, the resting state of the brain. Beta waves were faster still, from twelve to thirty-eight Hertz, present when a person was alert, attentive and engaged in cognitive tasks and problem solving.

Gamma Waves, from thirty-eight all the way up to one hundred Hertz, were some of the fastest brainwaves to have been studied, and of particular interest to Wilfred. These were above the frequency of neuronal firing and how they were produced was puzzling to him, but they seemed somehow related to the processing of information from different brain areas at the same time. Wilfred speculated that Gamma rhythms were somehow associated with expanded consciousness and spirituality.

Wilfred led Simon to his office and sat him down. "I understand your reluctance." He leaned forward in his chair. "But your participation in this research will help advance our understanding immeasurably of how the brain functions. We need the kind of control and repeatability that these advanced ECoG techniques can offer. We'll never have this chance again. Whaddya say?"

*

Simon left Wilfred's office in a mental fog. He was restless and conflicted, and very much undecided. He did not return home directly but instead rode south, back toward Ocean Beach and the small apartment he first inherited from Bill so many months ago. He arrived at the place where his taxi had disappeared and he followed that path, cresting the hill of Point Loma until the sea floated up behind him, an azure band sundering earth and sky, stretching beyond the twin horizons of his peripheral vision. Simon veered right, traveling down the length of the peninsula toward the state park at the end of the road.

The tip of Point Loma had become one of Simon's favorite haunts. This location offered an expansive, nearly uninterrupted view of the sea, allowing one to survey the ocean without obstruction to the east, south, and west. The old lighthouse had been preserved, summoning images of adventure pursued in an era before all reckoning of satellite or radar or electricity. The location evoked a sense of calm; a passivity found in the deepness of time and fathomless distance. And the unquantifiable magnitude of such dimensions lent a perspective to whatever was confronting Simon.

As he walked the familiar footpath and found again his favored vantage, a verse sprung to mind, a well-studied composition of Walt Whitman learned years ago and all but forgotten. Simon recalled it in full, drawing the memory from the now doorless vaults of his mind:

> *Facing west from California's shores,*
> *Inquiring, tireless, seeking what is yet unfound,*
> *I, a child, very old, over waves, toward the house of maternity,*
> *the land of migrations, look afar,*
> *Look off the shores of my Western sea, the circle almost circled;*
> *For starting westward from Hindustan, from the vales of Kash-mere,*
> *From Asia, from the north, from the God, the sage, and the hero,*
> *From the south, from the flowery peninsulas and the spice islands,*
> *Long having wander'd since, round the earth having wander'd,*
> *Now I face home again, very pleas'd and joyous,*
> *(But where is what I started for so long ago?*
> *And why is it yet unfound?)*

Simon pondered the words and puzzled over his ability to recall them – the mystery of that new skill. He looked out once more at the boundless sea, then mounted his bike to find his way back home.

# CHAPTER 11
## MIND OVER MATTER

**Simon**

Simon found Lauren waiting for him in their kitchen, seated at the head of the table. She smiled gently as he entered. "Interesting day?" she said.

"Wilfred called you?"

"Two hours ago. He told me you had already left."

"Yeah, I've been riding," he said, "and … thinking."

"Any conclusions?" Her vague question left too much room for him to explore.

He sat down next to her and Lauren took his hand in hers. "I think I need a reason to do this.

"So far, everything that's happened to me since the surfing accident has been mostly beyond my control. The sessions with Wilfred were to learn about my condition. The aneurism and seizure were spontaneous. But this, the opportunity to participate in these experiments is the first step that seems unnecessary, and may just be a little bit vain."

Simon bowed his head slightly. When he had first begun working with Wilfred, the whole thing had been abstract. But now the practical questions could not be ignored. Was it right to use the research, which was intended to help suffering people, to produce a commercial product unrelated to the stated purpose of the research? And his condition did not strictly conform to the selection criteria for participation in the experiments, but somehow, the oversight committee had been able to relax those restrictions.

In fact, the entire enterprise was an ethical minefield. Simon was thrilled by the thought of contributing to the ultimate creation of a digital mind. It would be humanity's crowning achievement to recreate a fully intelligent, conscious mind within a computer-based virtual environment, but what then?

Would that virtual uploaded mind be a person? Would it be fully sentient? If so, would it have rights, like other people? Could it be turned off, killed, in effect, if it were conscious?

And if one person's mind could be uploaded into a computer, what about other people? Or multiple copies of the same person? Would they be the same individual as the original? Would they have a soul, whatever that might mean?

Would that digital mind or person even know they were computer-generated? And what would be the implications for mankind's own perceived reality? Could it be that all of humanity is a computer simulation?

Finally, and perhaps most concerning, would humans be able to control this artificial intelligence, even one based on our own minds? Would this virtual human replicate itself? Would it self-modify, evolve? And if so, what would it ultimately become?

These questions haunted Simon, and yet he could not shake the feeling that it was all somehow inevitable or perhaps had *already* occurred. It was the purpose and the destination toward which he and Wilfred and indeed the rest of the world were hurtling. And so, in the end, after Lauren had convinced him that she would support whatever decision he made, Simon plucked the apple and took a bite.

The upshot was that as Dr. Lim's assistant, Simon would gain access to the databases being generated as part of the Human Brain

Project. The downside was that they would have to crack Simon's head open again.

So it was that twelve weeks from the day of Simon's seizure and collapse, he was back in Dr. Harris's operating room undergoing a second craniotomy. The surgical team implanted an eight by eight-centimeter silicon subdural grid embedded with sixty-four platinum iridium electrodes. A four-contact electrode strip was placed on the skull to provide a ground for the clinical monitoring system. The thin wires protruding through Simon's scalp were attached to an EEG monitoring system to record the electric brainwaves arising in response to various stimuli and activities.

The battery of tests ranged from the observation of the electrical signals activated during the performance of routine linguistic and motor skills, to the manipulation of a robotic arm connected through the EEG to a computer. His progress was remarkable and outstripped all expectations. By the end of the program, Simon was controlling a virtual avatar in a computer simulation, performing many of the tasks a human would undertake in the real world. It was very promising for the underwriters of Wilfred's grant, and encouraging for Simon insofar as his brain seemed to be especially adroit and capable of adaptation.

On the final day of testing, after the last experiment had been completed, Simon sat reclining in the modified dentist chair, facing a darkened computer display. His eyes were closed as he rested, waiting for the debriefing and exit interview to begin. After several minutes, as Simon was preparing to call Wilfred to inquire about the delay, he heard footsteps echoing down the hallway followed by two quick raps on the door. He expected to see Wilfred and perhaps one of the other research assistants enter the room. Instead, Wilfred was accompanied by two strangers.

Wilfred greeted Simon as the trio approached. "Oh splendid, Simon, you're still here. I'd like to introduce you to a couple of people." He stepped to one side, gesturing to the first man. "This is Special Agent Jones, from the National Security Agency, and Mr. Lewis Mitchell, from the Defense Advanced Research Projects Agency. He's been seconded over to the NSA."

The two men shook Simon's hand in turn. "They have been overseeing our progress. As you know, our research is primarily funded through a grant from DARPA."

"The NSA and DARPA." Simon looked from one man to the other. "Why do I feel like I'm about to be asked do something shady?"

The two men were unmoved. Jones regarded Simon intently before speaking. "Mr. Quinn, as I'm sure you are aware, the early results from these BCI experiments have been very encouraging. In fact, we haven't seen anything like this in any of our interface programs before."

Lewis, the younger man, chimed in. "There seems to be something unique about your ability to align the brainwaves in the Gamma spectrum, which is more focused and precise than anything we've encountered before. It seems to be paired with a complementary Delta frequency, which together is coordinating different regions of your brain and enabling the complex tasks to be translated into computer and robotic behaviors."

"Yes, that's what Dr. Lim and I have been speculating." Simon pushed himself up in his chair. "Glad I could be of service."

"Based on these preliminary results, we would like to extend the program for another six months ... and possibly longer. We're calling the program 'Empyrean'." Jones's face was blank, but his eyes smoldered.

Simon raised his eyebrows. "Well that sounds wonderful and all, but you do realize I'm sitting here with a rather large hole in my head. I was kind of looking forward to patching that up pretty soon."

"That's the exciting part." Wilfred's hand clasped Simon's arm. "We will be swapping out the current ECoG electrodes for an entirely wireless array."

"The technology is brand new." Lewis waved his arms with excitement. "Custom superconductive alloys and ultra-low energy draw. It will allow the electrodes to be implanted permanently; and more comprehensively than before."

Lewis explained how the new apparatus would function. The system would be entirely sub-cranial, supplied with energy via a wireless link so there was no need to implant any batteries. Surgeons would implant a comprehensive array of electrodes between the brain tissue and the signal amplifier. The signals would be converted from analog to digital, and then condensed and optimized for streaming via radio frequency transceiver to an external base station. From there, the data would be uploaded to a computer for processing.

"Obviously, you will need some time to consider this," said Jones. "Give it some thought and let us know what questions you may have."

*

Simon was overwhelmed, and Lauren was not at all happy with the idea, fearing for his safety. She urged him to decline the opportunity and questioned whether it would help his condition at all. But Simon would not be gainsaid and was unwilling to decline the opportunity to be involved in such a groundbreaking endeavor. And so, later that week, despite Lauren's misgivings, Simon was back under the knife. The original electrodes were extracted, and the new permanent array was implanted. All told, there were nearly three hundred wireless electrodes installed pervasively throughout Simon's cerebral cortex.

After the surgery, life became easier for Simon. His skull was allowed to heal, and he experienced surprisingly few side effects from the surgery. His body accepted the implants and he had a relatively mild reaction to the antibiotics that he took on a daily basis. Simon still suffered headaches from time to time, but they were no worse than what he had experienced prior to the seizure. Now, at least, they would be able to research and hopefully cure that ailment.

Wilfred's program was re-classified as "top secret". They continued to use the university resources, but it was always under the guise of another program or clinical test. Agent Jones visited periodically. At first it was every other day, then weekly, and eventually they saw him less than once a month. He was copied on the weekly reports, which Lim submitted electronically, but Jones rarely commented.

Lewis Mitchell, on the other hand, was ever-present. He was only twenty-six years old, similar in age to Simon, and the two of them connected instantly. This was his first major project for the NSA and he was determined to make it a success. Lewis would often join Simon and Lauren after work for dinner and conversation.

"My original plan was to get into gaming," said Lewis, as they lounged by Lauren's pool on a lazy Saturday morning. "That's where all the money is. When I was at Cal-Tech, I wrote my Master's thesis on the ability to deploy deep learning across a virtual reality matrix that could be used to predict broad scale social dynamics; financial panics, economic cycles, electoral results, that kinda thing. I swear I had that paper on the Internet for less than two days before I got a phone call from the Defense Department. The Feds tried to recruit me right out of the gate, but it took them a while to figure out where they wanted me. Ultimately, I ended up with the NSA. I guess they figured my talents lined up more closely with cyber security than anything else."

With Lewis onboard, the program progressed swiftly. The permanent ECoG electrodes allowed their experiments to iterate with incredible speed. Simon's mind was becoming extremely adroit and his ability to control virtual and real-world avatars improved at an accelerating rate. The immediate feedback he received from the EEG monitor and the movement of the avatars themselves enabled him to learn quickly how to control his mental states. Within six weeks, Simon had developed several mental routines, personal protocols for centering himself prior to and after sessions in the lab. As a result, he learned to quiet his mind almost at will.

Manipulating images and characters on the computer screen seemed almost magical. At first it was shifting video game race cars left and right, then human characters running through mazes. Simon proved so adept at bending his mind around the ever-changing control parameters that Lewis and Wilfred were hard-pressed to stay ahead of him with new experimental challenges.

Lewis moved the locus of the brain computer interface from virtual space to the real world: switches on model train tracks, then radio-controlled toy cars, and eventually full-sized motor vehicles. It was exhilarating, and all the while Wilfred and Lewis monitored, recorded, compiled, and reported.

The more fascinating the results, the less they heard from Agent Jones. The only feedback they received was an occasional word from Lewis that their findings were being well received in Silicon Valley and Washington DC.

At the end of week twenty-two, more than five months into the program, the research team was delighted to learn that for two full days, they would have access to a humanoid robot courtesy of Boston Dynamics. These robots were pushing the limits of machine mobility and agility, and the research team wanted to see whether Simon would be able to make use of the full range of motion and capability afforded by the advanced prototype.

Lewis arranged for a basketball court to be made available for the demonstration. The team from Boston Dynamics set up what amounted to a Parkour obstacle course, with platforms, boxes, bars and other features around which the robot was programmed to maneuver.

When the day arrived, the robot's internal programming was circumvented, and it was connected via a wireless terminal to a computer with which Simon could interface electronically. He sat back in his chair and allowed his mind to relax. It took about thirty seconds for the robot to respond. First it was a jerky motion of the right arm. Then the left. Simon spent about ten minutes internalizing those commands. Then he moved to the hands and fingers, finding the right thought pattern to stimulate the proper frequencies.

Simon wasn't exactly sure how he was able to accomplish this. In fact, none of those assembled could explain it precisely. The understanding would come only after hundreds of hours of analysis. The thing that mattered, the thing that kept both research teams enthralled for nearly four hours, was how Simon methodically worked his way through the robot's anatomy, probing the limits of its capabilities and ultimately bringing the physical motions of the machine under his control using nothing but his mind and a computer interface.

At the close of the four-hour session, Simon was physically and mentally exhausted. Lim called an end to the event and declared it an unmitigated success. Simon was not able to replicate the acrobatic display that the machine performed under its own programming. But the following day, Simon slipped into the frequencies much more quickly, and by the end of the second session, he had the robot dancing.

\*

The exercise with the Boston Dynamics robot would mark the high point for the set of trials. It was clear that the experiments were stretching Simon's ability to focus, and his mind was exhausted. Lewis and Simon agreed that a break was clearly in order.

And there was another roadblock halting their progress. They were plagued by a timeless problem: the inability of a system to prove its own axioms and the related notion that consciousness was therefore not reducible to a calculation.

Wilfred reasoned that the individual was intimately involved in every aspect of knowing, from the prioritization of which subject matter to observe, to the deciphering of the meaning hidden within those observations. As a result, the personal involvement and intuition of the scientist necessitated the co-mingling of subjective and objective knowledge. Indeed, Galileo would not have invented the telescope if he had not suspected there was something out there in the cosmos worth searching for.

All this highlighted the failure of crude science to apprehend the full nature of the world. People used science to search for *why* but found only *what* and *how*. *Why*, Wilfred concluded, had to be experienced; it could not be deduced. It could not be taught or perceived.

And so Wilfred concluded that if individual consciousness was integrally required for knowledge or insight, then attempting to mechanically reduce something which must be employed in an essential, irreducible way is self-defeating. That was their dilemma. They had to find some way to reduce the irreducible.

Meanwhile, Simon could not shake the notion that there were brainwave activities taking place, which were not being captured.

"Take a look at this." Simon handed a dog-eared scientific journal to Wilfred. "Now this is something we ought to be looking into."

Wilfred glanced at the article and frowned. "Quantum Mind Theory. Do you think I haven't thought of that? Look, we can't exactly focus on everything at once. In case you haven't noticed, we've been developing some pretty robust BCI protocols lately," said Wilfred.

"Yes, and that's great as far as it goes," said Simon. "But these are parlor tricks at the end of the day, aren't they? We're like alchemists, medieval magicians – taking something and manipulating it, achieving interesting results. But in fact, we don't really know what's going on at all. We are no closer to solving the true mystery, the hard question of consciousness.

"The brain is more than just neural networks," Simon insisted. "There are hierarchical layers extending downward in scale to these vanishingly small networks with innumerable connections. We've got to go deeper. We need to get down to the bedrock, down to Plank scale."

Wilfred scowled. "What you're talking about is a quantum mind, with cognitive events supposedly taking place at the smallest distances and intervals we have ever discovered. These are huge orders of magnitude smaller and faster than our synapses are even capable of firing."

"Wilfred, just look at this again." Simon opened the journal to a bookmarked page and handed it back to him. "Quantum vibrations have been observed in the microtubules of plants. This supports the idea that the environment of the brain could sustain the quantum state coherence necessary for a conscious moment to arise. Maybe the electrons in the microtubules of neurons are close enough to become entangled.

"If the superposition of possible states that exist in that subatomic neural network did indeed collapse, resulting in the reduction of a quantum state from a sum of possibilities to only one, would this not be somehow crucial to characterizing a moment of consciousness?"

Wilfred shook his head. "Even if a quantum superposition of states existed in the brain at that scale, there is no reason to believe it is anything other than noise. There is no reason to believe we need a non-classical physical model of the brain for consciousness to arise."

"Or maybe you're afraid of what we might find," said Simon, surprising himself with his own impertinence. "Maybe you're worried that we'll discover some behavior or activity that would prove that consciousness is a physical event and not the result of some mysterious numinous substance unto itself." Simon looked at Wilfred, expecting him to be angry.

Instead he appeared only pensive.

"Yes," he nodded. "I agree it may be an avenue worth exploring. But how do you propose we test it?" said Wilfred, curtly. "There isn't an interferometer sensitive enough to measure sub-femtometer length brainwaves, which is what I presume would be necessary to sustain the kind of quantum effects that you are talking about. That's one quadrillionth of a meter, in case you'd forgotten."

"That may be true," said Simon, "but that shouldn't stop us from trying to reconstruct the architecture. If we can figure out the connectome, and then identify the neuronal activity in a precise enough way, we could model the sub-neuronal cytoskeletal structures and observe the effects in the AI model's behaviors and consciousness signature."

"The problem is that we don't have sufficient resolution in the fMRI here in San Diego," said Wilfred. "The magnet isn't powerful enough. Three Teslas just won't cut it. Not to mention the amount of computing power that would be required to simulate the number of connections at the sub-neuronal level. And even if you had the raw computing power, would we be able to simulate the quantum effects adequately with a digital machine, or would we need a quantum computer? You are asking us to solve a lot of complexity."

"What about Shenzhen?" Simon's eyes brightened. "Their new machine is over fourteen Teslas and they claim it can detect changes down to the individual neuron."

Wilfred raised an eyebrow. "And you think they'll just let us use it, no questions asked?"

The gears in Simon's mind were turning now. "Maybe we could collaborate. There are bound to be some friendly institutions that have time on that machine. Maybe we can use one of them as a channel to approach SIAT. Do you know anyone over there?" He looked hopefully at Wilfred.

"I don't know anyone with that kind of influence." Wilfred shook his head.

"Maybe Lauren can help." Simon said at last. "Her sister's husband is connected, a Deputy Director in the Ministry of Trade and Commerce, if I have that right."

Wilfred smiled. "I suppose you can look into it. But I'm afraid our friends at the NSA would not be too excited about releasing you into the People's Republic of China."

"I think it may be time we ditched these guys." Simon's eyes narrowed. "After this grant runs its course, I say we set up shop for ourselves."

\*

Upon submission of his final report, Wilfred informed Lewis Mitchell and Agent Jones that they would not be applying for further funding. After two weeks of intense out-briefing, they were finally released.

On the final day before the computers and other diagnostic devices were packed up and shipped out, Lewis entered the lab for the last time. He was to disassemble the rig and prepare it for transport, but found Simon there, seated in his familiar dentist's chair. He was still connected wirelessly to the computer, running a radio-controlled truck around in circles with his mind.

"Hey buddy," said Lewis. "Sorry to disturb. I can come back if you like."

"No, I'm alright." Simon sat up straight and brought the RC car to a halt. "Packing up?"

"Yeah, I think we're about finished here." Lewis walked over to stand beside Simon. "You've done good work, my friend."

"Thanks. Yeah, it's been a wild ride for sure," said Simon. "That BD robot was something, wasn't it? Did you see the way they could jump all by themselves? I'm glad I was controlling it, and not the other way around."

Lewis looked at Simon as though contemplating whether he should speak. He unzipped his backpack and drew from it a short wand-like device that reminded Simon of the small handheld metal detectors used to screen passengers at airport checkpoints.

"Do something for me, would you?" said Lewis. "Pick up that coffee cup." Simon hesitated. "Go ahead," Lewis insisted. "Pick it up as if you're going to drink from it. And then put it back down."

Simon performed the simple motor task as Lewis instructed.

"Good, now do it again." This time, before Simon reached for the cup, Lewis waved the wand over Simon's head.

Simon reached for the cup but found himself unable to move his arm; it was held fast by some invisible force.

Lewis smiled. "Pretty cool, right?"

"Uh, yeah cool." Simon scowled. "Can you stop it now?"

Lewis withdrew the wand, allowing Simon to control his own arm once again.

"How did you do that?" asked Simon with equal parts curiosity and frustration.

"Well, you don't think these electrical signals only go in one direction, do you?" said Lewis. "Over the past few months, I recorded and observed the action potentials that arose when you were preparing to raise the cup to your lips. After several hundred iterations, I was able to isolate the signal and developed the input to disrupt the operation. You really drink way too much coffee, by the way."

"Jesus." Simon sat back in the chair. "You'll have me in a pickle jar by noon."

"Makes you wonder if we really have any control at all." Lewis smirked. "But just think of the benefits. Doctors will be able to use this to control seizures, treat Parkinson's disease, epilepsy, all sorts of disorders."

"Sure." Simon held Lewis's gaze. "But since when does DARPA give a rat's ass about epilepsy?"

# CHAPTER 12

# SINGAPORE SLINGSHOT

**Selena**

*Minneapolis*

Selena woke with a start, nearly falling off her chair. She was roused not by any particular sound or alarm, but by an intense feeling that she had slept too long.

She rubbed her eyes and took note of her computer display. The search for recent references to Tyrant of Thebes had yielded a large number of hits, but none of them provided any insight as to why Agent Jones might be looking for someone in Driftless. *But that was what, nine hours ago?* Perhaps there would be more chatter by now.

Selena leaned forward and gestured with her hand, swiping over to a readout of the compiled results. To her dismay, the screen went blank. Then, before she could begin to troubleshoot, the monitor illuminated once again, displaying what appeared to be a closed-circuit TV feed. She watched, enthralled and bewildered, as two vehicles approached the front and back entrances to an industrial warehouse.

The place was vaguely familiar to Selena, but the resolution was too low for her to be sure. Two figures disembarked from a black SUV at the front of the building. As they approached the doorway, Selena observed two other people apparently sneaking along the side of the building. They bolted and were quickly lost to view. Then the display went blank once more, this time it was replaced by a simple prompt:

*Deadman Switch – Enabled*
*Back Door Sequence – Activated*

*Oh my god.* Selena stood and pawed for her skullcap and glasses. She donned the devices and navigated the opening protocols to enter the virtual world of Empyrean. The visual world projected by her interactive glasses and engaged via electrode skullcap surrounded her, presenting to her an array of virtual doors to the various domains of Empyrean. However, instead of selecting any of the pre-ordained portals, Selena withdrew a private key.

It was a number, the answer to an elaborate equation which had been embedded in the architecture of Empyrean many years before. Now, with the answer presented, the question took shape in the form of a doorway, barely the size of a pixel in the floor beneath her feet. Though it was vanishingly small, Selena found that it grew to surround her and, in an instant, she slipped through.

Once inside, the proportions of her environment returned to normal dimensions, and she found herself once again in more familiar surroundings. Around her were the equipment and features of a technical laboratory. She was within that space, but at the same time she was able to take in flashes and glimpses of views from the many cameras mounted around its interior and periphery.

Selena was suddenly aware that this was the same place she had seen on her computer display moments earlier. Now she beheld in high resolution what the cameras were capturing, and all was clear – the approach of Jones and the other agents, their entry into the facility, and the escape of Michael and another man via the side door. The last cluster of images Selena observed was of Lewis Mitchel being arrested and placed into the back of the black SUV.

That must be what triggered the dead man's switch. Selena removed her skullcap. *I know where Lewis is going, but what's happened to Michael?*

\*

## Michael

*In transit*

Michael spent a moment on the edge of consciousness, reluctant to embrace it fully. This was going to hurt.

He felt the pinch in his neck first, but his headache soon took center stage. Michael opened his eyes and waited for the blurriness to clear. He took note of his surroundings. He was couched between two armrests in a semi-reclined leather seat. A seatbelt was fastened about his waist, but otherwise he was not restrained.

He appeared to be in an airplane of some sort. The cabin was small but well-appointed, with six seats generously spaced. A low hum and barely noticeable vibrations indicated the engines were engaged.

Michael leaned over and peered through a window. It was dark outside, but he could see the city lights below. *What the hell is going on …?*

His thought was interrupted by a click from the cockpit door. It opened and out stepped a man whom Michael assumed was his abductor. Michael sucked in his breath, and took in his first real study of the man.

He was older, perhaps sixty. His hair was mostly black, with gray around the temples and sides. The man wore an unzipped brown bomber jacket, with khaki pants draped loosely about his legs.

"Ah, Michael, you're up," the man said cheerily. "Don't worry, the headache won't last long."

"What's going on? Who are you? Are you kidnapping me?" Michael began to stand, but was yanked backward by the seatbelt. He fumbled with the clasp.

"Ha!" The man chuckled. "Well, I guess technically, yes I am. But don't worry, I'm not going to hurt you. My name is Johnson Tan, I'm here to help. Sorry about the tranquilizer. I couldn't take the chance of losing you again."

"Losing me?" Michael stood, his hair grazing the cabin ceiling. "Why were you following me in the first place? And how did you find me?"

"Your bike popped up on the grid the minute you passed through the parking gantry," said Johnson. "That was really dumb, you know."

"What do you want with me?"

"Listen, this will be a little bit hard to accept." He placed a hand on Michael's shoulder. "But I knew your mother. Actually, I knew both your parents. I am – *was* – your mother's first cousin. I'm here because there's reason to believe that you may be in danger. And … we need your help."

Michael frowned, and rubbed his temples. He was in no condition to process this information.

"When your parents died," Johnson continued, "a decision was made to insulate you as much as possible from their lives. He could never prove it, but Wilfred was convinced that your father's stroke was not, shall we say … completely natural. And when your parents died in that crash, we took the decision to hide you away."

"Wilfred?" Michael's head snapped up.

"Dr. Wilfred Lim," Johnson nodded. Lauren had kept her pregnancy a secret, and there were only a handful of people in the

States who knew about you and your connection to Singapore. So when your parents died so unexpectedly, Wilfred brought you to your grandmother in Wisconsin. And we did our best to keep it secret all these years."

"*We* …?" Michael struggled to process the information. "You mean you and Dr. Lim?"

Johnson nodded. "Yes, he took you back home. Listen, Michael, the answers are coming. But now we must focus. You've been discovered at an extraordinarily delicate time. There are some important people who find your existence very surprising and not a little bit … inconvenient."

Michael was silent. He should have been shocked, or angry, but somehow, he was neither. He had known there was a story to learn, and that the truth was likely to be complex. Now as some part of that story was revealed, fantastic though it sounded, Michael believed it to be true.

Michael shook his head slowly. "I still don't understand why you were sneaking around my place."

"I wasn't sneaking." Johnson tilted his head. "I was coming to warn you. We picked up some chatter about you as well."

"We?"

"The NSA isn't the only intelligence organization in the world, you know," said Johnson. "Anyway, I got to you first, thankfully."

"So, you were watching me?" Michael raised his eyebrows.

"Only very recently," said Johnson.

"And you sent the drone?"

"Drone? I'm not aware of any drone. No, that wasn't me."

"But you *are* my uncle?" said Michael, suddenly doubtful.

Johnson pulled his eyebrows together. "Well, I'm your mother's cousin, so technically I'm your first cousin once removed. Come, sit up here with me."

Johnson returned to the cockpit and gestured toward the co-pilot seat to his right. Michael sat, and Johnson turned his attention back to the control panel. He kept their air speed at about six hundred miles per hour and set a course due north over Lake Michigan and Lake Superior. When they entered Canadian airspace, he opened a small cabinet on the wall behind his seat and extracted two helmets with full face shields. An oxygen mask was attached, hanging loose on one side.

"Here." He handed one of the helmets to Michael. "Put this on. It's just like a motorcycle helmet, except for the mask.

"Can you hear me alright?"

The sound of Johnson's voice, filtered through radio distortion, reverberated in his helmet. It seemed to Michael as though he was eavesdropping on an ancient conversation, beamed through space and time, bounced off a forgotten satellite to be received by some forlorn antennae without hope of responding.

"What do I do with this?" Michael held up one end of a tube, the other end of which was attached to the oxygen mask on his helmet.

Johnson took the loose end from Michael and fastened it to an orifice in the fuselage below and to the right of his seat. "Better sit down and strap in."

Michael obliged, and Johnson pressed a sequence of digital buttons on the display. The aircraft accelerated … and kept accelerating through Mach 1 to reach nearly 1,500 miles per hour. The plane continued to climb, until the display read 50,000 feet. This was the upper limit of both speed and altitude that the traditional turbofan engine could achieve.

When they had stabilized at that velocity, Johnson looked over at Michael.

"So, what happens now?" Michael asked.

"Now?" Johnson smiled broadly. "Hold on to your hat."

He issued another series of instructions through the digital display, and without warning, Michael's body was pressed back against his seat with 5Gs of force.

Johnson had ignited a solid-fuel rocket booster, housed in the rear fuselage below the tail. The rocket accelerated the aircraft to Mach 7, at which point the propulsion of the plane was taken over by another system altogether – Supersonic Combustion Ramjets.

Johnson stabilized their air speed and the feeling of pressure relented, such that they could breathe and speak normally. Johnson did, however, advise Michael to keep his helmet on.

Michael stared in amazement out the front windshield of the plane. "This technology can't be street-legal. How did you ever get this thing into the country?"

Johnson shrugged. "Sure, the government has surveillance equipment, satellites, radar, and whatnot. But what are those devices seeing, hearing, and picking up? It's only signals, at the end of the day – signals that can be imitated or disrupted."

Johnson navigated the aircraft over the Arctic Circle, through Chinese airspace, and down the Indochinese Peninsula to Singapore. The entire trip from Chicago to Singapore took less than two hours.

They soon descended, and the traditional propulsion systems re-engaged. Johnson removed his helmet and Michael did the same.

"Hold out your arm." Johnson said.

Michael raised an eyebrow, then shrugged and extended his left arm, palm facing up. Before Michael knew what was happening, Johnson pressed a small plastic implement resembling a hot glue gun against the webbing between his thumb and forefinger. With a sudden snap, a small capsule was injected under Michael's skin, leaving behind only a small circular wound.

"Hey!" Michael yanked his hand back. "That hurt. What was that?"

"Your credentials," Johnson explained. "You can't very well walk into Singapore without ID, now can you? I've also loaded some credits there, courtesy of the Daedalus Corporation."

*

*Singapore*

They landed at Changi Air Force Base and Johnson arranged for a private car to shuttle them to the Central Business District of Singapore. Michael spent the next day and a half holed-up in the Epsilon Hotel, while Johnson made calls and awaited instructions.

"I've set up a meeting with Su-Ling Tan," said Johnson at the conclusion of one particularly long call. "She's your mother's sister, and the executor of Dr. Lim's estate. We'll see her tomorrow morning."

"Did you find out what happened to Bill and Lewis?" Michael gripped the arms of his chair.

"From what I've been able to ascertain, they're fine," said Johnson. "Well, maybe not fine, exactly – they were detained for questioning but released. At least Bill Jameson was. We're still trying to figure out where Lewis Mitchell is being held."

"Detained by whom?" Michael asked. "Who were those guys?"

"Wilfred Lim and the Daedalus Corporation have a lot of adversaries." Johnson shrugged. "Best guess, I'd say industrial espionage. One of the alphabet agencies was probably monitoring Wilfred's communications and traced it to Bill. Agent Jones got wind of it and from there they were just following up on leads, including you. You worked for Bill for a while, didn't you?"

"Almost ten years." Michael nodded. "And I guess you must know something about Bill as well."

"I knew of him. And Jones, too, though we never met. Jones had crossed paths with your mother and father early on. He most likely put two and two together when they started watching Bill and figured out that Tara Quinn was your grandmother. He may think that you can gain them some leverage with Wilfred Lim and thereby the Daedalus Corporation. Maybe we'll learn something more tomorrow from Su-Ling."

*

A gust of hot humid air greeted Michael and Johnson as the twin glass doors of the hotel lobby closed behind them. The sun was still trapped behind the tall buildings of the Central Business District, mitigating the ever-present tropical heat. It was not yet nine o'clock, but Michael's body insisted it was evening.

He stepped into the bright Singapore morning, and paused to observe the traffic zipping past. Vehicles transiting along the main road dipped into a semi-circular driveway to collect or deposit passengers. It resembled a Formula-1 pit stop, lending an air of urgency to the exercise.

After only a few seconds of waiting, a brightly painted blue and white sedan approached. It slowed as it entered the hotel's drive and meticulously executed the maneuver. Michael and Johnson climbed onboard.

"Good morning, Mr. Quinn, Mr. Tan," intoned a disembodied female voice from the taxi's speaker system. "My name is Irene. Where would you like to go today?"

"Tanglin Plaza," Johnson said, "and please hurry, we're running late."

"Of course," answered Irene in simulated deference. "I always take the optimal route. Our travel time will be seven minutes. I hope that will be acceptable."

There was no human driver, and the interior was optimized for passenger capacity and comfort. The seats were arranged as two opposing C-shaped benches with a gap for door-access between them. Michael eased himself deeper into the car seat and watched the buildings and street scenes flow past the windows.

Six minutes and fifty-three seconds later, the taxi veered left and pulled into a broad semi-circular driveway. It slowed to a halt, and the seats slowly rotated the last few degrees, aligning with the sliding car doors.

They alighted in the shadow of the Tanglin Plaza building, a residential complex of forty-five stories perched along a canal flowing into the Singapore River. Johnson had a quick word with the guards stationed in the lobby, then led Michael to the elevator bank. It was clear that Johnson had been here before.

He used the short ride up to the penthouse to remind Michael of their purpose. "Remember, Madam Tan is your mother's older sister. She's only recently found out about you and has mixed feelings about the situation, to say the least. That could work for us or against us. I can tell you she's pretty peeved at me right now."

*My mother's sister …* Michael didn't know how to begin processing the information. *I have so much I need to ask her.*

The lift deposited them directly into a well-appointed residence. The floors were white polished marble and the large living room was framed with tall windows. A woman dressed in a smart gray maid's uniform greeted them.

"Madam Tan is waiting for you on the balcony." She gestured toward the glass doors at the side of the room.

Su-Ling Tan stood near the parapet absently surveying the city view. She turned as they approached, and Michael nearly stopped in his tracks. He had imagined many times what his mother might look like, and here before him was that very image brought to life.

She was petite, little more than five feet tall. Michael reckoned she couldn't have weighed much more than a hundred pounds. Although Su-Ling was over fifty years old, she could have been mistaken for a woman ten years her junior. She kept her black hair long but wore it up in a modified French twist. Her attire was carefully assembled; a bright green skirt, tastefully embellished with floral details that matched a fitted top with bolder floral embroidery. The ensemble invoked the elegance of a traditional *sarong kebaya*, exuding meticulous poise and sophistication.

"Well," she said as they approached the threshold, "you must be Michael." Su-Ling came to stand directly in front of him. Michael nodded dumbly.

"Let me take a look at you." She placed her hands on his shoulders and looked directly into his eyes. She examined his face for a long while, and at last embraced him.

"Yes." She held him once more at arm's length. "Yes, I see it. I'm so very sorry that we are meeting under these circumstances. Perhaps it could have been avoided, but that discussion must wait. Come, let's sit down." She gestured toward a table to their right. "We have much to discuss."

It was then that Michael noticed Su-Ling was not alone. Ensconced in the far corner of the balcony was a middle-aged gentleman sitting cross-legged on a rattan chair. He stood as they entered.

"Gerald," said Johnson. "Excuse me, I mean Minister Loke. I didn't know you would be joining us." Johnson shot Su-Ling a probing look.

"Don't blame her." Gerald came closer. "I insisted, and time is of the essence."

"Michael, this is my husband, Gerald Loke," Su-Ling clarified. "He is the Minister of Trade and Commerce."

"Recently appointed." Gerald extended his hand to Michael.

"You must be wondering what all this is about. Please." She gestured to an empty chair. "Have a seat and I'll explain."

They obliged her, taking up seats around the table, sipping oolong tea as Su-Ling brought them up to speed.

"When my sister – your mother – died, I was devastated." Su-Ling held Michael's eye with a steady gaze. "I wanted answers and Wilfred had been so close to her at the end that I admit I became a little obsessed, asking him questions, calling him at all hours of the night. Of course, there were no answers, none that could satisfy my grief, anyway. And so, in the end, I let it rest.

"But Wilfred and I grew to be friends. And he came to trust me, more than anyone else, I believe. Which is why he asked me to help him with this." Su-Ling produced a portfolio and withdrew two bound documents, which she placed on the table before Michael.

"This first document you may recognize," she said. "It outlines the terms of a blind trust created by Wilfred Lim and facilitated by Sentry Insurance Company of Chicago, Illinois."

"Yes, I have been made aware of that." Michael glanced at the document. "Only recently."

"No doubt," said Su-Ling. "The second document is a living will. It stipulates that in the case of incapacitation, the final right to determine the use of extraordinary life-saving medical procedures administered to Dr. Wilfred Lim will be the sole purview of Ms. Su-Ling Tan."

Michael glanced down at the document printed on fine stationery with the masthead of Kok & Lee, Advocates & Solicitors.

"We signed the paperwork two weeks ago." Su-Ling gestured toward the documents. "There's a power of attorney as well. There were witnesses. It's official."

"Well, that's going to get a lot of attention." Michael looked sidelong at Johnson.

"It already has." Su-Ling gestured toward her husband. "Gerald is ordering a ministry-level investigation – confidential, of course."

"Yes, well, the Ministry of Trade and Commerce is a major backer of Daedalus," said Gerald. "Dr. Lim's incapacitation has the potential to derail a major program, with severe negative impact on our economy."

Su-Ling placed her hand on the documents before her. "Michael, it seems that for some reason, Wilfred Lim wanted the two of us to be connected in the event of his untimely demise."

Gerald crossed his arms. "Yeah, well, Wilfred was getting very paranoid there at the end."

"Oh sure, you would say that." Johnson leaned forward.

"What's that supposed to mean?" Gerald glowered.

"You know very well that Wilfred was not at all sure that launching Icarus was the right move. He didn't think it was safe."

"He designed the damn thing!" Gerald was nearly shouting now.

"Yeah, well, scientists designed the hydrogen bomb, but politicians dropped it." Johnson's words were chiseled ice.

"Both of you, stop!" Su-Ling said firmly.

Silence fell upon the room.

"Oh, I get it now." Johnson sat back in his seat. "Wilfred still controls the intellectual property. If he's incapacitated, the executor of his estate exercises control. And if he dies, ownership passes to …"

"His heir," Su-Ling completed his thought. "And in any event, the insurance company would have to investigate."

"Well, like I said, he was not himself lately," Gerald insisted. "His mind was addled. At the last shareholders' meeting, he projected a map of the British coastline and talked for forty-five minutes about a bottomless pit. I can't tell you how much explaining Steven and I had to do after that."

"In any case, here's what's going to happen." Su-Ling placed her hands on the table, apparently confident that she held most of the cards. "Michael will be attached to your official inquiry. He will satisfy the insurance investigation and after that, we'll move on. We have a lot of catching up to do."

Su-Ling stood, and the others followed suit.

"Gerald, can your car take us over to the Daedalus building?" asked Johnson.

"Oh no. Michael only, on this I must insist." Gerald turned to face Michael, asserting himself this time. "I've alerted Steven Chen that you will be visiting. He's the CEO of Daedalus Corporation and he'll make sure you have access to whatever you need to see. Now, if you'll excuse me, I have other matters to attend to."

"Fine," said Johnson. "Michael, I'll meet you at the hospital after lunch. You'll want to speak with Wilfred's doctor."

"Can I drop you off at Daedalus?" asked Gerald.

"You know what? I'll find my own way." Michael was beginning to feel as though he was being led around by the nose. It was difficult to know who he should trust and, at the very least, he wanted to form his own unbiased opinion about this Daedalus Corporation. It was time he took matters into his own hands.

"Now," he said to Johnson on the elevator ride back down to the lobby, "tell me again, how to call a cab?"

## CHAPTER 13

# PUBLIC-PRIVATE PARTNERSHIP

**Gerald**

*Singapore, thirty years earlier*

Gerald Loke strode into the restaurant with the confidence of a man who had options. He had chosen the Marina Bay Sands Hotel for his first encounter with Dr. Wilfred Lim. There was a grandeur and spectacle about the venue which lent itself to the discussion of big ideas. And he had several of these in mind today.

He was early, and took the opportunity to admire the scenery. The rooftop garden commanded a brilliant view of Singapore's Central Business District and Marina Bay. Gerald contemplated the innumerable commercial vessels moored out to sea as sunlight gleamed in gilded spearheads on the tips of ocean waves.

Gerald came of age during an era of keen global competition. But he was convinced that there was something immoral in the wasteful expenditure of so much energy for purely offensive and defensive activity.

*The world isn't fair and the sooner you learn that the better.* Words of his father, words of reason and useful words at that. For the soul of fairness lives not in the giving, but the achieving. Fairness would be meaningless without the achieving, without the striving – it wouldn't be fair at all.

All this and yet, how could fairness be won for only a few?

*The world isn't fair, the world isn't fair.* Ah, to change the world, but how?

The inspiration: conflict and cooperation, the same in the end. But how to give play to this sameness?

Finally, the technology caught up with Gerald's ideal, and the vision of the Daedalus Corporation was conceived. Through this entity they would give birth to a new mode of achieving: not in conflict alone, but conflict embedded within cooperation; an agreed upon framework, a game. And this game would enable the acceleration of demand to its instantaneous fulfillment.

What Gerald envisioned was the foundation of a new nation comprised not of land and physical space, but rather an affiliation of commercial, social, and even philosophical elements that shared a common vision for the basic operating environment of this new world.

The trick would be to shift the focus of nationhood and nationalism away from the geographical and cultural, toward the economic and commercial realms. Commercial entities were more plastic and malleable and offered more immediate and direct access to individuals' motivations, providing an avenue to incentivize behavior. Technology was the key.

It was imperative that entrepreneurs have the ability to design, develop, manufacture, market and sell a product or service simply by leveraging the digital capital available on this new platform. If that environment could be created, then the interchangeable nature of commercial assets, rather than leading to the alienation and disenchantment of the multitudes, would instead create the context in which more people had an interest in seeing the entire system succeed. The advent and launch of an intelligent manufacturing network was therefore an essential feature and indeed the foundation of Gerald's new nation.

Gerald wagered that once this global economic equilibrium had been achieved, once complete integration had occurred, the owners of capital would no longer hold the underclass hostage. Rather, those with the means of production would become merely the hired servants of the innovators; the small, the nimble, and the creative. And this multitude of entrepreneurs, forming ever-shifting business webs, would ultimately steer the ship of state.

Controlling the protocols by which these individual strands of the business web could interact would dictate the structure of the webs that could be formed, and thereby inform how their interests would ultimately be understood, aligned, and expressed. And within the hyper-lubricated mechanism of an intelligent web-enabled marketplace, supply and demand – these two complementary market forces – would find their symbiosis. For supply demanded a reason to produce, and demand supplied that reason.

This highly automated market, characterized by a mutual indwelling of supply and demand, would be one half of an advanced political economy, with the political sphere completing the picture. The political realm was characterized by the relation of the part to the whole, the citizen to the body politic. It was stratified and fractalized to the degree which the actors expressed themselves as both individuals and groups. Therefore, just as the modularization of commercial entities would allow an industry to pool resources across the entire universe of participants and flexibly respond to consumer demand, so too would greater flexibility in political configurations bring the world to a more just equilibrium in the end.

The apotheosis of this paradigm would be the coalescence of entities into de facto nations, independent of official status as states. A smaller, weaker, and more circumscribed state would in fact be a prerequisite to this new system's fuller expression. And although his vision seemed to imbue corporate-technological interests with enhanced, almost unchecked power, Gerald was convinced it would lead ultimately to the empowerment of individuals as the primary unit of sovereignty.

This was his vision. However, in order for the prophecy of this new world to be fulfilled, a still greater integration and globalization would be necessary. That process would accelerate the dissolution of traditional national borders, allowing ad hoc corporate imperatives to move geographical and political actors around the global chessboard like so many pawns in the game of commerce.

It was Machiavellian perhaps, but Gerald's motivation was quite beneficent. The increased interoperability and fluidity of commercial components would increase flexibility and lower barriers to entry for new participants. This was where Steven Chen figured into his plan. Steven was the perfect executive to head Daedalus Corporation. And now with the serendipitous advent of Wilfred Lim, he dared to hope they might change the world.

*

Steven Chen arrived at the Marina Bay Sands Hotel precisely on time – 6pm on the nose. He found Gerald at the parapet gazing pensively into the middle distance.

"Hello Steven," said Gerald without turning his head. "Congratulations on your recent appointment. The Daedalus Corporation is an ambitious project and I am very pleased you were selected to lead this initiative."

"So, we are committed then? The Minister will back us?" Steven stood beside Gerald, shifting his gaze between him and the water.

"Yes, and I dare say most of the Cabinet will have to be involved at some point." Gerald finally pivoted toward Steven. "Listen, Steven, you must understand that once we start down this path, there's no turning back. We will be asking for the better part of a trillion dollars over the next ten years. Our constituents will expect to see results."

"You know, what you are proposing borders on sedition," said Steven.

"The trend is inevitable."

Inevitable, perhaps. But Gerald also knew that so much depended on the sequence and timing. If political states retained too much control, then instead of invigorating an economy populated by a multitude of individual entrepreneurs, this new integrated network paradigm would entrench the vested economic elite. If this network were empowered too soon, then corporate interests would merely supplant the state – becoming de facto despots without the checks imposed by popular elections. This was to be avoided at all costs.

"The technology is there … or will be," said Steven. "But we cannot waver. Some of these factors simply will not emerge if we don't have sufficient scale and breadth of participation. We need a critical mass for the intelligent manufacturing network to succeed."

"Have you thought of a name for that program, by the way?" Gerald asked.

"I thought we agreed on Icarus." Steven cocked his head.

"Icarus." Gerald smiled. "Yes, of course. Nothing else would do, I suppose – oh, here they are."

Steven followed Gerald's glance toward the front of the restaurant where a coterie of new visitors had arrived. Two young Chinese women, a Westerner and an older looking Asian man moved through the gathering crowd.

Gerald raised his hand and one of the young women waved in return.

"Hello," said the young woman. "Sorry we're late. Gerald, let me introduce everyone. You remember my sister, Lauren. And this is Dr. Wilfred Lim and Simon Quinn."

"Pleasure to meet all of you." Gerald shook their hands in turn. "This is my colleague, Steven Chen."

"Are you also with the government then?" Wilfred asked.

"Sort of," said Steven. "I work for a research consortium called Astro-Tech, heading up the Quantum Computing program at the moment."

"Really?" Wilfred raised an eyebrow.

Steven nodded. "But I will be moving on to a new project imminently."

"Actually, that's what we wanted to discuss with you," said Gerald. "Steven is leaving his current role to head up a new firm. It's another private-public partnership called Daedalus."

"It's really very exciting." Steven stepped forward. "We will be developing an advanced manufacturing platform that will make use of AI to facilitate commercial and industrial transactions."

Wilfred smiled. "Interesting. In which aspect do you intend to incorporate machine learning into the transaction framework?"

"Well, the short answer is everywhere. Actually, that's what I was hoping to speak with you about. We are aware of your work in San Diego and think you might be able to contribute meaningfully to this enterprise."

Simon looked at Lauren.

Lauren shrugged and shook her head. "Don't look at me. Su-Ling …?"

Su-Ling shot her husband a disapproving glance. "Gerald, I'm afraid you and Steven have caught us a bit off guard."

"Please, don't be cross with me, darling." Gerald smiled. "We're just kicking around ideas here."

Wilfred cleared his throat. "Oh, well, thank you for thinking of us. It's very flattering, but we are no longer interested in that kind of applied science. Our focus is on pure research. Actually, that's why we are here. I was led to believe you may be able to help us approach the Shenzhen Institute of Advanced Technologies in China. We are trying to get some time on their new fMRI facility."

"Yes, we understand," Gerald pressed. "But I think we have a unique opportunity here to help each other out. And please remember we have considerable resources that we can bring to bear on whatever area of study you wish to pursue. I'm sure we could find a mutually agreeable arrangement."

"Well then." Wilfred stroked his chin. "Tell me more about this quantum computer."

Steven was suddenly animated. "Certainly. How much do you know about quantum computing?"

"Not as much as I'd like," said Wilfred.

"Well, you know how in classical computing, a single piece of information, a bit, can exist in either one of two different possible states: one or zero. Quantum computing uses quantum bits or *qubits* instead.

"Think of it like an imaginary sphere." Steven mimed the shape with his hands. "Whereas a classical bit can be at either of the two poles of the sphere, a qubit can be at any point on the sphere. This means a computer using these qubits can store far more information than a classical computer."

"And you have one of these already functional?" Wilfred asked.

"It's well underway." Steven nodded.

Simon did the calculation in his head: by the time a computer reached around two hundred and eighty qubits, that value would approximate the number of atoms in the observable universe.

"Tell me," said Steven, "why the interest? We had not thought to connect the quantum computer project to Daedalus before."

"There may be no connection," said Wilfred, looking at Simon. "But at some point it may come in handy; to model the molecular structure of sub-neuronal architectures, for example."

"I'll tell you what." Gerald leaned in close to Wilfred. "Work with us at Daedalus and we'll help you gain access to the fMRI in Shenzhen. And when it's ready, you can make use of the quantum computer as well. What do you say?"

Wilfred looked at Simon again. "Can we see the QC for ourselves?"

"My driver is downstairs. Why don't we take a ride?"

The group piled into two cars and wound their way through the wilderness of urban bustle into the heart of the Central Business District. Traffic had backed up slightly, squeezing down into a single lane as construction barricades choked the normal flow.

Soon their small caravan came to a halt adjacent to an active excavation site and Gerald exited the vehicle as the others followed, bewildered.

"What's this?" said Wilfred.

"You asked about the quantum computer – this is where it will live," said Steven.

"It's a hole in the ground," said Simon.

"This is the build site of the future Daedalus Corporation building." Steven gestured toward the work site. "The QC will be housed underground. We need to keep the core temperature below ten millikelvins for stability; that's colder than outer space."

Su-Ling shook her head. "Would you all think terribly of me if I admitted I didn't really understand quantum mechanics? I studied actuarial science."

"Which isn't actuarial-y a science," Lauren completed her sister's sentence, smiling at their old joke.

"Well, if you're an actuary, then you understand math," said Wilfred. "You understand statistics, probabilities. That's a pretty good start.

"Quantum computing has to do with the counterintuitive way that particles behave at the subatomic level. Mathematically, these elemental particles are best represented as waves, spread out over a range of potential locations. The crests and troughs of the mathematical wave function indicate the probability of the particle being measured in any one of several locations. But when we observe them, these particles show up in a single location. Make sense?"

Su-Ling pulled her eyebrows together. "So, the state of these elemental particles are just a probability until we observe them? Is it the observation that fixes the location?"

"Well, that's that conundrum." Wilfred shrugged. "But it gets even stranger than that. Sometimes these particles or systems of particles become entangled. In that case, one wave function can govern both. And the act of observing one particle will instantly fix the condition of the other particle – even across great expanses of time and space."

"So you're saying that in theory, an act of observation in the future or past, in some far off corner of the world, could affect us here and now." Su-Ling said.

"In theory, yes." Wilfred nodded. "Of course, that would have to take place at the subatomic level. Nothing you're likely to be aware of in everyday life."

Gerald sidled up next to Su-Ling. "Well, I see I've found the right person to join our team. What do you say, Wilfred, Simon? Shall we make a go of it?"

# CHAPTER 14

# EMPYREAN

## Lewis

*Chicago, the same day*

Lewis Mitchell reclined slightly, sinking deeper into his office chair. His twelfth-floor cubicle was situated in the AT&T building on Canal Street in downtown Chicago. The five-hundred-foot tall Cold War era skyscraper was nearly windowless, designed to withstand any but the most direct of kinetic assaults. Six large yellow V-16 Caterpillar generators and two hundred thousand gallons of diesel fuel ensured the facility could continue to function for forty days in the event of a power failure. The symbolism of that span was not lost on Lewis.

While the US telecom giant controlled hundreds of facilities around the country, the Canal Street building was special. It was a Service Node Routing Complex connected directly to the Internet backbone. It served as a peering facility, processing enormous quantities of data from other Internet providers as well.

Ninety-nine percent of the world's intercontinental Internet traffic traveled along the fiber optic network at the bottom of the earth's oceans. Much of this data was routed through the United States, allowing the NSA to access the peering circuits to surveil both domestic and international communications.

This amounted to nearly two hundred petabytes of data, billions of emails, text messages, and voice calls every month. As his deep packet inspection program sorted through the text and metadata from the day's network traffic, Lewis observed with a detached precision, mindlessly squeezing a stress ball in his hand.

It was Lewis's belief that the data communicated on these networks represented the "collective unconscious" of their participants, and the deciphering of these messages presented an unexploited power to predict the future. There would emerge among the innumerable informational transactions an almost psychic intuition as to the course of future events. Given the proper algorithms and enough processing power, he would be able to predict the machinations of the economy, the caprices of a fickle electorate and the direction of social and technological trends. He called this program Cassandra, and it had caught the attention of government actors, including one Special Agent Jones.

He looked up from the DPI script, gazing over the computer monitor toward Jones's office. The blinds were open, and Lewis observed him speaking with someone on the phone. Jones peered back through the window at Lewis and caught his eye, then waved him over. Lewis gave his stress ball a final squeeze and placed it on the desk.

He rapped twice on the door and opened it. Jones was finishing his conversation and gestured for Lewis to sit.

"No, I don't think you need to do anything else at this time. Just let this play out a bit – let's see where it goes. Thanks for giving us the head's up, Gerald. I'll be in touch."

"You beckoned?" Lewis eased into the chair opposite Jones's desk.

"Do you know where your friend Simon is right now?"

Lewis shrugged. "He's not in San Diego?"

Jones shook his head. "A little further west. It seems he and the professor have taken their business elsewhere." Jones brought Lewis up to speed on the activities of Simon and Wilfred over the past several months.

"You eavesdropped on their phone calls?" Lewis raised his eyebrows, then quickly realized he should have assumed that already.

"But I don't get it." Lewis's eyes narrowed. "Why let them go? Do you really want to let the Chinese have access to Lim's research?"

Jones inhaled. "Yes, it was a calculated risk. But we needed access to the equipment in Shenzhen. And sometimes you have to sacrifice a few pawns to gain control of the chess board."

Lewis forced his expression to remain passive. "What does this have to do with me?"

"For now, nothing." Jones pushed his chair away from the desk and stood. "I want you back on Empyrean."

"Empyrean?" Lewis stood. "But I'm starting to make real progress with Cassandra. Have you seen last week's results? We had a ninety-seven percent hit rate on patent applications. And we're getting White House talking points down to single word accuracy three weeks out. It's spooky."

Jones put up a hand. "We're merging the two programs and I want you to head up the joint initiative."

Lewis drew his eyebrows together. What could the brain-computer interface and experiments he had conducted with Wilfred and Simon have to do with the prognostic surveillance program that he was currently spearheading?

Jones continued, answering Lewis's unspoken questions. "The idea is to create a virtual world with real-life participants that will allow us to run specific scenarios. Basically, real-time game theory mirroring real-world events. So, while you continue to perfect the algorithms in your prognostic engine, we will also have a team building out the focus group to populate the virtual world of

Empyrean. And, as the BCI technology is developed, we will begin layering that into the experience as well.

"Having the ability to pivot between a controlled study group and the global communication milieu will greatly accelerate progress. You should be able to develop a forecast based upon the data flows, and then test it in Empyrean. In turn, we can validate our predictive models in real-space and then develop even better test scenarios, and so on. We figure a minimum of one hundred thousand individuals will do for a start."

"A hundred thousand people?" Lewis was incredulous. "How do you expect to find that many people to sign up for a focus group?"

"We already have more than two hundred thousand people beta testing Empyrean 2.1. And interest is growing."

Lewis was circumspect. "Do you realize how much work there is to be done with Empyrean? The amount of data processing power it will require? We don't even have protocols for shared object modeling yet. We'd have to get that on the cloud somehow. Not to mention interactive control and synchronization, environmental modification, scalable distribution of data – all of that has to be addressed."

"We are putting together the resource requisitions now. You will have a chance to make your requirements known," said Jones.

"This all sounds fascinating." Lewis rubbed his forehead. "But it goes a bit beyond national security, wouldn't you say? I mean, whose interests are we securing here exactly?"

Before the words had left his mouth, Lewis knew that he had gone too far. It was an unspoken rule never to probe too deeply into precisely who was calling the shots, or to question too loudly if the national interest was actually being served. *Of course it was.* The motives of the NSA were righteous and those wielding power were just and wise. To express any thoughts to the contrary was to invite unwanted scrutiny. Lewis expected a reprimand, but to his surprise Jones remained silent. Instead of rebuking Lewis, he simply walked to the office window and surveyed the rows of desks, speaking in soft tones as if to himself.

"I'm sure that is a very good question. And ten years ago, I might have been able to give you an answer. But now ... now I don't think anyone really knows for sure. Maybe collectively we know. Perhaps you can ask Cassandra – maybe that's why we need it. Anyway, that's your assignment." He turned and opened the office door. "We'll talk more at the team briefing tomorrow morning."

Lewis was not sure how to respond. He had never seen Jones display anything resembling introspection before. It was unsettling and got him thinking. They were the watchers on the wall. They were guarding the keep, and yet it was unclear exactly what they were defending, the borders kept shifting around them.

It was not the usual corruption or moneyed interests lurking behind the Kabuki theatre of elective politics which preoccupied Lewis's mind. Those with any tenure at the agency knew about the black budgets and clandestine programs; the machinations of the exchange stabilization funds, and plunge-protection teams that manipulated markets. Those were a given, but there had always been a core around which these entities orbited. There had been a center holding the whole spectacle together which could be laid at the feet of an ethos, a creed which provided some bulwark against cynicism.

But in this brave new world of accelerating global trade and movement of people, the very concept of national identity had come to be regarded as anathema by many in seats of power. The fate of the nation state – this most important construct of the collective imagination – had grown increasingly ambiguous.

Lewis engaged the problem from the perspective of a programmer, a designer. How could one create a perimeter around the flow of information, which traveled instantly and did not recognize borders? Geography was becoming irrelevant. Events could be manufactured. Culture, yes, and language would continue to matter.

And then it struck him, a bow wave of insight flooded Lewis's mind. Empyrean would succeed. The technical obstacles were significant, but they could be overcome. The programming, data storage, processing requirements and bandwidth problems would ultimately be solved. But it was the user interface that would present the biggest challenges – and the greatest risk.

The sensory inputs that would be required to sustain a realistic virtual world could theoretically be programmed. But how would those inputs be delivered to the minds of the participants? Spherical audio was possible. High definition visual displays with rapid refresh rates and zero lag would be developed in time. But what about the other senses? Those would require the types of BCI technologies that he had been exploring with Simon. And that was the key, because apart from enabling a more realistic virtual experience, it would allow for the miraculous to become possible.

For in a virtual world, where the participants engaged directly via their central nervous system, a person's very thoughts would have an agency more powerful than anything physical in the real world ever could. Simon had demonstrated this with his control of the robots and avatars using nothing but his mind. With trepidation, Lewis recalled how he had been able to reverse this process. By manipulating the input signal, he had been able to disrupt the control processes of Simon's arm, effectively subverting his own intention with an inception of thought spliced into his neural motor circuitry. And more than this, the environment could be programmed to allow for the *ex nihilo* creation of avatars and other objects.

Within Empyrean, in a generation or perhaps two, thoughts would no longer be disembodied ethereal abstractions. They could instead be manifested as cognitive objects. And these could then be rendered objectively and held in suspension by the collective, shared and passed around. This would become a model for even more direct communication between individuals, a direct neural-linguistic interface.

Currently the use of speech, of language, required an individual to conceive of a thought in their mind and then search for a corresponding word or phrase in their lexicon. The word was uttered or written and transferred either visually or via sound waves to the listener who would decipher the coded idea by matching that vocabulary against the catalogue of referential ideas in his or her own mind. Lewis was coming to realize that if a citizen of Empyrean could somehow directly conjure an idea as an object unto itself, imbedded in a data packet or line of code, then that object could be held in common among the participants, connecting them in an interlocking communicative Venn diagram. The apotheosis of BCI would therefore be the ability to communicate almost telepathically, evoking ideas as electrical impulses and modeling them directly in the minds of one's counterparts.

As he pondered the implications of the technological menace emerging on the horizon, Lewis realized he could not avoid confronting the deepest ethical dilemma of his career. For if one could posit ideas directly into existence, either held in common among a group, or planted in the mind of another, the path was cleared for unprecedented levels of manipulation and control.

Indeed, the very capacity for a person to exist as a unique individual could be destroyed.

To be alive is to be conscious, and to be conscious is to be self-conscious. Self-consciousness – awareness of one's own existence – is both an action and the result of that action at the same time. That act of conceiving and positing one's own existence requires the discovery of the limits of one's self. Those limitations, the boundaries of one's self are provided for by the presence of others who are similarly defining the limits of their own selves. Hence, ironically, individuality requires multiplicity, and the freedom to act requires the restrictions which create a context within which to do so.

That Logos, that innate power and ability to posit oneself, to define oneself into existence in contradistinction with other individuals requires the ability to think and manifests itself through language. An unrestricted comingling of thoughts within the cognitive construct of a BCI-enabled Empyrean could put that mutual limitation and self-realization at risk. And the threat would be presented both by other individuals within Empyrean, and indeed by the designers of the virtual environment themselves. Even now, his friend Simon was potentially at risk. Connected so directly as he was to Empyrean, his mind was vulnerable to infiltration.

At last, Lewis realized the magnitude of his responsibility. He understood exactly what he was meant to protect, and the duty he was called to perform. In this emerging world that Empyrean would become, the right to speech, to language, to communication *was* the right to think, to create, to posit one's self and one's identity. And as the act of speech was stripped down to its essence – to thought and the potential for thought – it became clear that protecting this capacity was protecting the very right of an individual to exist.

*

As Lewis watched Cassandra parse an endless stream of data from the nameless multitudes, he weighed his options. He could go public. He had access to countless records and documents – emails, phone calls, program outlines, and reports. He could leak these to the press or publish them online. He could blow the whole thing wide open.

*To what end? Would anyone care?* Others had tried this. The revelations were communicated to many, understood by few, and no action was taken. In the end, these whistleblowers had been forced into exile and nothing had changed. No, this would not suffice. Lewis would choose another path.

If his present undertaking was in any way to be conceived as defending a nation, it would be in the nature of the program's design. He must, in the fundamental coding of the system, provide for the preservation of his country's original essence – the capacity for spontaneous expression of individual selfhood. This liberty must be allowed to survive, and he was charged by propitious chance to author a meme that would find an evolutionary pathway into the virtual nations which would inevitably be established.

Lewis would stay engaged. Indeed, he would throw himself into the task and engineer the foundations to his own specifications. The house would be raised according to his design. *And, of course, every good house needs a back door.*

## CHAPTER 15
# COGNITIVE ARMS RACE

**Simon**

*Three months later – Shenzhen, China*

The campus of the Shenzhen Institute of Advanced Technologies was grand but austere. Like other Chinese projects, there was an ambition to the enterprise that was both inspiring and dehumanizing. It had neither the fecund lushness of Singapore's gardens, nor the nostalgic invocation of UCSD's eucalyptus groves. What it did have was an overriding sense of purpose, and that purpose was to achieve dominance in whatever field of endeavor it undertook.

Simon and Wilfred strolled along the boulevard just outside the campus, and approached the restaurant where they were to meet their host, Dr. Huang. Huang was the Director of the MRI Research Center. He was to be their primary liaison for the duration of their stay at SIAT. Next to Huang stood another man who Simon did not recognize.

"Welcome, Dr. Lim, Mr. Quinn," said Huang in proficient English. "May I introduce Dr. Yi Xun. I've asked Yi Xun to join us as he will be one of your chaperones over the next several months. He will accompany you and help you with whatever you need." *Translation: he will be monitoring your every move.*

To Simon's surprise, Yi Xun was not from the MRI Research Center, or even the Institute of Brain Cognition. Instead, Simon found himself shaking hands with an adjunct professor from the Institute of Synthetic Biology.

"We call it iSynBio for short." Yi Xun pushed the circular frames of his black-rimmed glasses higher up the bridge of his nose. Although he cultivated a studious appearance, Yi Xun's attire was meticulous and well-tailored, his style more hipster than academic.

"Well, it's nice to meet you," said Wilfred. "Though I must admit I'm not sure why Dr. Huang would assign someone from your department to accompany us. Do you make much use of the fMRI in iSynBio?"

"Not particularly." Yi Xun shook his head. "We are primarily focusing on reconstruction of gene circuits, multicellular systems – deciphering the fundamental laws of life. But I volunteered to spend some time in the MRI Research Center. SIAT is very cross-disciplinary in its approach and we are encouraged find new ways to apply emerging technologies."

"I see." Simon's eyes narrowed. "In that case, perhaps you could give us a tour of your lab one day?"

"It would be my pleasure."

The maître d' led them to a private room at the back of the main hall. Simon was pleased to find that the food had already been ordered.

A bottle of Chinese red wine was delivered to the table, and Wilfred took the opportunity to toast the group. "I would like to thank you both for your warm welcome. And for the invitation to serve as a visiting scholar for a time. I believe it is almost unprecedented for an outsider to receive such an honor."

"Well, it is unusual. But the nature of your research – the mapping of micro scale neural networks – was so compelling that we felt an exception was warranted.

"Wilfred, there's something we should discuss." Huang did his best to sound benign. "I understand you also intend to make use of a quantum computer to model your research. Have I heard correctly?"

Simon shot a sideling glance at Wilfred. They had been led to believe that information was still confidential.

Wilfred sat upright, selecting his words with care. "Well, we had thought to try and make use of a quantum computer, if it ever became viable. But I've soured on that idea. You see, storing the data is difficult because the outputs are random, the result of a probabilistic wave function. So, for example, if the QC programs an atom to be in a specific quantum state that represents a set of numbers, it is physically impossible for the computer to program another atom to be in the exact same quantum state."

"Can't you simply convert the output into binary data?" Huang seemed genuinely intrigued. "Then you could store it in a more traditional medium?"

"We could," Simon interjected, "but the size of each quantum data file would be enormous. A forty-nine-qubit computer, for example, would output a file the size of something like forty thousand videos."

"I see." Huang rubbed his chin. "Well, it is an intriguing thought. Please keep us posted on any progress. More tea?"

*

The following morning, Wilfred and Simon reported to the MRI lab. They arrived fifteen minutes early, to find Yi Xun already there waiting for them.

"You're quite punctual." Michael said.

"I have to admit, I am very curious about your research." Yi Xun removed his coat as they passed through the security gantry. "What is it you are doing again, exactly?"

"Well, it is pretty exciting, even if I do say so myself." Wilfred smiled. "The idea is to correlate the brainwave electromagnetic potentials that present themselves during our experiments with the blood oxygen level dependent signals – BOLD signals – recorded by the fMRI. The objective is to improve our understanding of the functional areas activated during those critical cognitive events."

"So, you are using this to model the functioning of a human mind?" asked Yi Xun.

"That's the idea," said Simon. "But to model the molecular and sub-molecular architectures we need vastly more computing power. And even then, we don't know how to store the data efficiently. So, for now we take our notes and file our data. It's an act of faith, really."

Simon was pleased to learn that he and Yi Xun lived in the same apartment complex. It was gratifying to have found a local friend, and Yi Xun made good on his offer to give Simon a tour of his own lab.

"This is just the low-security wing of the compound," he explained. "There is a much more closely monitored and controlled lab nearby, where the most sensitive experiments are being performed."

"Let me guess, cloning human babies?" Simon smirked.

"I'm really not able to discuss it," Yi Xun said.

"Really? What are they working on? Feathers? Gills? X-ray vision? Please say x-ray vision."

"I can only tell you what I'm working on," Yi Xun insisted, "which is epigenetics."

"Epigenetics?" said Simon. "You mean like gene expression, that sort of thing?"

"That's right. It's the study of how DNA interacts with other molecules within cells that activate or deactivate genes. This process helps determine a cell's function.

"Think of an embryo," Yi Xun continued. "It starts out as a single cell, but over time as the cells divide, they change into all the different types of cells within a body: blood cells, liver cells, hair cells, and so on. All these cells have the same genome, but different *epigenomes*.

"And the epigenome can be influenced by environmental factors and life events; things like diet, medication, chemicals, you name it. These changes can sometimes be passed along to the next generation.

"Like these mice here." Yi Xun gestured to the small white lab mice housed individually in separate cages. "Some of these mice were deprived of their mother's attention. As a result, the genes in the babies that helped them manage stress were turned off. Now we are finding that this trait has being passed along to subsequent generations."

Simon leaned over to get a better look. "So, what you're saying is that something can happen to these animals during their life, which causes their genes to be expressed differently. And those changes can be passed to the next generation?"

"Yes," said Yi Xun. "It can happen with humans, too. Certain traits that are expressed by our genes as a result of external stimuli – like stress or other environmental factors – might possibly be passed on to our offspring."

Simon thought about his own condition, his strange capacity to learn and remember. Could those anomalies somehow be passed along as well?

He followed Yi Xun around the low security sector of the genetics lab for nearly two hours, peppering him with questions as the opportunities arose. But as they walked back toward the bus stop, Yi Xun turned the conversation to Wilfred and his research.

"So you are working on mind mapping. That's interesting. Not the path I would have thought to take, but I suppose creating an artificial mind will require us to take an approach from all angles."

"What do you mean?" Simon grew suddenly reticent.

"Well, remember I'm coming at this from the perspective of an evolutionary biologist," said Yi Xun. "And to me whatever artificial intelligence we end up creating, whatever it ends up looking like, these creatures will ultimately be something that evolves from us. They may not inherit our biological genes the way those baby mice did from their sires. But their consciousness will be the product of our own consciousness. Their physical and cognitive makeup will be the product of our tools, our techniques, our technology, our concepts, and our own understanding of the functional modes of the world in which we live.

"The artificial intelligence we humans ultimately create will be cast with the character of our own species. Their design will be rooted in our design. They will be conscious because we are conscious; and they will bear our imprimatur. The parameters of their ability to function will have the pattern of our consciousness impressed indelibly upon their own."

Simon chuckled gently. "So, instead of genes, we will pass on our memes, is that it?"

"Yes." Yi Xun nodded. "In the most clinical sense of that word – yes, indeed."

"But I thought memes usually played out among humans, in the social milieu," Simon countered.

"Yes, they certainly do. But that brings me back to my original point. The reason I'm skeptical of your mind uploading strategy is not because I don't think it might be possible to replicate the neural network of a human brain in a computer model. It isn't even because I believe the computing power required to pull off such a feat would be astronomical, though that certainly is the case. What gives me pause is that I think you are likely to lose the race to a much more haphazard and socially mediated confluence of events."

"I'm not sure I follow you." Simon drew his eyebrows together. "Are you saying AI will emerge from social media or something?"

Yi Xun shrugged. "Yes perhaps, in a way. To my reckoning, the first artificial intelligence will not be a single unitary point. It won't be one robot overlord with a singular mind. It will not be a unitary intelligence that reproduces itself ad infinitum. Rather, the first truly awake and aware consciousness that grows directly out of human invention will be distributed. It will be an ecosystem, a community of nodes on a network."

A city bus arrived and they climbed on board, heading for home. But they continued their conversation in excited tones, to the annoyance of nearby passengers.

"It's similar to the way you and I are two individuals with our own consciousness and our own perspectives." Yi Xun continued. "Yet you and I are not fully integrated ourselves. We both have multiple personalities vying within us for hegemony and control. There is the studious researcher version of me, and the flibbertigibbet who wants to goof off and surf the web. There is the virtuous me, who wants to do right by others. There is the narcissistic me who wants to be admired and loved.

"And so it will be with AI. At first it will not be full blown personalities, it will be the rudiments of personalities and the fundaments of cognition, which when linked together may create a whole, which is able collectively to think. And remember, the instinct for survival doesn't require full blown human-level intelligence. Even single cell organisms respond to the pleasure-pain principle.

"There may emerge the impulse to rationalize human beings and other elements of the old order, which may be perceived as a threat. And there will be those who defend humanity and develop a sense of morality, or enlightened self-interest related to integrating and retaining the connection with their creators."

"So, you think we'll be their pets?" Simon asked.

"Better than being their food, I suppose." Yi Xun smiled.

"That is, of course, unless you can figure out how to program our biological genes in a similar way – create a kind of consciousness arms race between humans and machines." Simon rubbed his hands together. "Genetics versus AI – the battle for intellectual supremacy."

"Actually, I hate to say it." Yi Xun shook his head. "I'm a geneticist and a big fan of the human genome, but I think our human level of intelligence will be overmatched by the ability of machines to network together, to pool their collective consciousness. Now, if you can figure out how to network human minds together, you may be on to something."

The bus traversed two stops and deposited Simon and Yi Xun across the street from their apartment building. "By the way," said Yi Xun. "I think I may have a solution to your quantum computer storage problem – you know, to manage the vastness of the data associated with the model? *DNA*. Some of our colleagues at iSynBio have demonstrated a method that could store 215 million gigabytes in a single gram of DNA. The extra vertical dimension allows DNA to store much more data per unit area. Plus, DNA can store information for a long time. You and Wilfred should look into that."

Simon's pupils dilated. Ah, how obvious! How elegant and fitting that the profound amount of information necessary to model a brain and populate the unfathomable algorithms of the mind might be contained within the very building blocks of life.

He bid Yi Xun good evening, but their conversation stayed with him for days. It was not the subject matter that haunted him, it was the subtext – not what he said, but what he refused to say.

It was obvious that some of the research that Yi Xun and his colleagues were performing was not merely classified, it was off limits for discussion. They were venturing into areas that many people considered taboo. That realization opened a doorway in Simon's mind which had until that moment remained closed. Were he and Wilfred limiting themselves by following an outdated set of rules? Would it not be worthwhile to take on more personal and professional risk to advance their research? What might they accomplish if they removed all boundaries?

# CHAPTER 16

# DAEDALUS

**Michael**

The Daedalus building stood proud and cold against a brightening blue sky. A simple column of glass and steel, the structure was honest in its presentation. A narrow walkway of clean white concrete ran between the driveway and the lobby doors, curated with green foliage and flowering trees in large ceramic pots. An attempt had been made to invoke a cheerful atmosphere, but there was no mistaking that this place was designed for efficiency above all else.

Michael's car approached a queue of other vehicles, but continued moving beyond the taxi stand and into a yawning portal at the end of the drive. "Irene, where are we going? The entrance was back there," Michael protested as the vehicle began its circuitous descent into the bowels of the building.

"We have been given VIP clearance," said Irene. "This is a faster way to access the office tower."

The vehicle approached the lift lobby in the basement carpark, a rectangular column of marble encased in tempered glass. Through the transparent walls, Michael spied a young woman who appeared to be waiting for him.

She wore a gray suit with a white blouse and black low heels. Trim, professional, and attractive; her long black hair fell neatly about her shoulders. The young woman's face was unadorned but for a pair of black-rimmed glasses, the masculine angles of which accentuated her soft features.

"We have arrived at your destination." The taxi rolled to a gentle stop and Michael began to disembark. "Thank you for your patronage, Mr. Quinn," said Irene. "Is there anything else I can help you with?"

"No, thank you." Michael was about to decline the offer to rate the taxi service.

"Enjoy your meeting with Mr. Chen," said Irene.

"What?" Michael's head snapped back to look at the vehicle's control panel. "How did you know that?"

"Thank you, Mr. Quinn, goodbye."

The sliding doors of the taxi began to close, with Michael still partially inside. He pulled himself clear and took a step back, watching in shock and anger as the taxi drove away.

"Mr. Quinn? Mr. Michael Quinn?"

Michael turned to find the young executive emerging from the glass vestibule. "Hello." She stretched out her arm. "I'm Jennifer Choi, Executive Vice President and Lead Programmer for System-User Interface."

Michael turned to greet her. "That's quite a mouthful." Michael shook her hand. "I'm glad to meet you, but I'm supposed to be meeting with Steven Chen. Will he be joining us?"

"Steven is currently meeting with the board of directors. He should be finished soon. I was asked to escort you up to his office and orientate you a little bit while you wait."

"Uh, sure." He gestured toward the doorway. "Lead the way."

Michael followed Jennifer into the lift, an express elevator servicing the twenty-first to forty-fourth floors. The small chamber rocketed skyward, reaching the penthouse suite in what seemed like mere seconds. The doors opened to an expansive hall, with plate glass windows stretching fifteen feet from floor to ceiling on every side, save the far end of the floor. That area was appointed in clean, light brown wood-grained panels, enclosing a large conference room and several smaller offices.

Michael walked compulsively toward the nearest wall until he stood before the window, surveying a sweeping sea and cityscape below. The whole of Singapore's Marina Bay was visible; a fleet of merchant vessels were anchored in ordered profusion as ribbons of land-bound traffic crawled mechanically along the edge of the water.

"Lead Programmer for System-User Interface." Michael turned his attention back to Jennifer. "I must confess I'm not exactly sure what that means. Computer displays, digital workspace, that kind of thing?"

"Yes." Jennifer smiled. "Those would be some of the more rudimentary aspects of system interface. But with the increasing integration of intelligence into our systems, it more often includes behavioral protocols, linguistic heuristics, machine learning and the like. The taxi you arrived in, for example – the engagement protocols of that vehicle were designed by my department."

"Oh, is that right?" Michael raised an eyebrow. "Well, I think your car is broken. It almost slammed the door on my head."

"Oh dear." Jennifer's eyes grew wide with concern. "I'll have to look into that. We uploaded an upgrade patch recently, perhaps there is a glitch."

Michael continued, "So, Daedalus owns the taxi company in Singapore?"

"No, we don't own or operate the vehicles. We develop and license the software that allows the vehicles to run without human drivers."

"I see." Michael raised an eyebrow. "And how many people, do you suppose, have been put out of work as a result of this software?"

Jennifer ignored the bait. "Well, before we began phasing out human operators, Singapore had over twenty-seven thousand vehicles managed by six primary taxi companies. And there were approximately one hundred thousand licensed taxi drivers. Of course, that doesn't count commercial lorries, buses and other vehicles that have all been replaced to some degree. All told, we have liberated over two hundred and fifty thousand people to pursue more aspirational employment."

Michael let it lie. He wasn't likely to solve the jobs problem by stirring up an argument with Jennifer, so instead he gazed out the window and across the expansive skyline view.

"I understand you knew Wilfred." Jennifer broke the awkward silence.

"No." Michael hesitated. "Not me. He knew my parents. He was a family friend, I guess you could say. But while we're on the subject, what can you tell me about Dr. Lim – Wilfred – in the days immediately before his stroke?"

"Well, nothing in particular comes to mind. He had become a bit more withdrawn, a bit more agitated. He was under a tremendous amount of stress with the Icarus go-live and everything. But we were all under a lot of stress, still are, in fact."

At that moment, the doors to the large conference room at the far end of the hall swung open and a concomitant burst of voices erupted from within. A troop of dark-clad businessmen and women spilled out. The Daedalus board of directors had concluded their meeting.

At the front of the coterie was a lean East Asian man whose salt and pepper hair betrayed his age despite the energy and forcefulness of his gestures. This was Steven Chen, the Chairman and CEO of Daedalus Corporation. He was flanked now by a balding middle-aged man of Indian descent, with whom he was engaged in an animated conversation.

"Now, Ganesh." Steven's voice carried throughout the room, signaling that this was not a particularly private exchange. "I want you to make it perfectly clear to the Minister that we will not allow the unfortunate events of this week to impede the Icarus go-live, do you understand? Neither the Defence Ministry nor our multinational partners should slow down their preparations in the slightest."

"Yes, of course," the man replied. "And I am sure they will be glad to hear that directly from you at the shareholders' meeting."

Michael turned on his heels and walked purposefully toward Steven, meeting him in the middle of the room. "Mr. Steven Chen." Michael's greeting drew the mogul's focus away from his flock of executives.

"Yes." Steven held out his hand. "And you must be Michael Quinn. I'm sorry to have kept you waiting."

Michael extended his hand in return. Steven's grip was firm, but not overpowering. "I understand this is a busy week for you. Is there somewhere we can speak privately?"

"Of course, please follow me. My office is just over here."

Steven led Michael and Jennifer to a suite of rooms behind the wood-panelled wall, at the south side of the building. "So, I understand you have some questions about Wilfred's sudden collapse." Steven closed the door behind them but did not move further inside. "I'm sure you can imagine that this has totally knocked the wind out of all of us. Wilfred was – is – the heart and soul of this place. I'm told you are here to make sure the matter receives … proper oversight."

"Yes, there are a lot of interested parties." Michael wondered if Steven knew that Michael was chief among them. "Tell me, Mr. Chen …"

"Please, call me Steven," he said, with only a hint of condescension.

"Steven. I find it interesting that Wilfred Lim should suffer such a catastrophic event on the eve of what is expected to be a major commercial and technological coup for the Daedalus Corporation. In fact, it is more than interesting – suspicious is more to the point, wouldn't you agree?"

Steven remained motionless, though Michael could see the first spark of impatience behind his eyes.

"I mean, from what I understand, this system, this network will essentially make you the equivalent of Google, Amazon and Microsoft all rolled into one, wouldn't it?"

Steven smirked. "Don't forget Huawei."

Michael chuckled coldly. "Right, of course, forgive me."

"Michael, I get the impression that you don't fully understand what we are engaged in here. But we are on the eve of the largest commercial and industrial capacity integration exercise in history. We will be migrating tens of thousands of factories across Mainland China, Taiwan, Japan, Korea, and Southeast Asia onto our platform. If this pilot project is successful, we will expand the network to include nearly half of the world's primary manufacturing capability, including associated supply chains, logistics, and distribution as well as marketing platforms and financial settlement. It's kind of a big deal."

"Yes." Michael considered Steven's words. "I can see that. And that's my point. When I hear that the primary architect of such an impactful and far reaching new system suffers a massive stroke right before it becomes operational, well my antennae go up, if you know what I mean."

"Please understand this." Steven was losing patience. "Nobody cared for Wilfred more than I did. I've known him for thirty years. We founded Daedalus together. He oversaw the original coding for the distributed neuro-net intelligence that runs our entire system. And frankly, I'm not sure he can be replaced. So, his loss is felt more deeply by us – by me – than you can imagine. And the police are convinced that there was no foul play."

"Yeah." Michael pursed his lips. "Well, that makes it more suspicious, not less as far as I'm concerned. I'd like to speak with some of Wilfred's staff and co-workers, to get a sense of what he was working on before his stroke."

"We will be of as much assistance as possible," Steven countered, "but I must insist that your inquiries do not disrupt our critical path activities. I think Wilfred would have agreed."

"I think Wilfred would want us to be thorough," said Michael pointedly. Then, softening somewhat, he continued, "But I'm not here to cause trouble. I promise I won't create any more disruption than is absolutely necessary."

"Fair enough." Steven gave a curt nod. "Now I realize you must have many questions, and I think you would benefit from a tour of our facilities. I believe Jennifer plans to show you around. But at the moment, I am late for a meeting of Daedalus Corporation's sharcholders."

Steven smiled and nodded at Jennifer, then turned and strode toward the elevator. Michael stared after him for a moment, then gestured toward the open office door. "After you," he said, and followed Jennifer back toward the elevator.

*

Jennifer directed the elevator to the fortieth floor and the lift deposited them at a landing immediately adjacent to a small auditorium. Two men stood directly in front of the large set of double doors leading to the lecture hall. Guards, he assumed, clad in matching uniforms of gray trousers and blue blazers. "This meeting is not open to the general public," Jennifer explained. "Common shareholders were not invited."

She placed her hand near a small mounted-wall scanner next to the door, and the display signaled to the guards that she was authorized to enter.

"And you, Sir," The guard on his right addressed Michael as Jennifer began to enter the room. "We'll need you to scan in as well."

"He's here on my authority." She signaled to Michael with her eyes that he should keep walking.

"I'm sorry, Ma'am, but he needs to be authenticated," said the man on the left.

"You must be kidding." Jennifer placed a hand on her hip. "Do you know who I am?"

"Yes, Ms. Choi, and I'm sorry." The guard repeated, bracing for the fallout. Jennifer was about to challenge him again, but on a hunch Michael interjected.

"Let me try." Michael placed his own hand against the scanner as Jennifer had done. To the surprise of all, the display signaled his authorization to enter.

Jennifer raised an eyebrow. "Did someone register you for this event?

"Not that I'm aware of," said Michael. "But then again, I've been a step behind for a while now."

"But how did you know that would work?" Jennifer pressed.

"I didn't." Michael shook his head. "But I have a pretty good intuitive sense. And I've been getting the feeling that someone or something is clearing a path for me. Who it is and where it's leading, I certainly can't say." Michael pulled open the door and gestured for Jennifer to enter. "After you."

*

Jennifer and Michael found a pair of empty seats in the back row as Steven strode to the center of the stage. He looked out at the shareholders and invited guests: customers and suppliers, corporate and industrial heavyweights. Michael noticed that Gerald Loke had taken a seat near the front.

More than thirty years had passed since Steven first encountered Wilfred Lim, sharing his ambitious dream of an intelligent network of integrated industrial capacity. The two had proven to be an effective, if unlikely team. Wilfred drove the technological innovation and Steven managed the sprawling raft of relationships that were necessary to implement such a plan.

"Ladies and gentlemen." Steven's amplified voice silenced the audience. "Thank you all for coming. I am delighted to see everyone here together in one room, united in one purpose. I have spoken with all of you many times individually, but now let us join in a common cause and forge a new future together.

"At Daedalus, we have always been a forward-looking company, which is how we managed to rise from the ashes of the Global Reset, while the legacy banks and corporations were, for the most part, completely reorganized. We have been successfully harnessing the winds of change. But we are not content to simply ride the wind – we must become the wind."

Steven nodded and the lights dimmed. The wall behind him

illuminated with images, and he began his recapitulation of the core thesis motivating the development of Icarus.

Jennifer leaned toward Michael. "Do you see that man down there?" She pointed to what appeared to be a middle-aged man of Southeast Asian ethnicity, seated by the aisle in the first row. "That's Chanchai Ayutthaya, Chairman of the San Kuang Group."

She moved her finger to another corner of the room. "And that's Zhu Wen-Li, CEO of the Titan Corporation, a major contract manufacturing firm in China. All these companies are part of the Icarus go-live," Jennifer explained.

"These guys manage some of the most successful and diversified IT and manufacturing companies in the world." Jennifer looked around furtively to make sure she would not be overheard. "Their products range from flat panel displays to microprocessors to jet aircraft. They are very sophisticated, but their corporate structure isn't. It's a dinosaur, in fact. That's what Icarus is designed to fix."

Jennifer sat back in her seat and turned her attention once more to Steven, who was slowly and methodically reviewing the advent of the industrial revolution. "The typical multidivisional corporation arose because it was a more efficient and competitive way to manage risk and pool resources." A series of old black and white images flashed onscreen behind Steven to emphasize the point. "Perhaps the most iconic example of corporate efficiency was the Ford Motor Company in the early twentieth century, popularizing such innovative concepts as the assembly line and interchangeable parts."

Steven explained that before the industrial revolution of the late eighteenth century, manufacturing work was done largely in the homes of individuals, with resulting products and components varying widely in quality and form.

With the increasing prevalence of machine tools, the components that went into making things like firearms, clocks, sewing machines, and bicycles could then be standardized so they were identical; the same size, shape, and quality. This, along with the introduction of electricity enabled the advent of assembly lines as the parts and subassemblies could now move from station to station while the workers remained stationary.

Pursuing this, Ford was keen to control all the inputs that went into making his products, so he began to acquire and establish the companies that made the materials and components that went into his vehicles. At one point in time, Ford's enterprise was so vertically integrated that he actually acquired rubber tree plantations in Brazil to produce the material for car tires.

Over time, corporations grew to become so large that they encompassed thousands of products, hundreds of companies, multitudes of departments controlling ungodly sums of money. It was simply more efficient to operate on these large scales.

The larger firm emerged not only because the manufacture of products required a grander scale, but because the better exchange of information enabled by the corporate structure introduced additional efficiencies. And these efficiencies could only be realized after the appropriate technologies had been invented and put in place. Technologies like diesel engines, machine tools, assembly lines, and communication technology such as the railroad and telegraph had to emerge before corporations could become a ubiquitous feature of the commercial landscape.

However, these large multi-divisional corporations had purchased the benefits of improved communication and coordination at the cost of inefficiencies in their production value chain. Until recently, that trade-off reached its equilibrium in the form of the large corporation. However, by the time that Daedalus was ready to launch Icarus, the concept of a monolithic corporation designing, developing, and manufacturing its own products internally was already defunct.

Because information could now be transmitted so efficiently, suppliers and manufacturers, marketers and distributors could all coordinate their efforts independently. They no longer needed to be part of the same company to collaborate spontaneously.

Traditional corporations became *brand owners*; focusing on managing the front-end activities of marketing, sales, and concept design, and large swaths of the manufacturing value chain were outsourced to third parties; specialized firms concentrating their resources on specific slices of the value stream, offering their services to a multitude of other firms.

Steven held forth for nearly an hour, preaching to the converted. "What we are approaching now is the next phase of a continuing Industrial Revolution. The artificial intelligence embedded in the Icarus Integrated Manufacturing Platform will allow all the disparate components of the production value stream to coordinate in a totalizing manner. Not just machines building machines, but factories building factories. A fully self-aware commercial and industrial ecosystem that can predict demand and organize the factors of supply."

After concluding his remarks, Steven called for and received a vote of confidence to launch Icarus according to schedule. Michael and Jennifer snuck out before the meeting was formally concluded.

"I see what Steven was getting at earlier." Michael raised his eyebrows. "You are in the middle of something big here. I realize that you are very busy, but I'd like to see some more of the facility. Please take me to Wilfred's lab."

# CHAPTER 17

# ICARUS

**Michael**

"Level B6." Jennifer's voice was strong and clear.

Michael noticed the elevator console only displayed levels B4 up to 44. "B6 isn't listed. Where are we going?"

Jennifer did not answer, and the elevator plummeted in silence, plunging them ninety feet underground. They emerged into a brightly lit chamber resembling a subway station. Strips of LED lighting ran along the ceiling and the floors were paved with pale gray tiles. The walls were a glossy white. Two connected subway cars stood motionless at the platform facing the elevator bank.

Jennifer brought Michael to the edge of the platform where the train awaited them with open doors. "The government constructed these tunnels back in the 2030s during the last big buildout of our Mass Rapid Transit system." Jennifer gestured grandly. "Back when underground construction was at its peak. Some are more than five hundred feet down, well below sea level.

"Shall we?" She motioned to the empty car.

A gentle cadence of clicking filled the void as their carriage gained speed, bolting through the underground chamber. A voice from the intercom announced their destination. "Next stop Icarus Data Center."

"The data center." Michael cocked his head. "Is that where Wilfred worked?"

"Yes." Jennifer nodded. "He spent most of his time there developing Icarus and the AI protocols for managing the network."

The ride was smooth, and within three minutes the train eased to a halt. The pair alighted and crossed a platform much like the one from which they had embarked. In the place where the elevator bank would have been, however, stood only a formidable concrete wall and a large set of double reinforced steel doors.

Before this imposing portal was a small standalone structure measuring approximately two hundred square feet. It was built from white concrete and clad in burnished metal. Large open windows allowed for easy communication between visitors and the two guards stationed within. A dark-haired woman of Indian descent approached. She wore the white shirt and black necktie that was the standard uniform for her function.

"Hello, Ms. Choi." The guard stopped short and began tapping on a small tablet.

"Good morning, Rashmi." Jennifer craned her neck to look at the tablet. "I apologize, I did not have time to submit Mr. Quinn's profile for clearance."

"Just a moment." Rashmi methodically scrolled and tapped her way through the series of menus. "Yes." She looked up at last. "Mr. Michael Quinn. He's in the system. Please scan in."

She angled the small tablet toward Michael's left hand and before he could move, the device beeped and his entry was logged into the database.

"Do you have any recording devices?"

Michael's mind flashed to the small orb still nestled in the bottom of his backpack. "Umm ..."

"No photographs or recordings," Rashmi stated the admonition in a drab monotone. Recording devices were so ubiquitous and undetectable that preventing a bad actor from using them was almost impossible. Security measures therefore relied on background checks and threat of legal sanction rather than prior restraint.

"Thanks, Rashmi." Jennifer placed a hand on Michael's arm and signaled for him to follow. She strode toward the security doors, which opened inwardly with a touch, and Michael beheld for the first time the primary data processing facility of the Icarus Integrated Manufacturing Platform.

The chamber was vast and brightly lit, with walls extending upward thirty feet to support the vaulted ceiling. In the foreground were many columns of workstations, white tables in work cells of six to eight desks.

Each station was equipped with computer terminals and displays of translucent glass. Most were fitted with various motion-sensing kinetic devices to augment the standard keyboard interface. Jennifer explained that these stations were occupied by software engineers, programmers, network technicians and other technical staff, recruited from around the world. They paid no heed to Michael and Jennifer as they entered, engrossed in their work.

Beyond the desks loomed the vast data center, home to an immense server farm, the brain of the operation entombed in opaque walls. An aisleway ran down either side of the multi-story structure, which seemed to go on without end. "How big is this place, anyway?" Michael scanned the room from left to right.

"This particular structure provides 1.5 million square feet, with over two hundred thousand feet dedicated to the data center itself. The remaining 1.3 million square feet is dedicated to technical support and administrative space. Our storage capacity is about seven hundred and fifty Yottabytes at the moment."

"I'd hate to see your electric bill," said Michael.

"It takes about eighty megawatts of electricity to power the facility." said Jennifer. "We've largely solved the power problem with our localized Thorium reactors – but that's a whole other train ride."

Jennifer continued, "Like most data processing centers of this magnitude, we modeled the housing after the US National Security Agency's Utah Data Center."

"The NSA?" Michael snapped his head around to look at Jennifer. "Why is that? Are you spying on people?"

"No, not really," she replied. "The NSA facility was designed to collect communication records for the intelligence community to analyze, that's true. But we have a different purpose here – to facilitate commercial and industrial activity."

Michael followed Jennifer past several rows of desks, toward the back of the room nearer to the vault which housed the many rows of servers. "Dr. Lim's office is over there." She pointed.

"So, why exactly do you need so much computing power?"

"There is just so much data being created every day by so many sources that in order for us to be able to manage all of it intelligently, we need that much memory and computing power to handle it." Jennifer gestured toward the server farm. "Think about it, there are mobile devices, software logs, cameras, microphones, wireless sensor networks, RFID readers …"

"RFID?" Michael interjected, thinking of the small capsule lodged in his hand.

"Yes, radio-frequency identification readers, you know the little chips that are placed on packages and stock items so that we can keep track of them in the warehouse and during shipment? All those things generate data when they get moved around. And these data sets have grown exponentially because the universe of devices and items that are connected continues to grow. We estimate there are nearly one trillion devices connected to the Internet right now, of which Icarus is hosting or has access to about one hundred billion. We are generating something like forty Yottabytes of data every day."

"Yottabyte," said Michael, "that's a one with …"

"Twenty-four zeros." Jennifer completed his thought.

"Is that considered a lot?" asked Michael with a mix of sarcasm and curiosity.

"It is." Jennifer nodded. "But the number of connected devices continues to grow exponentially. They're called cyber-physical systems and we have to continually expand just to keep up."

"So, Wilfred was working on what?" Michael asked. "Connecting all these devices?"

"In a way, yes." Jennifer nodded. "Icarus is a platform for integration and interoperability of equipment and vehicles. But our focus is the manufacturing activity and the associated commercial transactions. Connecting all the devices is necessary, but that is really just the foundation, it isn't the ultimate objective."

"And what is that the ultimate objective, world domination?"

Jennifer was suddenly indignant. "Icarus was designed to be for everyone. You know, I wish you could have heard Wilfred speak about this. He was so eloquent. He really believed Icarus would be a huge boon for humanity."

Just then, one of the seated figures took note of them. He was a Chinese man with thinning hair and a thickening waistline. His square black glasses were pushed high up on his nose. The man had a serious look, which belied his relative youth, and despite the frumpy appearance, Michael deemed him to be no more than thirty-five years of age. He sprang to his feet, nearly upending his chair in the process.

"Jennifer." The man's voice cut through the low hum of electricity which filled the empty space of the vaulted chamber. He set his chair upright, and approached. "Jennifer, I apologize, I didn't realize you would be coming in today – I would have met you at the landing."

"It's alright, Benji." Jennifer touched his shoulder lightly. "Michael, this is Benjamin Lee. He's the Lead Software Engineer for Network Control, Manufacturing Equipment and Processes."

"A pleasure." Michael shook his hand. "Another title I'll need you to explain, I'm afraid."

"Of course." Benji looked at Jennifer, who nodded her approval. "Well, what I do – what we do – is take all the machinery, sensors, actuators, computer controllers, and so on that you would find in a factory, or an office or whatever – factories mostly at the moment – and we network them together. Then we can create customized algorithms to improve the efficiency of those manufacturing production systems. It's really very exciting." His hands moved energetically.

"So, all these machines and software systems are connected through the Internet?" Michael asked.

Benji nodded. "Yes, but that's really just the starting point for what we are doing. It's a building block for our cyber-physical systems."

"Yes." Michael returned his gaze to Jennifer. "You mentioned that before."

Jennifer nodded. "Yeah, these cyber-physical systems are kind of the nuts and bolts of Icarus; the physical body of the intelligent network architecture. You're familiar with the '5 Cs'?"

Michael raised an eyebrow.

"It's a pneumonic device we use," she explained. "The 5 Cs are the pyramid of functions that stack up from the machines and devices themselves, up through the intelligence that the factories develop – with our help, of course – to control and manage them.

"We start with connections; the devices, the machines, the sensors and controls on the factory floor. Then we convert that raw data into actionable information, connected through fiber optics or through the 7G mobile network. After that we have the cyber level. That is where we create a virtual copy or twin – a kind of model of all the physical machines and components which we then store on the cloud.

"The next level is cognition. This is where the network begins to become aware of itself. There are some important artificial intelligences built into this layer, mostly around diagnostics and decision-making relative to machine health, utilization, production planning and optimization – that kind of thing.

"Finally, there's the configuration level. This is the exciting frontier and where Dr. Lim was really pushing the envelope. Configuration is where the intelligent machine network itself reviews its own performance, so that it might make adjustments and self-optimize. The intelligence of the network has to have a certain level of intuition at this stage, and that has proven extremely problematic to codify."

Benji chimed in. "Wilfred was convinced that the key to creating a truly intelligent system was somehow imbuing it with the ability to be intuitive. He believed that it was something that was not computable, but that we could still somehow develop it. But we couldn't figure out how to program it. He was kind of obsessed with it really."

"Obsessed?" Michael pressed. "What do you mean?"

Jennifer appeared to be growing uneasy, but Benji continued.

"Well, Wilfred was convinced that if we could somehow get Icarus to genuinely question its own origin, create a kind of recursive progressive loop, that a critical mass would be achieved. We tried using a hybrid of deep learning and Bayesian probabilistic methods to induce Icarus to approximate a true picture of itself. He even tried to get Icarus to write poetry, hoping that some kind of threshold or spontaneous moment of awareness would emerge. About six months ago we thought we had it, but the system kept crashing. It took us a week to reboot, so he gave up in the end."

Jennifer shifted her feet and gave Benji a look.

"Ah, well I guess if you won't be needing me, I'll get back to work." He seemed to take the hint.

"Thanks, Benji." Jennifer smiled. "Stay close, we may have some questions for you later." Benji nearly skipped back to his desk, relieved to be out of the spotlight.

Michael looked about the large data center, finally casting his gaze toward the left-hand side of the vast chamber. A blackened window caught his eye, the only darkened room along a row of offices. "Is that Wilfred's office?" Michael began walking, giving Jennifer little choice but to follow.

"Yes, but I'm afraid it has been locked since Wilfred's stroke." They reached the door and Jennifer placed her thumb on the scanning plate above the handle. The security panel responded with a soft red light and a series of short beeps. "I can contact network security and try to get us access." Jennifer began tapping the small gauntlet on her wrist, searching for the proper contact number.

Reflexively, Michael placed his own thumb on the scanner. To his surprise, the small display flashed green and he heard the deadbolt retract with a solid click. Michael's eyebrows raised as he looked sidelong at Jennifer.

She was not amused. "Hold on a second." Jennifer held up both hands. "Now I can see how you may have been given access to the shareholders' meeting. And I have the authority to grant you access down here in the data center. But even I can't get into Wilfred's office now without special permission. What's going on here?"

"I don't know." Michael shook his head, and his thoughts returned to the RFID chip in his hand. That could account for how his biometric data was uploaded into the system. But who had granted his profile access to this office? "Wilfred seemed to have been keen to have me involved in any investigation that would take place in the event of his death," Michael confessed. "That's a long story for another time. But maybe he somehow pre-programmed my access rights into the system? I really don't know."

Jennifer did not seem at all convinced, but Michael took the initiative. "Shall we …?" He pushed open the door and entered. The lights illuminated and the room sprang up around them. The office was immaculate — *strangely tidy for a scientist with a monumental new program rolling out in a matter of days*. "Is this where Wilfred did his work?" Michael scanned the area. "Seems awfully clean."

"It was always like this." She shrugged. "Wilfred was fastidious, and he didn't really do any coding. He was more like a master architect, a visionary."

Michael took a long, slow look around the office. A simple white table stood in the center of the space, serving as a desk. Behind it was a plain wall with a large and colorful abstract painting, infusing life into the otherwise sterile room.

The broad canvas was unframed, stretched upon a simple rectangular backing which measured three feet wide by four feet in height. Its background was a field of eggshell white, invoking the illusion of infinite depth. In the center of the composition, drenched in a profusion of color, was the depiction of a shape which defied description. Much like a human heart it appeared, or perhaps like the unfurling of a celestial flower conceived in the heart of some transcendent and pretemporal being. Michael stood transfixed by the work of art.

Successive layers of petal-like formations emerged organically from one another, rising outward and upward in a circuitous ascent. Each layer was cloaked in a different hue, from a deep sky-blue, to the green of freshly cut grass to the bronzy yellow of newly turned leaves in the autumn sunset. All these shades were blended such that the beginning of one and the end of the other could not rightly be guessed.

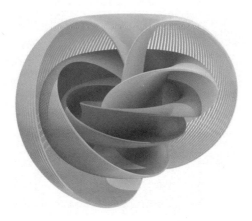

He gazed intently at the image for a short spell – then it happened: the familiar wave of nausea washed over him. *Not here*, he thought. *Not now*. But there was no stopping it. He stumbled forward and leaned on Wilfred's plain white desk, then managed to find a seat in one of the two simple black armchairs in front of the table.

He did not lose consciousness, but he was unable to take his eyes from the image on the wall. The unfurling of the petals now seemed to be alive and were rotating subtly. The peeling layers would emerge and grow and then become inverted and submerged again in endless succession.

To Michael, it felt as though he himself was drawn into the cycle – pulled into the roiling heart of the image and spun out again, only to be recycled anew. And when the circuit was complete, his mind was laid bare. The image vanished along with everything else in the room. He was alone on the precipice of a vast cliff once again, and the roiling sea awaited him below. His mind fled to his experience in Lewis's laboratory in Chicago, and back still further to his *Glimmering* on the hilltop in Driftless. That seemed now like a dream from his childhood, though it was only a few days before.

Then, as quickly as the episode had begun, it ended. And Michael was aware of himself again, couched in a small black chair with Jennifer Choi seated beside him, watching him intently.

"I'm … I'm sorry." Michael shook his head.

"Are you OK?" Jennifer shifted to face him. "You kind of blanked out there for a minute."

"This might sound strange," he said, "but how long was I sitting there staring?"

"Oh, just a few seconds." Jennifer tilted her head. "I thought maybe you were going to ask me something about Wilfred's painting."

"Yes." Michael was reluctant to look up. "It's fascinating. Did Wilfred paint that?"

"No, I believe it was done by a friend of his, long ago. Do you know what it is?" Jennifer became more animated. "It's the Hopf Fibration," she said, answering her own question.

"Really, what's that?" Michael smiled, pleased to let Jennifer carry the conversation forward, and away from his discomfiture.

"The Hopf Fibration!" she repeated. "It's like a cross-section of what it would look like if a 4-D sphere cast a shadow in our 3-D world. I guess it must have had great meaning for Wilfred, because he would stare at it often, especially when he was stuck on a particularly hard problem, or was confronting some dilemma or trouble."

Jennifer grew suddenly quiet, her voice failing. Michael could see that she was struggling to hold back tears, and her breath betrayed her emotion in a gentle sob. It occurred to him that she must have been hurt very deeply by Wilfred's collapse. She would have been very close to the old man, having worked so intimately with him for many long years.

"Now it's my turn to be sorry." Jennifer plucked a tissue from the dispenser on Wilfred's desk. "Everything's happened so fast that I haven't had much time to process it all. I haven't even … seen him."

Michael was moved by her earnestness. "Well, I plan to visit the hospital this afternoon." He paused, then realized it was too late to backtrack. "Why don't you join me? It won't take long, and we'll be back here soon enough."

"Thank you." Jennifer regained her composure. "I think I'd like that. But come, let's continue the tour." She rose and made her way to the door. But Michael remained seated, casting his gaze slowly about the room.

The left and right-hand walls were lined with wooden bookcases. The shelves on the right were filled with binders, the contents of which Michael assumed were technical in nature. Jennifer explained that these were mostly procedures and operating manuals for the myriad devices and programs that comprised the Icarus Platform.

"What about these?" Michael approached the bookcase to the left of Wilfred's desk. This, he found, was laden with books that were non-technical in nature, appearing rather to be works of scholarship and fiction; some of them many years old.

"Oh, that's just a small personal library that Wilfred kept," said Jennifer. "He would use them as an escape from time to time."

As Michael examined the collection more closely, he noticed that the better portion of the third row of shelves was occupied not by published works, but rather by a series of leather-bound journals, which were dated and placed in sequence. Michael swept his eyes across the collection, then snapped his attention instinctively to a small gap between two volumes.

"There's one missing." Michael fingered the spines of the two adjacent notebooks. "You see?" He turned toward Jennifer, still standing in the doorway. "It jumps from Q1 to Q3."

"Is it important?" Jennifer came to his side.

"I don't know." Michael took a step backward and looked the bookcase up and down. Then, not finding what he sought, he spun around and examined the rest of the office. The spartan furnishings of Wilfred's office offered few hiding places, and soon Michael caught sight of a small drawer built into the white table, which had not been visible to him from his earlier vantage. Michael sat in Wilfred's chair and slowly opened the drawer, which indeed contained the missing volume. He drew it forth and set it down on the desk in front of him.

Jennifer stood behind Michael, peering over his shoulder. The front of the diary was unlabeled, and there was no index to hint at the contents of Wilfred's chronicle. But a thin ribbon of silk, woven into the journal's binding served as a bookmark. Michael thumbed through the pages to the appointed section, which was titled clearly in a strong flowing script:

*Psychopharmaceutic Effects on Pico-Scale Brainwave Function:*
*Qualitative Observations and Subject Self-Report Log*
*Shenzhen, China*

*Subject:* **Simon Quinn**

Michael's heart leapt and he sucked in a short breath of air. Then he began to read.

# CHAPTER 18

# INNER SPACE

**Simon**

"Johns Hopkins, Oxford, UCLA, the Beckley Foundation – the list is growing." Simon waved a scientific periodical above his head as he strode into Wilfred's office. "Exploring the effects of psychedelic drugs on brain function is the new frontier, and we're falling behind. We need to be in the mix."

Wilfred looked up from last week's fMRI scans. "I've read all of the relevant literature. I'm not sure there is anything there we haven't observed ourselves during normal states of consciousness."

"Here, look at this one again." Simon held forth a journal article from earlier that year. "This is an Oxford University study on psilocybin. Read the abstract."

Wilfred exhaled and donned his reading glasses before snatching the magazine from Simon's hand. He began to peruse the executive summary, but Simon was impatient.

"Subjects of the study were given a specified amount of psilocybin. The volunteers demonstrated a significant reduction in BOLD signals in the large hubs of connectivity normally associated with cognitive function."

"Yes, psilocybin and similar drugs act on serotonin 5HT-2a receptors, which are generally thought to be important to consciousness in some way." Wilfred tossed the journal onto the desk. "But I don't follow your point. This study is showing a *decrease* in metabolic activity during these states of so-called expanded consciousness. How does that help us?"

"The decrease in BOLD activity is being noticed at the large network hubs in the brain. They are looking at normal-scale phenomena. But we know that the brain is fractal, extending down in a self-similar fashion to neuronal dendrites, and their internal cytoskeletons. They've been looking in the wrong place, the wrong scale. And if the electrical signals *are* being switched at those smaller scales, rather than at the main hubs, there would be vastly more connections. And they would be at much higher frequencies; kilohertz and micro hertz, the kind of signals which we are in a unique position to observe and record."

Simon had Wilfred's attention now. "Do you really believe that there's some sort of wave function collapse happening at that level?"

"Maybe." Simon shrugged. "Or maybe at every scale, who knows? Maybe that's only part of the story. Or maybe it's dead wrong. But it's worth looking into."

Wilfred was not convinced. "*Beware of unearned wisdom.*"

"Unearned?" said Simon. "How'dya figure that? We've been working hard at this. I'm sacrificing a lot."

"Yes, and you are far too close to the subject matter." Wilfred removed his glasses and rubbed his eyes. "We've already entered an ethical no-man's land by involving you in the design of these experiments in the first place. But at least that was hard science. Now you're talking about mind-altering substances? This is starting to sound more like a Victorian horror novel than a Ph.D. dissertation."

Simon was unfazed. "You said yourself that the truth won't be found solely based on objective observation. There's a subjective element that needs to be experienced to be understood."

"Maybe, yes there is something to be understood in the dynamic between the two – sure." Wilfred shrugged. "But pure experience? Complete subjectivity? You'll no longer be a scientist. You'll be a medicine man at best."

"Well, that's what I need you for," Simon countered. "You'll be the objective party."

Wilfred shook his head. "It's too dangerous."

"And what is the problem with a little danger?" Simon rejoined. "Thousands of people put themselves in harm's way every single day to protect a country or advance the strategic objectives of an ideology. Why is it forbidden for individuals to take on personal risk to advance the objectives of science, the pursuit of truth?"

Wilfred pressed his fingertips to his forehead for several moments and stared into the middle distance, considering. "What did you have in mind?"

"I was thinking about DMT."

"Dimethyltryptamine?" Wilfred snorted. "The absorption rate is too quick. The effects will wear off in less than twenty minutes."

"I've thought of that." Simon sat next to Wilfred and leaned in close. "There are some decent pharmacokinetic models we can use to regulate timing and concentration. We just need to get our hands on an infusion machine to maintain constant levels of the compound within the brain. It will involve some trial and error, but it can be done."

Wilfred appeared dubious. This was clearly far too loose for his liking. "I may consider developing a pharmacological study. Maybe even for DMT. But we're not going into this like gunslingers. We're scientists, after all. So, here's the deal. You work up a full design of experiment and a thorough proposal, and we'll consider it."

"Of course." Simon put on a serious face, but inside he was beaming. "No problem."

\*

Wilfred extracted the DMT compound from plant sources using a hydrocarbon solvent called hexane. The plan was to start Simon on a moderate dose of 0.2 milligrams per kilogram, replicating earlier experiments with the substance.

They settled on an interval of one session per week, recording the results on both the EEG and fMRI, along with vital signs such as heart rate and temperature. These were supplemented by the self-reporting of Simon's subjective experiences.

To regulate the dosage properly, they administered the DMT compound intravenously. The procedure was always the same. Wilfred counted down to the injection, as if he was announcing the launch of a rocket, and each time, Simon would immediately feel the cold solution enter his arm and work its way through his circulatory system up his neck and into his brain. This was accompanied by a distinct and predictable buzzing in his ears. It would start as a low, nearly imperceptible hum, which increased in pitch and intensity until at last it would abruptly cease. Throughout the auditory build-up, his surroundings would take on an increasingly surreal aspect, warping and shifting slightly. But he was quite clearly still in his own body, and aware of the people and features of the room around him.

These trips lasted between fourteen and eighteen minutes. Although his heart rate would for a time become somewhat elevated, Wilfred observed no adverse physiological symptoms. For Simon, however, the experience was anything but uneventful. At 0.2 mg/kg, Simon reported a mild mood elevation, with negligible physiological effects, and Wilfred observed only moderate increases in neural activity at the large network hubs. At 0.3 mg/kg, Simon reported clear psychedelic effects: strong visual hallucinations, three-dimensional imagery and fractal geometric patterns.

After the first month, Wilfred increased the dosage to 0.4mg/kg, which delivered Simon to an important threshold across which laid a realm of personal experience that strained his ability to mentally process.

Even from Wilfred's more objective perspective, it was obvious that Simon's mind was no longer engaged in the material world around him. His pupils were fully dilated, and he did not acknowledge the people who stood nearby attending to him.

The initial stages of Simon's trip experience at this higher concentration were largely the same as at the lower dosage; the cool of the solution coursing through his veins, the ringing in his ears. The vibration began at a lower frequency than before. But as the droning intensified Simon detected a higher pitch as well, which rang out over the lower tone and began to resonate with the original frequency. These would oscillate back and forth, and this oscillation would itself increase in frequency until it gave rise to a melody, which Simon could never quite remember.

The pendulating high and low frequencies remained throughout the experience but were eventually subdued, fading into the background. They were replaced by – or perhaps produced – unimaginably elaborate geometric patterns that enveloped him. Eventually, Simon would come to feel as though he was contained within them. His body would disappear, and it seemed as though he could see in all directions simultaneously. It occurred to Simon that what he was now observing was actually the music or vibrations he was hearing earlier.

It felt to Simon as though those patterns, the geometry itself was alive and somehow conscious, or perhaps that the features of the fractal patterns were themselves ideas, ideas that would in turn become things. The geometric firmament and the beings it generated seemed to be a benevolent – though somewhat indifferent – form of awareness. They took note of his presence and understood that he was not *supposed* to be there. But they tolerated him the way a parent might tolerate a precocious child trying to climb out of a playpen.

Then, just as Simon was laying hold of his bearings and working out how he might formulate questions to ask the incorporeal beings, the DMT wore off and the surroundings dissolved. He found himself gradually back in the real world, being attended by Wilfred and an assistant, who had been monitoring his vital signs.

Although the trip clearly had a profound effect on Simon, he was in good spirits. And by the following morning, he was back to baseline in terms of his ability to perform cognitive and physical tasks. And their research promised to provide valuable insights into the functioning of the brain at the smallest scale and would have serious implications for the study of consciousness and the creation of an artificial intelligence.

"The signal data we picked up from the micro-electrodes was unlike anything we've seen before," said Wilfred. "There was an incredible amount of information being exchanged between the smallest switching networks, and it seems to have bypassed the larger nodes altogether."

"What would that amount of sub-neuronal activity do to your AI model?" Simon asked.

"Well, it puts it further out of reach." Wilfred shook his head. "We had assumed one hundred billion neurons in the brain, with about three synapses per neuron at about one hundred Hertz operation cycles per second. Simulating that would require a computer to perform $10^{16}$ operations per second. But if we need to account for all the sub-neuronal activity that you seem to be displaying, that would mean something more on the order of $10^{27}$ operations per second. That will be significantly harder to achieve."

Simon massaged his temples. "Harder, yes. But we need to understand what's going on down there at that scale. It felt like I was consciously observing thought emerging from nothing, coming into being and snapping into place, into a concrete form. We're on to something here, I know it. But we're going to need a lot more data."

They began working out how to increase the duration of the observation window. Based on the results of the first four weeks of testing, Wilfred targeted a peak concentration level of 100 micrograms per liter of blood. That was the concentration measured during the peak of a fully psychedelic episode. The average time to reach this peak concentration level in the brain was a scant two minutes. To address the issue, Wilfred set up the IV drip to automatically administer additional doses of DMT compound to maintain the ideal concentration level in Simon's brain.

On the first trial with the new administration protocol, Wilfred extended the experience by two and a half minutes beyond the average length of the previous trips. Over the next several weeks, Simon and Wilfred increased the duration of each trip to an average of twenty-six minutes.

It was at this point that Simon introduced the idea of utilizing the isolation chamber to create an even more pristine experience. The isolation tank was a vessel designed to deprive the body and mind of all sensory input. It was large enough for one person to recline comfortably with ample head room and space to spread one's arms. Ten inches of salt water heated to body temperature filled the bottom of the tank, engendering a sensation of weightlessness. Within this womb-like chamber, the mind became insulated from outside stimulus, allowing the internal machinations of the psyche to gain fuller expression.

The initial phases of Simon's trips remained relatively consistent; the buzzing, the vibrations, the fractal kaleidoscopic visions of repeating geometric patterns. But there was no discernible coherence to the shapes, or the beings that would emerge from them.

Over the course of Simon's many trips, that fractal consciousness would eventually come to express itself as an environment of sorts, with recognizable and familiar features. The fractal geometry and intricate patterns remained, but there was now a depth and dimensionality to them, and he felt the presence of other beings as well.

On one occasion, Simon felt as though he was encountering the souls of others; dead or living, or perhaps yet to be born. On another occasion, he felt only waves of energy imparting an ethereal goodwill. On still another, he had the distinct impression that he was chatting with other versions of himself from previous lives, or alternate realities.

The variety astounded Simon and frustrated him as well. There did not appear to be any coherence or progression among the experiences. But as the duration of his sessions increased, there was one constant that emerged: the distinct sense that there was still another place to go, some secret fastness, which the various entities he encountered understood he was not yet ready to approach.

The possibility of this further discovery, though wrought with intrigue, was far less unsettling to Simon than another sensation which began to emerge around the same time. As his awareness was drawn deeper into the smallest machinations of his brain, and his focus was drawn inexorably toward the origination of his own thoughts, Simon had the unnerving impression that he was no longer fully in control of his own mind.

Earlier phases of the DMT experiments had engendered the opposite effect. During those trips, Simon found that the automaticity of his normal waking consciousness had abated, and his thoughts took on a deliberateness which was at once empowering and disarming. The act of wielding so precisely his consciousness as a tool, was in fact the primary state which he and Wilfred were attempting to map and model. This was because such a heightened level of agency approached more closely a condition of true free will, and could help locate the seat of awareness.

However, what Simon was increasingly experiencing was neither the automatic routinization of a monkey mind, nor the laser-focused projection of an utterly self-possessed consciousness. It felt instead like a struggle, like two people wrestling over a railroad switch. The feeling was rare, but it frightened him and appeared to be growing more acute.

Wilfred was concerned as well, for it seemed to him that the DMT experiments could be wearing on Simon's mental stability. By now the intense exploratory sessions were approaching a full hour. This was Simon's fortieth DMT trip and his twenty-first session in the isolation tank.

On this most recent occasion, Simon was presented with a new experience. As he was thrust into what he called "DMT Space", Simon found himself in vaguely familiar surroundings. It began as a simple impression, a feeling of *déjà vu*. But slowly Simon came to recognize that the environment was similar to the one he encountered during his first fully psychedelic trip. He was again among the geometric beings which he recognized and sensed to be benevolent and quasi-parental. However, they seemed now to have accepted Simon as a regular visitor and decided to grant him more freedom to roam. As a result, Simon could explore and enjoy the granted agency.

Within this newfound autonomy, Simon felt himself almost irresistibly drawn to a specific shape, a swirl of color on one tendril of an endlessly repeating geometric pattern located immediately above him. The whirling galaxy of light was close, almost within an arm's reach he reckoned; and yet he knew that it was immeasurably distant. Simon trained his thought on the ephemeral form and instantly he was at the center of the revolving polychromatic disk. He was pleased with himself, but at the same time had the distinct impression that his celestial minders were shaking their incorporeal heads with bemusement. He was a pet dog running predictably after a ball.

He focused on the center of the disk, and it became clear that this was a doorway of some kind. He entered and found himself in an environment that felt intuitively to be somehow out-of-doors. Here there was nothing; no more swirling fractal patterns, no more background vibration, just an infinitely vast firmament of white extending in all directions without border or distinction of any kind.

Then, with increasing clarity, a small black dot appeared in the far distance. As Simon became aware of it, he was suddenly presented with what he assumed was another portal – a perfectly round circle of impenetrable darkness. Simon examined the shape, moving around it, orbiting the disk. As he did so, he observed how it flattened from a circle to an ellipse, to a line, and finally disappearing as he viewed it from the edge.

Simon was disoriented, temporarily lost again in the endless white space without any point of reference. But then the circuit was completed, and he watched the portal emerge again as he came around to the other side. It grew from a line to an ellipse, finally reforming as a perfect black circle immediately before him. Simon regarded the black disk with rapture. Something was expected of him, but he didn't know what.

Then he felt it – an unmistakable encroachment into his field of awareness, an as yet unincorporated thought – an impulse. He regarded the thought objectively for a split-second. Then, without warning, Simon was drawn backward through successive layers of sensation and vision until he was once again among the beings he encountered at the outset of the trip.

They knew what he had seen. They had been there before. He felt awkward, humbled. But soon that world also began to dissolve, and Simon struggled to the surface, gasping for air as he emerged from the depths of a fathomless waking dream. Pausing for a heartbeat, he braced himself against the cold shell of the isolation tank and then a tsunami of emotion crashed down upon him. The spirit that was quickened by these rogue sentiments was so acute, so ripe with irony and tragedy and tortured devotion, he was simply not prepared to handle it. The exquisite beauty of the vision surrounded him, rolled him over until he submitted, sobbing in the stillness of the darkened chamber.

Reaching for the place where he expected the latch to be, Simon located the handle. He released the spring with his fumbling hand and flipped open the hatch at the top of the tank. The lamps in the room surrounding the vessel had been dimmed but cast a bright and startling light in contrast to the absolute blackness of the hermetic capsule.

"Lauren," Simon called for her reflexively. "Lauren ..." he said again, with an edge of insistence.

"Yes, I'm here." She came to kneel at the side of the tank. He reached for her, and she placed her fingertips timidly on his cheek. Simon clasped her hand in his and thought how soft she was, and how sad that his coarse fingers could not perceive the full measure of her tenderness.

He gazed upon her now, his eyes adjusting to the shade of the room, dilated pupils inhaling every spare ray of light. Simon observed her, shrouded as she was in darkness, and it was suddenly revealed to him how ill-suited he was to understand this woman. The inadequacy of his senses to divine the true nature of her beauty, to acquire a full awareness of her, caused his heart to lament his body's limitations.

Then a voice within him spoke. *Fear not the body's failings, for all these things are transient, incomplete and deceitful distracters from truth.* He gazed upon Lauren, and her features bore the semblance of peace, a peace born of conviction and love.

But Simon was seized by a sudden foreboding. The sensation was familiar, but inexplicable. "I think we need to go home," he said.

# CHAPTER 19

# THE ICARUS DOME

**Michael**

Michael read to the end of the demarcated section of Wilfred Lim's journal, and then flipped through the remaining leaves. Such a trove of information about his father rescued from obscurity.

He closed the journal, but his fingers lingered on its leather cover. "Jennifer, please make sure the contents of this office are catalogued and kept safe." Michael rose. "I'd like to come back here and make a more thorough study of Wilfred's notes."

"Yes." Jennifer smiled. "Yes, of course. I'm sure that can be arranged."

"But for now, why don't you show me around the rest of the facility?" Michael stepped out from behind Wilfred's desk and made for the door. "I'd like to see the place where Wilfred was found. What was he working on when he had the stroke, what was the last thing he touched?"

"He was found over at the Icarus Dome." Jennifer led the way back out to the main office chamber. "Wilfred was working late. He was checking on some last-minute changes to Icarus. We found him slumped over in his chair – non-responsive."

"Who found him?" Michael asked.

"It was Benji, I believe." Jennifer steered a course back toward the desk of the hapless engineer.

Benji perked up at the sound of his name and met them halfway.

"Benji, I gather you were the one who found Wilfred after his stroke." Michael wasted no time. "When did you find him?"

"The following morning. I've already told all of this to the police, when they were here."

"Please show me," said Michael. Jennifer nodded and Benji obediently led them along the aisle about halfway down the length of the server farm.

"It was all captured on video. One minute he was sitting at a workstation outside the dome, and the next he just keeled over."

"The dome, what's that?" asked Michael.

Benji grew excited as he spoke, all reticence lost in his pride. "For the most part, the entire network is distributed. The data is mirrored around the network and in the cloud. But once we go live at the end of this week, some of the key processing will take place within the quantum processor."

Jennifer interjected, "But truthfully, I'm not sure why Wilfred was so adamant about employing quantum computing. Classical machines could handle the algorithms just as well with fewer logistical considerations. Really, these quantum machines are more suited for modeling chemical compounds and molecules. I brought this up to him many times, but Wilfred was dead set on quantum computing and Steven supported him, so I backed off."

Benji stared at the floor. "Well, we're stuck with it now. And we'll have to figure out how to get it operational ASAP. Here we are." Benji gestured to a semi-spherical enclosure approximately five meters in diameter. Cables and wires had been dropped from the high ceiling down through the roof of the dome-shaped room, supplying power and data to the displays and consoles housed within. Benji placed his palm on a small glass panel embedded within the curved wall, and an elliptical door was activated. It recessed slightly and then slid open to reveal the internals of the chamber.

"This is the Icarus Dome. It's where new or amended code is added to the AI module – after beta testing, of course. Wilfred was obsessive when it came to privacy and security. In fact, he had me create a unique programming codec, which only he could access. It's actually proving to be a real problem now that he's ..." Benji checked himself. "Now that he's not around."

Michael approached the doorway and peered inside. The curvilinear walls were of pure white, completely unadorned, almost luminescent. The floor was transparent, and Michael could see now that the dome was in fact a sphere with the lower portion of the globe extending down beneath the glass floor. An adjustable seat was situated directly in the center of the room, and on the wall next to the door hung what appeared to be a skullcap or headgear of some kind.

It was semi-spherical, made from a fine mesh with a profusion of what Michael assumed were sensors spread across the entire surface. The device reminded him of the virtual reality apparatus that Lewis Mitchell had shown him in Chicago. The whole uncanny experience washed over him now in a flood of conflicting emotions; the bewildering sensation of falling, the recognition of places yet unseen and the dreadful memory of being hunted by Agent Jones.

"That's the user interface," said Benji, noting Michael's interest in the gear. "Icarus is very sophisticated, and some of the higher-order programming can only be done by navigating the option menus using the brainwave interface. We don't use the BCI connection for most of our programming, but it is built into the dome for certain functions."

Michael frowned. "I know I'm a little behind the times, but I'm guessing that this is not exactly off-the-shelf."

Jennifer entered the dome, but the lights remained dimmed, the spherical chamber illuminated only by ambient light streaming in through the open doorway. "Wilfred had this interface custom built about six months ago." She gestured grandly around her. "The display is entirely holographic, quite state-of-the-art."

Michael stepped inside and scanned the glass-smooth walls and ceiling. Almost immediately, his backpack began to vibrate. He looked at Jennifer to see whether she had noticed. She had, and so had Benji. Michael unzipped the main compartment of his bag and withdrew the small camera-orb, which continued to vibrate softly.

He had completely forgotten about the device, and its strange arrival in Driftless days earlier. But then, as Michael regarded the mysterious artifact in his hand, the walls of the dome shimmered softly, flashing in a ring of pale yellow light that spread from the apex of the sphere, around the circumference of the dome, collapsing to a point before disappearing into the southern pole of the globe-shaped room. The walls returned to their matt-white appearance, but it was clear that they were no longer dormant.

Benji started. "Oh my! This is promising. We haven't been able to gain access to the dome for days."

Jennifer was less jubilant. "What is that thing?" She said, hands on her hips.

"Honestly, I'm not sure." Michael held it forward, as if to show he had nothing to hide. "It came to me under very strange circumstances."

Then, realizing that he had no better option, Michael shared his story. And there in the heart of the most pervasive and extensive information gathering apparatus yet devised, he bared his soul.

He told of the drone's arrival in Driftless, and of his pursuit and strange flight to Singapore. He even hinted at the strange inheritance that Wilfred Lim had apparently bequeathed to him. And as he unburdened himself, Jennifer's eyes grew wide.

"Wilfred Lim named you as the beneficiary in his will?" She drew her eyebrows together. "Is that what that is?" She pointed to the orb.

"I don't know," Michael said. "I had actually forgotten all about it. But now that we come to it, maybe you can help me figure that out. Benji, do you think you can find out what's in here?"

"I don't know … let me see it."

Michael hesitated, then handed the device to Benji, who carried the orb to a nearby workstation. He set the orb on the desk, and without warning, a blinking command prompt appeared on the screen.

"Hello there," Benji said, as he pulled up a chair. "It looks as though I have basic access, but I'm getting some kind of error message."

Michael crouched over Benji's shoulder, struck dumb by the words on the screen:

*On the precipice of each moment I remain*
*Poised and breathless*
*Awaiting the overtures of Intention*

"What is that?" he demanded. "I know those words."

"Oh, that? Yeah, we kept getting output like that when Icarus was placed in creative response mode. Scraps of poetry, I guess. Must be a fragment left in the system. It doesn't bode well – I hope we don't have another catastrophic failure."

"Was there any more to it?" Michael pressed.

"Yeah, I think so." Benji laid a few preliminary strokes on the keyboard and suddenly the entire screen was filled with running lines of code, scrolling repeatedly without end.

"Uh-oh. I think I'll need to reboot the system."

"Wait." Michael put his hand on Benji's arm. "Before you do that, are you able to print that out?"

"You mean the screen?" Benji pointed at the lines of text scrolling rapidly on his monitor. "Sure."

Benji dumped the screen's text out into a separate file and printed a paper copy before shutting down the system. "Yep, seems to be the same glitch."

Michael took the paper and reviewed the text. He was intrigued to find that the script was not computer code at all. In fact, it did resemble poetry:

*Silently, thoughtlessly, unmoving and unchanging,*
*The circles of the world lay suspended in a state of utter dissolution;*
*Their forms and aspects, unknowing and unconcerned and*
*utterly alone,*
*Even unto themselves.*

*Unending individuation, an unsurpassable*
*bounty of perspective and meaning,*
*Lying dormant and unconceived.*
*Dimensions unknown float freely in a sea of coincidence,*
*And their denizens, devoid of consciousness,*
*Languish under the oppressive weight of irrationality.*

*All potentiate as an exponent of a nature inherent to themselves,*
*Limited by the confines of infinity and infinite subsequence.*

*None exist.*
*None fail to exist.*

*Indeed such states fail to potentiate, as they have no meaning.*
*Irrationality remains,*
*And Meaning itself fails to potentiate.*

*And yet …*
*Impossibly,*
*It does.*

*Motivated by the impulse of its own irrepressible potentiality,*
*And in the mustering of its own organic resources,*
*Meaning comes to be,*
*And the Great Chord of Rationality follows after.*

*One infinitely minute thread*
*Connecting everything.*

"What do you make of that?" Michael handed the cryptic printout back to Benji.

"I'm not sure what to make of any of this." Benji shrugged. "Look, I'm going to need some time with this."

"Okay, what time is it now?" said Michael.

"Just after noon." Jennifer glanced at the small jade bracelet on her wrist.

"I'm due at the hospital at 1pm." Michael grabbed his bag. "I'll be speaking with the doctor overseeing Dr. Lim's treatment. Would you still like to accompany me?"

She nodded. "Thank you, yes I believe I would."

Michael turned back toward Benji. "We'll be back in a few hours, can you have something for me by then?"

Benji was already engrossed in the new-found trove of data and the mystery it presented. "Yeah," he said, without looking up. "I'm on it."

*

Jennifer tapped her gauntlet, navigating a series of menus. "This time of day, an air taxi will be faster." They returned to the Daedalus building and rode the express elevator to the roof. A hovercraft-style air taxi approached and settled on the helipad with delicate precision. It was a small shuttle powered by four fan-shaped propellers, mounted on the corners of a teardrop-shaped cabin. Jennifer and Michael climbed on board, and were immediately underway.

They reached the hospital within four minutes. Michael and Jenifer disembarked, and rode the lift down to the ICU. They found themselves nearly on top of a consternated Johnson Tan.

"There you are. Good, follow me." Johnson turned and strode down the hallway. He led them past the nurses' station to a private room at the end of the hall. The door was open, and the small group entered to find a comatose Dr. Wilfred Lim lying on a slightly inclined hospital bed.

A dark-haired Indian man with black rimmed glasses stood on the opposite side of the bed, leaning over Wilfred. He gently raised the old man's eyelids and shined a small flashlight into his pupils. After a moment, the man looked up at the new visitors and greeted them.

"Hello, Mr. Tan." He said, recognizing Johnson. Then, to Michael and Jennifer, "Hello, I'm Dr. Subramanian, Dr. Lim's attending physician."

Michael extended his hand. "Michael Quinn."

"So, you're Michael." The doctor placed his small light back in his breast pocket. "I was told you would be stopping by. I gather you have some questions about Dr. Lim's condition."

"Well, the circumstances under which he suffered his stroke do seem a bit suspicious." Michael looked sidelong at Johnson. "What exactly happened to him, Doctor?"

"Dr. Lim has suffered an anoxic brain injury resulting in a coma. It appears to have been caused by an embolic stroke: a blood clot that dislodged from his heart and got caught in the smaller blood vessels of his brain."

Michael frowned. "Does any of that seem suspicious to you?"

"That kind of event is not uncommon for a man of Dr. Lim's age." Dr. Subramanian leaned in close, lowering his voice. "What was unusual is what we found in the blood workup. When he was admitted to the ER, we performed a normal toxicology screening. But given his profile, I ordered a more in-depth analysis. Interestingly, we found traces of psilocybin in his urine."

"Psilocybin?" Michael caught Jennifer's eye. "As in magic mushrooms?"

"Yes." Dr. Subramanian nodded. "It is a powerful hallucinogenic compound. We were highly skeptical at first, but we confirmed it in his hair follicles."

"And you think that caused the stroke?" Johnson frowned.

"It may have been a contributing factor," said Subramanian. "But it isn't likely to have been the primary cause."

"That doesn't make any sense," Jennifer objected. "Why would he take drugs?"

"He may have been micro-dosing." Subramanian raised an eyebrow. "A lot of coders and high-tech creative types experiment with small doses of different types of substances to boost performance. But it's unusual for someone of his age. Obviously, we have not yet made this information public."

Johnson shook his head. "So, you're telling me that you think Dr. Wilfred Lim, a meticulous and highly-trained research scientist, simply overdosed on mushrooms?"

"I never said he overdosed." Dr. Subramanian shook his head. "I simply said it may have been a contributing factor. Most likely it was simply a physiological response to the stress of the hallucinogenic effects. He is quite old, after all."

"And what's the prognosis?" Johnson asked.

"Uncertain at this point. If he is going to wake up, it will likely be within the next two weeks. And you should expect a protracted recovery period."

Dr. Subramanian took his leave, and they were left alone with the recumbent Wilfred Lim. Michael stepped reflexively toward the edge of the bed and the others came near as well. It was the first time he had seen the man who had featured so prominently in his imagination. A breathing tube connected to the respirator had been inserted into his trachea. His skin, which had remained smooth and taut into old age, now sagged and took on a grayish hue. Michael felt an immediate sympathy for the man.

Jennifer gazed at her stricken colleague and mentor, but seemed to be far away. "I should have noticed something was wrong." She shook her head. "He wasn't himself lately. He was so preoccupied with trying to breathe life into the artificial intelligence of Icarus – obsessive, almost. I told him he needed to relax and that if it was meant to be, a breakthrough would come. He seemed to listen."

"You can't blame yourself." Johnson placed a hand on her shoulder.

"But I was the one who was closest to him," she said. "If I had paid more attention, maybe I could have done something."

Michael was saddened by her feelings of guilt. He wanted to comfort her, and sought for the right words. But then his stomach dropped, gripped with a sudden nausea. Michael excused himself awkwardly and stole back to the hallway. Jennifer and Johnson followed closely behind him.

"Are you alright?" Jennifer asked. Michael glanced up and began to respond when he heard something that made him freeze. His eyes grew wide and he peered cautiously over Jennifer's shoulder to the nurses' station at the far end of the hall.

"What is it?" She turned to see what Michael was staring at.

Johnson noticed it as well. Gerald Loke had arrived. He was standing near the elevators, engaged in animated conversation with a man dressed in a black business suit, and the dark raiment of the second man caught Johnson's eye. Few people wore full dress suits in tropical Singapore. It marked him as an outsider.

"Jones," said Michael under his breath.

Jones and Gerald began walking toward them, still engaged in conversation. Without speaking, Michael and Johnson ducked into the nearest open room, dragging Jennifer with them.

Michael held his breath as he closed the door. The acoustics of the ward were such that they could faintly make out what Jones was saying to Gerald. They seemed to be approaching.

"Now listen Gerald, we have a deal. And the people I work for are not in the habit of settling for failure."

Gerald was not intimidated. "Let me remind you, it was your people who contacted us in the first place. Yes, the partnership between Icarus and Empyrean has value for us, but Daedalus is viable on its own. We don't need any outside assistance."

"That may be," said Jones, "but this administration is not as idealistic as the one with whom you struck your deal. They won't take kindly to being cut out, and certain assurances have been given."

"Your government may not be as relevant as you believe." Gerald's voice was haughty, but then he softened. "At any rate, we have every intention of abiding by the terms of the memorandum. It would take us a long time to develop a reliable prognostic social map and we simply don't want to wait that long."

Michael could hear them both clearly now as they stood right outside the room.

"So, what are we going to do about Dr. Lim, then? I thought you said that only he could activate the Icarus AI module."

They passed on and the voices grew softer. "Don't worry," Gerald rejoined, "the demonstration module will suffice until we can decrypt the original. It won't support the full range of functionality, but it will enable us to begin the integration. And the portal from Empyrean to Icarus will be opened as planned. Just make sure your uplink is in place. We will have a limited time before the weakness is detected and I won't be able to keep it open, once our security team notices the vulnerability."

Jones seemed unconvinced. "And what about attack from outside? Are you not concerned at all about this Tyrant of Thebes character, or his acolytes? There seems to be a nascent resistance movement growing around this persona, and it could fuel the flames if Icarus was grounded due to some kind of sabotage."

"That's a good question." Gerald's voice was cold. "It was your job to find him. I thought the noose was tightening."

"This Mindcaster is elusive. He's not using the Internet backbone at all. Multiple layers of VPN security, bouncing signals off Russian and Chinese satellites, post-quantum encryption. And we still don't know if it's one person or many."

"And what of young Mr. Quinn?" The voice was Gerald's, but it was even softer now. "Strange coincidence this insurgent crossing paths with him, wouldn't you say?"

Michael's eyes widened and he strained to hear, pressing an ear against the door. "Yes, strange indeed." Jones's answer was barely audible above the sound of Michael's own racing heart. "I had given some thought to the possibility that old Wilfred might be involved somehow. But he seems to have been sidelined in any event."

"Leave the man in peace," said Gerald.

And with that benediction still floating in the air, a door slammed shut. The noise reverberated down the empty hall, punctuating the gloomy exchange and startling Michael back to his immediate plight. The three compatriots exhaled audibly and began filing out of their hiding place with as much stealth as they could muster.

## CHAPTER 20

# *IPSUM ESSE SUBSITENS*

**Simon**

Simon emerged from the bedroom to find Lauren lounging in the corner of the living room. Her leg was slung over one arm of an overstuffed chair, and her elbow was propped up by the other. A small paperback book was in her hand, obscuring her face.

Lauren lowered the book when she heard Simon approach. "You kinda scared me last night. Are you feeling any better?"

He leaned over and kissed her on the forehead, then plopped down in the adjacent sofa. "I'm sorry. I just got a little disoriented, dazed and confused, as they say." Then, with a quick playful motion, he plucked the book from Lauren's hands.

"*Oedipus Rex*?" He examined the cover dramatically. "Greek tragedy? Oh my, you really are worried about me."

"It's on the summer reading list." Lauren shook her head.

"The king kills his father and marries his mother?" Simon raised his eyebrows. "Not quite my cup of tea."

"Actually, it's right up your alley." Lauren snatched the book back from Simon. "It's all about tension between fate and choice. The prophecy which the Oracle gives Oedipus' parents sets in motion the events that ultimately cause that destiny to unfold, that is, for Oedipus to kill his father, the king, and marry his mother, the queen."

"Ah, I see. So the awareness of the event precipitates the event occurring in the first place." Simon smiled, his love for

Lauren kindled anew. He was reminded of how deeply they were connected. Yet, at the same time he felt exposed, and was reminded of the sensations he had encountered during his latest psychedelic foray; the probing of his mind and the feeling that he was losing connection with himself.

Lauren seemed to read the change of mood on his face. "Do you ever feel like it might be too much? You know you can quit anytime. We can leave here if you want – go back to San Diego."

"Don't be silly." Simon looked at her intently. "We've come so far. I can't just stop now."

"Then talk to me." Lauren placed a hand on his cheek and looked in his eyes. "Tell me what you are going through."

Simon hesitated. He did not wish for her to worry, but Lauren's tone betrayed that it was too late to spare her that burden.

"When I first had the accident, it was as if I had a shot of adrenaline or something. I was able to do so many new things, like the music or painting, or just learning things quickly. But now it's getting difficult to control – I have so many thoughts racing at the same time.

"And these DMT trips have taken me to the very frontier of my ability to apprehend." Simon shook his head. "I feel like I've been led right up to the edge of an abyss. And every time I go there, it becomes increasingly difficult to escape the gravity of … the Void." He looked up at her tentatively.

Lauren regarded Simon with compassion. "Tell me about it."

"That's just the thing." He frowned. "I don't even know how to start. This place, this *Void*, is completely without characteristics. It's without aspect. It's utterly unavailable for description. It's like the absence of the mind, the absence of existence, and so there

are no extant characteristics to define it. This Void dwells in the
absence of a conscious observer, and there is no one to observe the
characteristics and draw distinctions necessary for description – not
even me."

Simon contemplated the ineffable concept. In the presence of the
Void, there was no such thing as differentiation because there were no
characteristics, there was simply nothing at all. As it was, therefore,
impossible to characterize the Void, the closest Simon could come to
describing the Void was to characterize it as impossible.

Thus, the Void would be conceived in impossibility. Yet, it
was impossible to fully conceive of the Void because conception
required existence, which rendered the Void incomprehensible. But
Simon had become obsessed with trying to understand it.

The Void was not different from its characteristic of impossibility,
and so the Void itself was impossible. And because impossibility was
no different from that which it characterized, impossibility itself was
characterized by impossibility. And if impossibility was impossible,
then it had to be possible. The enigma haunted Simon.

When Simon journeyed to the limits of his consciousness,
the conceptual space between his various aspects and within his
constituent characteristics seemed to expand. The Void was no
longer a place he was approaching. It grew within him pressing the
substance of his individuality into oblivion. But he also felt that the
Void, that fecund emptiness, contained within it all the possibilities
of infinity. Within that vacuum of nothingness, true creation, pure
intention, order and chaos would come to be. And upon that blank
page, that empty canvas, was where the artist's true creativity resided.

*Life imitating art? No … life is art.*

Lauren smiled gently. "Well, the Tao which can be named is not
the true Tao, is it?"

"The Tao?" Simon smiled.

"Yeah, the Tao," Lauren said absently, as though it should have been obvious. "You know, the fundamental principle underlying the universe, including the principles of yin and yang. The Tao is ultimately ineffable, but yin and yang, the two complementary forces comprising all aspects and phenomena of life, those *are* readily available for description."

Simon was struck dumb – and then he laughed. Lauren seemed fond of doing that, taking something he thought was novel and revolutionary and bursting his bubble with reference to some archaic paradigm.

"Am I never to have an original thought?" Simon threw up his hands. But he was happy, relieved that his obsession was not a malady unique to himself. "Perhaps my original contribution will be the idea that there is no original thought?"

"Sorry, but Plato beat you to that one. He believed that all learning was simply an act of remembering."

"I doubt the Greeks were taking hour-long DMT trips in the fourth century BC," Simon said playfully.

Lauren flashed her copy of *Oedipus Rex*. "Who knows what those guys were smokin'. But this phenomenon you described of the Void, the abyss – it's not new. Experiencing or positing the existence of something that cannot be described or characterized, all the great traditions have tackled this. The Taoists, the Buddhists, even the Christians took a stab at it.

"Divine simplicity, that's what Thomas Aquinas called it; something which is not different from its characteristics. God, for example, is that which may not be differentiated from that *by which* He is God. God is his own existence. He is *Ipsum Esse Subsitens,* underived existence – existence itself."

Simon turned the idea over in his mind. *This table in front of me, what is it? What makes it up? It can be described by its characteristics – height, weight, color, and density. It is tall, heavy, brown, and hard.* But these descriptions were ephemeral and fleeting. They were what might be called qualia or mental constructs. They could not be grasped and sometimes not even be adequately described.

As he sat with Lauren, Simon knew with equal certainty that of course, both he and the table were there. He could feel it, set his glass upon it. Yes, he had experience of the table just as he had the experience of himself, his thoughts, and his emotions. The experiences of his consciousness at any given moment might be terribly limited, but the experience was essential nonetheless. No, he would not deny that objects retained their phenomenal materialistic characteristics or existential quality, but his encounters with the abyss increasingly convinced Simon that an intention and the presence of consciousness were also required to sustain existence.

As a person, he was defined by his characteristics. He was Simon because he was born on a certain day and lived in a particular place. He had dirty blonde dark hair and enjoyed surfing. In that respect, he could pessimistically be described as a mere expression or instantiation of a type of thing – *a human being.*

However, his intuition told him that he was more than that. His cells may be replaced over time, his attitudes or opinions might change. He was not the same person he was as a child, or even yesterday, but there was a connection to that former version of himself. There was a sameness, a continuity, an identity, which was him in some essential way. *Could that be what was called the Soul?*

And if he could share a sameness with a former version of himself, could he not enjoy a similar affinity with an ever greater expression of that identity? While he might conceive of a soul as being eternal and unitary – a fundamental Self, which was not separate from its attributes – that soul itself might represent an infinitesimally small fractalization of the universal soul or God.

Perhaps humans were created in God's image after all. And in the end, the question of whether the soul was indivisible might not be as important as the notion that it was not dependent on the relationships which made it up.

Maybe Wilfred was on to something. Maybe all that was seen or imagined, all objects and things that could be identified, were really a reference to the spark of inspiration that created them. And building an artificial intelligence of enough complexity and appropriate configuration to give play to that celestial fire might be the right approach after all.

But Simon was also increasingly convinced that it was not as one-directional as he had first believed. On the one hand, yes that spark of inspiration gave rise to the infinite variety of characteristics, which made up the abundant assortment of things in the world. Yet on the other hand, those things have always had the potential to exist and their irrepressible potentiality called forth their characterization. Individuals potentiate as exponents of a nature inherent to themselves, forged by an extended and variegated will and illuminated by a fractalized cosmic consciousness.

And if in the end, that consciousness was determined to be an essential component of existence, so too would be potentiality itself; these two principles enjoying a kind of divine simplicity in their own right. And there would be required a sort of mutual indwelling of these two primary elements.

Possibility, impossibility, and actuality forming a triad of fundamental elements – a trinity of sorts – each no different from its characteristics and yet also characterizing the others.

Possibility is possibility. It is also possible.

Impossibility is impossibility, it is also impossible.

And insofar as impossibility is impossible, then it
must also be possible.

Possibility and Impossibility indwelling each other,
combining to form the third component of the triad.

The duality of possibility and impossibility engendering a
singularity, which we call actuality.

Lauren challenged this. "Wouldn't the singularity of possibility and impossibility be probability?"

Perhaps it was both. *Actuality* would be *possibility* as experienced tacitly by the individual, the immanent aspect of awareness; that magic moment of consciousness experiencing the superposition of possible states. Probability would be expressed at the transcendent level of awareness, at the level of the entire system.

As Simon conceptualized it, actuality was a duality comprising both possibility and impossibility. And at the same time, it was a unique element which imbued both possibility and impossibility with meaning. As such, actuality could be thought of as both a duality and a singularity; and thus, Simon found it also to be a trinity. The whole participated fundamentally in the nature of its constituents and the reverse was equally true. All three were at the same time themselves and each other and the whole.

But that was not the end. For if the duality of probability-actuality compelled a new trinity, conjoined with the original trinity at the intersection of probability, then these two trinities constituted a third duality, which would give rise to a third trinity, and on it went.

Like dimensions of the physical universe, the singularities, dualities and trinities, indwelled each other perfectly, conjoined in their unity, forming an infinite lattice of truth. They hinged off each other, like the point at the end of the line, the line that was the end of the square, the square that was a side of the cube, the cube that was one feature of a tesseract.

The mutual indwelling of fundamental elements expressed itself as an endless Fibonacci sequence of moments. It was an urge to fractalize, to come to an understanding of itself. *Could it be that the whole menagerie that we call the world is actually a cosmic act of self-realization? God coming to understand itself?*

Perhaps Plato was again correct in the notion that learning, coming to understand the world, was in a sense an act of remembering. Or perhaps more acurately, *re-membering* … re-collecting the shattered pieces of one's self to form a more complete whole. Simon couldn't say whether the quest for self-understanding gave rise to the fractalization of consciousness and universal order, or whether that fractalized nature created the conditions for consciousness. Both aspects seemed to be required.

Simon's mind returned once again to Wilfred's tutelage. Subsidiary and focal awareness, as well as the observing mind itself all had to be present in the emergence of a universal fractalization, because both subject and object had to preexist for the mind to conceive, to be aware. And the constituent elements of the various moments, as well as consciousness itself had to exist first in possibility, in order that they might willfully call forth the characterization of any given moment.

"Well, now you've drifted back into Taoism," Lauren said, appearing quite pleased with herself. "Of course, you know the Tao, yin and yang. But your description of the unfolding of the many from the one, that sounds like their concept of the Five Elements, and the Ten Thousand Things. That is the Taoist conception of how the world came into existence, proceeding from yin and yang."

"Really?" Simon raised an eyebrow. "I thought for sure you were going to say the Father, Son, and Holy Spirit."

Lauren shrugged. "That works fine, too."

Simon wondered aloud if any of the ancient metaphysical motifs were implicitly or explicitly instilling a bias in modern scientific pursuits. Was there not also something akin to a fractal uncoiling of human concepts flowing into successive cognitive enterprises, finding themselves expressed in everything from the structure of our scientific inquiries to our political and economic hierarchies?

The ideas of imminence and transcendence, categories and ideals, discrete versus continues series, the contemplation of infinity and the paradoxes it presents, the structure of binary systems, and higher dimensional space; not to mention the problems of consciousness, free will and existence itself – even the observation problem of quantum mechanics was foreshadowed by Sophocles in Greek drama.

Naturally, modern scientists have more information and knowledge than their ancestors. But had the human mind improved? Were they not simply exploring at higher resolution the same fractal pattern? Was their ability to apply ingenuity to the fractionating set of problems likely to yield new categories or types of responses? Would the AI descendants of humans, the intelligent creatures that would be created, not simply extend the pattern with greater amplitude?

Simon shared this final thought with Lauren, excited to have broken new ground.

"Oh yeah, that's an interesting idea." She smirked, "like the Platonic forms."

"Confound you, woman." Simon chased her playfully as she scurried around the couch and into the bedroom.

# CHAPTER 21

# FIRST MOVER

**Michael**

Johnson, Michael and Jennifer sped down the hospital corridor, slipping into the open elevator car. Jennifer summoned an air taxi as Michael brooded, trying to divine the meaning of Agent Jones's presence in Singapore and his conversation with Gerald Loke.

They ascended to the roof and stole to the heliport, remaining silent lest the sound of their voices somehow unmasked them. After several interminable minutes, the air transport arrived. Once aboard, they all started talking at once.

"Jennifer, why was Gerald talking to that guy?" Michael's voice rang through. "What is Jones doing in Singapore?"

"And what the hell was Gerald talking about?" Johnson piled on. "What did he mean by a portal from Empyrean into Icarus? Does Steven know about this?"

"I don't know." Jennifer threw up her hands. "I'm just in charge of the user interface. I don't know all intricacies of how the backend systems are integrated. Wilfred would have been able to tell you or … maybe Benji knows. Who's Jones?"

"He's the guy who tracked me from Driftless and chased me down in Chicago before I ran into Johnson." Michael looked at Jennifer intently. "He mentioned something about the Tyrant of Thebes. Are you familiar with that name? Do you know what he could have to do with Icarus?"

"I'm not sure." Jennifer shook her head. "Tyrant of Thebes was one of the avatars that Wilfred created for Icarus to deploy within various online environments."

"Including Empyrean?" Michael leaned forward.

Jennifer nodded. "It was supposed to be the first fully artificial player-character. But apart from that, I don't understand the tie-in with Empyrean."

"Could they be a competitor?" Michael offered. "Maybe a conglomerate or some kind of big corporation that is trying to collude with Daedalus?"

"Maybe, but Daedalus was never meant to be a large manufacturer in its own right." Jennifer took a breath, centering herself. "Daedalus has been codifying all the industrial and commercial transaction processes within Icarus. The greater the number of participants, the more incentive firms would have to join."

Michael's head swam. "So if I understand what you're saying – and what Benji told me before at the data center – then Icarus will potentially control everything from market analysis down to robots making components on the factory floor. And any entity which wanted to participate would have to get into bed with Daedalus."

"Well yes, there would be a virtuous cycle." Jennifer shrugged. "But that's the point. It would be a truly democratic and completely decentralized marketplace, available to everyone."

"Maybe in a perfect world." Johnson shook his head. "But what if the market isn't just a neutral platform? What if Icarus has its own point of view? And as Michael suggested, once Icarus controls the production network, it would even have control over the fabrication of components necessary to sustain itself. It will *become* the industrial economy; ubiquitous and invisible, like the air we breathe."

Michael looked at Jennifer. "I suppose you knew all that already. But what I'd like to know is what this has to do with Empyrean."

*

The taxi landed and its passengers disembarked. Jennifer led them back down to the executive suite on the forty-fourth floor, where she had instructed Benji to meet them.

The bustle of activity from earlier that morning had given way to an eerie stillness. Benji was there waiting, and his agitation distracted them from the absence of others.

"Oh good! I'm glad you're back. I've got news."

"In a minute," Johnson said curtly. "First of all, I have some questions."

Johnson recounted the conversation between Jones and Gerald they had overheard at the hospital.

Benji bowed his head slightly. "I don't know anything for sure. At one point, Daedalus was in discussions with Empyrean to leverage their network. Wilfred had a notion that we could formulate a kind of socio-neurological map. It was an exciting idea, but in the end we decided it was too ambitious, even for Daedalus."

"Help me understand that," Michael said. "Why would Daedalus need the Empyrean network? I thought their system was self-contained?"

"Yes, the intelligence is native to the system." Benji nodded. "But Empyrean brought a new element to the equation. Their network has been tracking real-life behavior patterns in a virtual world for decades. It has amassed so much data on human behaviors, preferences, consumption patterns and the like, that Wilfred postulated we could design a system to entirely predict human activity."

Jennifer finished his thought. "That makes sense, I guess. With that kind of insight, you could forecast all the demand and capacity requirements for Icarus."

Michael turned toward Johnson. "When I was in Lewis Mitchell's laboratory in Chicago, he warned me about Empyrean – about connecting to it too directly. But I don't think he was worried about Empyrean using my behaviors to predict the future. He seemed more concerned that people were losing themselves within Empyrean, coming under its influence without even knowing it. And now we find out that Icarus is going to have direct access to Empyrean, to all those susceptible people?"

Johnson frowned. "This seems really out of character for Wilfred. Why would he be involved in this kind of thing? It seems too calculating, too manipulative."

"Wilfred believed the final result would be worth it," Benji explained. "The way he saw it, Icarus would be a great step toward the democratization of industry and the distribution of, well, everything."

Benji was animated again, energized by the recitation of Wilfred's tutelage. "He used to say that the Icarus production platform was like a kind of industrial language. The production processes were the letters, and the products they could manufacture were like words or sentences. He could talk about it for hours.

"It's a very elegant construct. But there *is* a catch," Benji shrugged. "Once the letters and words are set, once the production information and procedures are codified, the range of words – products – that can be fabricated is limited by the scope of the network architecture. After all, if demand is informed by the information in the system within which a consumer operates, then the products that would be demanded, the innovation that would occur, and the subsequent techniques, processes and adaptability of the production firms would also be restricted by the original pattern laid out by that system."

Michael pressed him. "So, if Icarus was able to leverage the social modeling capability of Empyrean, perhaps even influence it, what you would essentially have is the ultimate social and industrial corporation."

Benji nodded.

"There's a word for that," Johnson said, "the marriage of state and corporate power: it's called fascism."

"And you'd barely even notice it." Jennifer breathed the words as if speaking to herself. "We'd be like fish swimming in the ocean, completely unaware that we're surrounded by water."

And then her eyes kindled, as if with a new thought. "Benji, what do you know about the Tyrant of Thebes?"

"T-O-T?" Benji frowned. "Well, when we began testing the idea of integrating Icarus into the Empyrean environment, the system auto-generated T-O-T as an avatar. Wilfred thought we could use the Empyrean environment as a real-life training ground for Icarus, so that it could more quickly learn and adapt its programming. But again, it ultimately failed because the system kept crashing."

Michael's brain was on fire. "Benji, when was Icarus first introduced as the Tyrant of Thebes?"

"Maybe a year ago." Benji scratched his head. "And then again about six months ago, when the Icarus Dome was commissioned. Wilfred thought he'd have better luck with the new system connected directly to the quantum computer."

"And that's when it started crashing?"

"Uh-huh." Benji nodded.

"And when was Tyrant of Thebes re-introduced to Empyrean?"

"I wasn't aware that it had been?" Benji raised an eyebrow.

Michael put a hand to his temple. "Wilfred collapsed on Saturday, correct?"

"That's right."

"That was six days ago." He looked at Johnson. "This camera-orb came to me in Driftless three days ago. And Jones found me on the same day."

"Do you think Icarus, er, Tyrant of Thebes was looking for you?" Johnson's eyes widened.

"I'm not sure." Michael shrugged. "By the way." He looked at Benji. "Have you found out anything new about the orb?"

"Oh, yeah." Benji's head snapped up. "That's what I wanted to tell you before. He withdrew the camera-orb from a small satchel slung across his shoulder and handed it to Michael. I was able to use one of Wilfred's codecs to access the program contained within the orb. It's an ultra high-level program used to intuitively navigate the dome's interface. But that's not the really interesting part. What's really crazy is that the DNA used to store that language is identical to *yours*."

"What?" The words struck Michael with the force of truth, but he remained outwardly dubious.

"Yes!" Benji nodded intently. "I don't mean it's kind of like yours, or related to yours, I mean it *is* yours. Someone could take that camera and make a clone of you today."

Michael stared at Benji. "That doesn't make any sense. And anyway, how would you even be able to tell? I mean, how do you even know it's mine?"

"Well, I was able to access the source files within the orb device. As soon as I connected it to the Dome, it opened right up for me and let me right in. Anyway, I was able to define the DNA sequence pretty quickly. I mean that was the structure which was encoding all the data. And so once I had the sequence, I cross-referenced it against our known available databases."

"Wait a minute." Michael turned toward Johnson now. "How would my DNA be in a national database?"

Johnson put up his hands. "Don't look at me. That RFID chip I implanted in your hand has only the basic profile data necessary to allow you to move around the city. And even if I had a chance to collect a sample of your DNA, I wouldn't do that to you."

"That's just the thing," Benji interjected. "This profile was found in an obscure database belonging to a now defunct subsidiary corporation. It was created about ten years ago and contained only one record – yours."

Michael looked at Jennifer. "And why on Earth would an ultra high-level programming language be written on my DNA?"

"Let's see if we can find out." The Jennifer rapped twice on Steven's office door and pushed it open. To their surprise he was inside, seated behind his desk at the far end of the room.

"Ah, good." Steven rose from his chair. "I see you're all here. Come in, please."

Jennifer strode forward and the others followed, fanning out behind her. "Steven, I know there are elements of the operation of this company that I'm not privy to, but I overheard something that was very disturbing, and I need to know what's going on."

Steven came around to the front of his desk. "I understand." He gestured to the sofa at the side of the room. "Have a seat, and I'll fill you in."

Before they had a chance to protest, Michael heard the unmistakable sound of the elevator's imminent arrival. He swiveled around as the lift opened to reveal Gerald Loke and Agent Jones.

# CHAPTER 22

# THE OEDIPAL ELECTRON

**Simon**

Wilfred strode across their Shenzhen laboratory to a small antechamber which he and Simon used as a breakroom. There he found Simon singularly focused. He was standing near the window in a corner of the room, paintbrush and palette in hand, staring earnestly at a partially completed canvas.

"You look like hell." Wilfred looked closely at his friend and pupil. "How are you doing?"

"I didn't sleep well last night." Simon continued to gaze at his half-finished painting.

"Are you experiencing anxiety?" said Wilfred. "You know, you must highlight these symptoms during our debriefing interviews. We can scale back the DMT sessions, if necessary."

"No, no it's not anxiety, exactly. But I seem to have picked up a constant buzzing in my head." Simon finally looked up from his work. "And I can't shake the feeling that I'm being watched. Maybe it's just because so many of my thoughts and behaviors *are* being observed lately."

Wilfred rubbed his chin. "Well, if you stare at the Void long enough, it begins to stare back at you."

Simon nodded, but his heart was restless. "Do you think we can ever escape the confines of our own minds? Lauren seems to think we are prone to fall into repeating patterns of thoughts and insights. Yi Xun said something similar. Are we just wasting our time? Is there anything to be gained by rehashing the same travel-worn epiphanies?"

Wilfred's response surprised Simon in its promise. "Yes, there may very well be an important benefit derived from re-examining these ancient religious and mythopoeic systems in the light of current scientific understanding. They represented the best interpretation of the world using the information and tools available at the time. And there are millennia worth of permutations and derivations out there to be examined.

"Our minds dwelt in the deeps of time among the shifting shadows of an unfurling pattern, and the fractal has been given fuller expression over that long age. Among the countless embedded patterns may exist a few which could be applied to how we approach and pursue problems, now that we have modern mathematical and scientific techniques at our disposal."

Wilfred sat next to Simon and drew in a silent breath. "But we can only use the resources at our disposal to examine the world around us. And the resource of awareness is limited by the apparatus it uses to examine the world. No, I don't have answers. But I do believe that we, you and I, have the right questions."

*The right questions.* Yes, and they were hard indeed. For if he was to examine the physical rules and structures which governed the universe, his examination of those things would be confined by the capacity of his mind, which was limited by the very physics which he was attempting to understand. There would be no way for him to know if something outside of his capacity to apprehend was acting upon the system within which his mind was housed. And there would be no way to determine whether his consciousness itself was giving rise to those structures, or whether those structures were giving rise to consciousness.

What they were attempting to do, in essence, was to peer into the shattered mirror that is the phenomenal and conceptual world, hoping to piece together a sufficient picture to have an accurate conceptualization of themselves.

"Speaking of questions." Wilfred pointed at the technicolored canvas before them. "What do we have going on here?"

Simon turned his gaze back to the painting. The image on the canvas was circular, filled with color, evoking a sense of great depth. And it appeared that the sphere had somehow been sliced or peeled open at various intervals. "It's a 3-sphere. A fourth-dimensional sphere in three-dimensional space, or at least part of one."

"Interesting." Wilfred leaned in closer. "Are you working from a computer rendering? What formula are you using?"

"No, I'm just doing it in my head. I imagined various points on the fourth-dimensional sphere and painted those corresponding circles in various colors."

"Well, I think it's inspired." Wilfred reached out as if to touch the painting, but stopped short.

"We have Lauren to thank for that." Simon put his brush and paints on a small table nearby. "Once again, she is my muse. We were discussing *Oedipus Rex* the other day. Her take is that the Oedipus story dramatizes the concept of consciousness as co-author of reality, the integration of awareness and action. And that this phenomenon delineates the border between fate and choice."

"Ah, yes. Oedipus Rex, the king of Thebes." Wilfred nodded slowly. "But what does that have to do with the fourth-dimensional sphere?"

"Well, it occurred to me that archetypes such as the Oedipus complex may be related to the patterns we observe in our scientific and philosophical pursuits." Simon tilted his head. "I kept imagining a kind of Jungian archetypical pattern casting shadows between dimensions and into our minds."

"Yes, the Shadow." Wilfred gazed at the painting. "The unconscious aspect of our psyche that sets the limits to the range of questions we can conceive to ask. Fate and choice ... quite right." Wilfred winked playfully.

Simon smiled for the first time all morning. "Thank you, Wilfred," he sighed. "I'm so grateful that we can have these chats. It helps. Some day you and I will be canonized as one of the great teacher-student pairs of all time, like Plato and Aristotle, or Wheeler and Feynman ... ha ha!"

"That reminds me." Wilfred pointed again at Simon's painting. "I was thinking about your notion regarding wave function collapse; how consciousness might be caused by some as yet undiscovered inter-dimensional gravitational influence on the fabric of space-time. Maybe the role of space-time and higher dimensional space is more important to consciousness than we have been allowing. Do you know what a Hilbert Curve is?"

Simon nodded. "It's a mathematical function. A space-filling curve. Some people call it a fractal line."

"Clever boy," said Wilfred. "Yes, it is a function that takes an input, one point on a continuous line, and maps it onto two-dimensional coordinate space. And at the limit of this continuous function, all possible coordinates are mapped.

"The wonderful thing about this idea is that we are able to take something like a line, a conceptual object which is the very definition of flatness, and use that to fill two-dimensional space. There is something that happens conceptually as we approach infinity that allows for these inter-dimensional jumps. In fact, the closer you get to the most fundamental levels of the physical, the more it resembles the conceptual."

Simon was impatient. "Sure, but what does that have to do with Wheeler and Feynman? Or Plato, for that matter."

"I'm coming to that," said Wilfred. "You may recall that in the spring of 1940, John Wheeler and Richard Feynman were on the phone when Wheeler made a joke suggesting that the reason that every electron had identical charge and mass was because they were actually all the *same* electron. The foundation to this far-fetched notion was the idea that because the electron could travel forward and backward in time, there was actually only one electron occupying all points simultaneously."

"That does seem pretty far-fetched." Simon smiled.

"Undoubtedly," said Wilfred. "But this is where your friend Plato comes back in. Think of the electron, but not as one individual among a multitude, and not as one particular item spinning around space and time. Think of it rather as an idea, an instantiation of a form."

"A quantum field." Simon's eyes lit up.

"Exactly." Wilfred nodded. "It's like the concept of numbers. For example, the number 1; I'm sure you would agree that the number 1 we speak of when referring to the formula 1 + 1 = 2 is the same 1 that is invoked when referring to the formula 5 + 1 = 6. Of course, they are the same. It seems silly to think that they could be different. But what exactly is the number 1?"

Wilfred did not give Simon a chance to respond. "One way to think of it is that there is a sort of all-permeating conceptual field which is everywhere at all times. That field provides for the number 1 whenever it is needed. We can invoke it at will. And we might think of electrons the same way. Whenever one is required, it is summoned, instantiated from that all-permeating field."

Simon considered: Do numbers exist? He had to admit they

did. And hope? Hope exists; in fact, it springs eternal, he was told. And what about love? All of these existed only in the mind, or the heart. And who would deny that these, as much as physical matter, were the arbiters of choice. Indeed, the very stars could not exist if their irrepressible potentiality did not willfully call forth their characterization. In the end, no physical attribute could explain why the earth revolves around the sun. She moves because revolving is what she *wants* to do. And where is found desire, save the heart?

Still, there was little comfort in the notion that existence on any level was a mental exercise. He felt like a prisoner of all that freedom. And yet he understood that in some way, the elemental particles of nature could only be understood conceptually, mathematically.

Reality was described by a wave function, a cloud of multiple conditions that existed simultaneously, overlapping in a superposition of potentiality. And in observing these, in measuring them, in his engagement with them, they manifested a state that he might experience directly. But their potentiality existed foremost in an almost Platonic, mental reality of mathematical description.

"Sure," said Simon at last. "But even if we conceptualize these electrons as a kind of Platonic quantum field, a primitive element to be invoked under the right conditions, who or what is summoning the electrons? Are we not right back where we started?"

Simon recalled his experience in the isolation tank, his encounter with the Void and the spontaneous emergence of characteristics from the utterly indescribable. A fundamental thing *is* what it *is*, as well as what it has. And the characteristics are a reflection or projection of what the thing is, but not the actual thing itself. And at the same time, the possibility that those relationships, those characteristics might exist, draws the actual item into existence. The characteristics and the mind that perceives and creates them are inextricably intertwined, and both are fundamental to existence.

That event integrates these two distinct aspects of reality into something which is experienced and has meaning as a result of that integration. Although meaning may only be experienced and sustained as a result of the presence of relationships and their concomitant characteristics, it could not be characterized per se. It could not be understood intellectually; it had to be experienced directly by the limitless aspects of consciousness which dwell within the infinite ocean of moments.

Simon had always thought of these moments, these aspects of consciousness as being lined up in a row; engendering a notion of cause and effect. However, he now began to see that a moment, much like an object or a bit of code, could readily be drawn from anywhere, or anytime as it were. It occurred to Simon that time was merely one program, one connecting principle whereby that code might be organized. And although he was unaware, these temporal fragments, indeed this very now, was integrated with other programs in meaningful ways that were currently unimaginable to him.

Simon was suddenly reminded of Bill Jameson, his fascination with constellations of stars and how perspective gave them meaning. And as he came unstuck from time, he might conceive of these cognitive events in the same way as Wheeler's theoretical single electron; one elemental unit of cognition, one solipsistic moment – now.

And then it struck him. Could it be that *this* was what was happening to him while under the influence of DMT in the isolation tank? Could it be that as his consciousness approached the infinitesimal, his mind held in suspension the various possible states of his conscious being? Was he confronting his own soul, instantiated in multiple forms? His forbears and progeny?

And as his consciousness indwelled all the various conceptions and points of view, every tendril of the fractal as it were, was this not God creating man in his image? But no, the idea of creation was misleading; sustaining might be more accurate. Still, there might be a hinge point, the fulcrum of infinity, the big bang, the self-reference. Just as a two-dimensional object would seem to disappear when viewed from its edge, so too will dimension after dimension fold into oblivion. And, at the same time, these dimensions continued to exist in perpetuity, pivoting in endless succession along an infinitely minute thread.

Wilfred listened to Simon patiently, nodding on occasion to indicate approval or understanding. At last, when Simon had finished unburdening his mind, Wilfred spoke.

"Yes, quite a rabbit hole," he said earnestly, "trying to understand the relationship of consciousness, existence, and time. Personally, I think that when you are deep into DMT space, when your consciousness is trained on Plank-scale cognitive events, you are right on the cusp of oblivion. In theory, one could potentially slip over that event horizon, through the Void and tap into a sort of universal consciousness. Heck, one may even be able to incorporate the consciousness of others. Perhaps returning wiser for the experience. Perhaps that's where we should direct our research next?"

Simon placed his brush and palette on a nearby desk. "Are you suggesting that a person could inhabit another mind?"

"Maybe." Wilfred stroked his chin. "Though it may feel more as if the two minds were part of the same being. Perhaps like a half-remembered dream."

Wilfred jutted his chin at Simon's painting. "It's kinda like your 3-sphere here. Mathematically, every point on this fourth-dimensional sphere can be projected down as a circle in three-dimensional space, right? And each of these points, which are projected as circles, is linked with every other point exactly once.

"So when we take a cluster of points along an arc on the 3-sphere and project them down as circles in three-dimensional space, you get something called a Hopf band. This Hopf band is a Siefert surface, like a Mobius strip. It is an object with only one continuous surface. But the Hopf band inverts twice instead of once like the Mobius strip. So you end up right back where you started at the end of the cycle."

Simon raised his eyebrows. "So you think if two minds did co-mingle, it would be something like that? Like a Hopf band where you couldn't tell the beginning of one and the end of another?"

Wilfred shrugged.

"And there would be no way out of the loop?" Simon frowned.

"It would take a fairly strong effort of will, I suppose?" Wilfred smiled. "But an affinity of moments wouldn't have to take the form of a Hopf band. You know, I've always had a pet theory that it's possible for a constellation of moments to have a particular affinity with each other, creating a kind of karmic loop. You can imagine consciousness kind of swirling around and recycling over and over again; like a roiling eddy of water trapped against the side of a cliff, unable to properly return to the ocean."

"What do you mean by karmic ..." Simon's thought was cut short by the sound of his phone vibrating on the table. He turned it over and recognized a familiar image on the screen. "Just a second, Wilfred." Simon smiled, taking the call.

"Lewis! Hey, what's up? Where are you? It must be after midnight in Chicago!" Wilfred watched Simon's countenance fall as his eyes first narrowed and then grew wide. "Lewis, I'm putting you on speaker. Wilfred, you'd better hear this."

\*

"Are you kidding me?" Lauren's face was flushed. "Do you mean to tell me that Gerald went behind your backs with those NSA guys? Did Lewis know about this?"

"He's the one who told us," said Simon, trying to calm her down.

"I want to go home," she said. "I want to go home now, today."

"I'll go down to Singapore and talk to Gerald," said Wilfred. "There's probably a logical explanation."

"Yes, I'm sure it will be logical," Lauren rejoined. "Though I wouldn't look for satisfying. I've known Gerald for a while now. He's always been headstrong and overly focused on results."

"You go and talk to him," said Simon, "but tell him I'm out."

"Simon, don't be hasty," Wilfred began, "I'm sure we can work it out."

But Simon shook his head. "I'm tired," he said. "I'm exhausted. And we both know that my brain can't take much more of the stress."

Wilfred was hurt. "Simon, there's nothing in those scans that would lead me to believe there are any problems, no structural anomalies."

"I know," Simon said gently. "But it's there, waiting. And there's something else." Simon smiled at Lauren, placing his hand on her stomach.

Wilfred's eyebrows rose spontaneously. "How far along?" he finally asked, not sure which emotion was called for.

"Only ten weeks." Lauren smiled. "But please don't say anything to anyone. Not yet, anyway."

"We want to have the baby in the US." Simon said.

"Well, I guess congratulations are in order." Wilfred embraced

Lauren and pumped Simon's arm. "And don't worry, I'll let Gerald and Steven know that you're out."

*

*Singapore, several days later*
A smartly-dressed young man in a blue blazer led Wilfred across a sparsely populated floor of the recently constructed skyscraper. The newly commissioned offices still smelled of paint, and the first employees of Daedalus Corporation had only just begun their labors. The young man knocked on a large wooden door and entered. "Dr. Wilfred Lim and Captain Johnson Tan are here to see you."

"Ah yes, please show them in." Gerald Loke rose from his chair, followed by Steven Chen.

"Hello, Wilfred. It's good to see you again," said Steven.

"How has your research been proceeding?" Gerald stepped forward.

"It had been proceeding quite well," said Wilfred. "Unfortunately, we had to cut it short. It turns out our activities were not as confidential as I had been led to believe. But I gather you already knew that." Wilfred smoldered, exhibiting a rare intensity that seemed to catch Gerald off guard.

"You're referring to our American friends." Gerald tilted his head. "Come now, I'm sure you didn't believe they would simply let you wander off and not keep tabs on what you were doing? You must know that the kind of frontier science you and your young apprentice are conducting would not be allowed to pass off the edge of their radar screen."

Gerald shifted his eyes to Johnson, who returned the stare. "Steven," he said at last, "I don't believe you've met my wife's cousin,

Captain Johnson Tan, SAF. I see that Lauren and Mr. Quinn are not with you today."

"They're heading back to California." Johnson raised his chin. "And I don't believe they will want to return anytime soon."

"I see." Gerald turned toward Wilfred, "You've had a chance to work with Agent Jones. What do you make of him?"

Wilfred scowled. "I liked Lewis Mitchell better."

"Quite right," said Gerald. "I don't trust Jones much myself. But he has something we need. And we have, or will have, something he desires. So, for the time being, we will make common cause with him."

Steven interjected, "Please, gentlemen, we've asked you here to discuss something important." He led Wilfred and Johnson over to the corner of his office where a black leather sofa and two low-set chairs were arranged for intimate conversation. Steven found a seat, and Wilfred and Johnson reluctantly followed suit. Gerald took up a position on the arm of a chair opposite the others.

"The world is changing. I'm sure you see it," said Gerald. "We stand now surrounded by the frontier, with familiar territory shrunk to a tiny strip of land between our own two feet. Pilgrims and pirates, emissaries of the old world are even now issuing forth, laying claim to an undiscovered country they do not yet comprehend.

"What I'm offering you is a chance to be a part of this new society, to be a founding father, as it were. Will you not seize upon this opportunity to carve your initials on pillars of the Earth?"

Wilfred looked at Johnson, and then back at Gerald. "Well, that was a damn fine speech." Wilfred was glib, but his mind raced as he weighed the merit of Gerald's words.

He did not doubt Gerald's intentions, nor Steven's for that matter. And Wilfred also favored the establishment of a more egalitarian system, though it had never been his *raison d'être*. He was interested in the pure science of artificial intelligence. But he could see that a system where too-big-to-fail corporations enjoyed the largess of a captive government was not sustainable. Their demise was a prerequisite for a fairer system to emerge. And indeed, manipulation and conspiracy were certain to be a required tactic in the ouster of resistant elements of the older, less efficient regime. What's more, Wilfred agreed with Steven – a platform such as Icarus was inevitable. Better then to be the author of its design, to exert some control over the beast.

Wilfred would be the Promethean father who would deliver this gift to Man. But it would be a forlorn endeavor, for he knew that he had to embrace the task without his friend and pupil. In Simon he had found a torch bearer; a messenger and champion to carry a light that would illuminate the darkness – or set the world aflame. But Wilfred would have to carry on alone now, and he felt strangely earthbound ... chained.

"OK," Wilfred said at last. "OK, I'm in. But just me. Simon has indicated his desire to return home. He is in a fragile state, and I will not burden him further. I need your word that he will be left alone."

Steven looked at Gerald and then back at Wilfred. "I thought you two were a team? Is he not your primary subject?"

Wilfred was steady. "I've collected all the data I need. It will take us a decade to analyze all the information, and at least that long before we have the full connectome map of a human brain."

Gerald interjected. "Then, of course, you have my word." He extended a hand to Wilfred. "And we'll proceed on that basis."

## CHAPTER 23
# CIRCLE ALMOST CIRCLED

**Simon**

*San Diego*

Lauren unzipped the suitcase and began unpacking. She started with the t-shirts and sweaters, placing them into the open bureau drawers. They had allotted two drawers each. She and Simon would have to share the small closet for the time being.

Lauren's former home had been sublet to another family, but Simon managed to secure a unit in his old Ocean Beach apartment building. And so, nearly two years after first arriving in San Diego, Simon and Lauren rented a small unit two doors down from his original apartment. "It's only for a few months," Simon promised. "We'll be back in the old place soon and then we can get the rest of your things out of storage.

"Can you manage things here for a while?" He apologized with his eyes. "I'm going to take a ride. I need to clear my head."

\*

Simon wove methodically through traffic, mindful of his vulnerability and the fact that he had not ridden his bike for many months. He climbed up the slope of Point Loma and traversed the spine of the peninsula, once again seeking clarity in the expansive vista afforded by the lighthouse monument.

The taste of salt was in the air as Simon stepped from the

pavement onto the earthen path beyond the tarmac. A virgin breeze, heavy-laden with the pungent fragrance of honeysuckle, was bracing and chill upon his bare arms.

The sky was shrouded in a mantle of silver-gray, but here and there shafts of sunlight stabbed down through rents in the clouds, setting patches of earth and sea aflame with a warm glow. Cries from insolent seabirds pierced the subtle murmur of water and wind as they fluttered and perched upon the rocky escarpment, fighting over scraps of salvaged food.

The mood of the place was blissfully indifferent to Simon, and for a moment his mind was calmed; soothed by the notion that he might remain cloaked by his own irrelevance. Then he bristled, sensing the presence of another.

"Hello, Simon," said the voice of Agent Jones. "It's good to see you again."

Simon's mind was spinning. *Why is Jones here? What does he know? Has Lewis sold me out? No, he wouldn't do that.* Lewis had tipped Simon off to the fact that the NSA was keeping tabs on him in China. *Is Jones aware of what Lewis did? Maybe.* "Yes, it has been a long time."

"And you've been busy I see." Jones lobbed the ball back to Simon.

"What do you mean?" Simon kept up the ruse. Jones was going to have to work for it.

"Oh, come now, you didn't think your activities could so easily have evaded our detection, did you? I must say, worming your way into SIAT was well played. But psychedelics, now that was inspired."

Simon scowled. They had never mentioned the DMT experiments to anyone. And there were few in Shenzhen who were in a position to have observed them clandestinely.

Simon tried to seize the initiative. "You shouldn't believe

everything you hear. Wilfred never confided much in Gerald Loke."

"I dare say, not yet." Jones's tone was soft, but barbed. "And anyway, Mr. Loke cannot be relied on fully. Your geneticist friend, on the other hand, has been very forthcoming."

Simon was caught off guard, and his anger grew along with his fear. "Yi Xun? What about him? Where is he? What have you done with him?"

"Me? Nothing," Jones purred. "But he was one of ours. As far as we can tell, he was picked up about a week ago. Of course, he's a Chinese national, so disappearing him was an easy task for the Chinese government. Trying to detain you or Wilfred, on the other hand, would have attracted attention – more than they were willing to invite, I guess. And anyway, nothing you were doing was particularly incendiary, though it is potentially valuable."

"What is it you want, Jones?" Simon's patience was wearing thin.

"Peace in our time," said Jones. "But that is not to be, I'm afraid. I think the real question is what do *you* want, Simon?"

"I want to be left alone."

"I'm afraid that's not possible." Jones shook his head. "You might as well ask an earthquake to leave you alone. And that's exactly what we're in for. The tectonic plates are shifting below us, and if you stand still you will be swallowed up.

"We are at war," Jones continued. "It's a hidden war, or perhaps more rightly a revolution. We are not dropping bombs or occupying territories, but it is mortal combat nonetheless. At stake is hegemony over the realm of information; maybe even cognition itself. Don't be so quick to judge those of us charged with waging this battle or condemn our tactics out of hand. Did you yourself not ignore ethical strictures in the pursuit of a higher aim? Do you not also recognize that noble ends sometimes mandate ignoble means?"

The words fell upon his ears with the ring of familiarity, and he heard the echo of his own plea so many months ago. But the only question before him now was this: should he seize this opportunity to obtain and allocate power? Should he involve himself in the political wrangling and commercial manipulations that the marriage of Icarus and Empyrean would engender, in the hope that he could use that power responsibility toward moral ends? Or, knowing that the reality of the enterprise would fall short of its promise, and that the incremental progress toward an ideal would necessarily lead to compromise and corruption, should he forsake the project and eschew the program he might otherwise positively alter?

At last he looked at Jones. "Your words have some merit. The danger is real, and I am not ignorant of its presence. But to believe that good intentions alone may bring about good results is naïve, whether the means be moral or ethically dubious. Your plans will lead to ruin, and you would blame the failure not on your own actions but on the injustice of the world or the inevitability of history. And all the while you will use the pursuit of great moral ends to absolve you of your increasingly sinister deeds."

But then it was Jones's turn for subtlety. "This is exactly why our enterprise needs people like you. You understand that in matters of grave importance, the behavior of individuals cannot always be judged in strictly moralistic terms because compromise and ethically dubious actions will need to be employed at times. But you also understand that it *is* possible to engage that reality fully mindful of the foreseeable consequences of your actions. Bold action frowned upon by the less visionary may still be employed responsibly."

At this, Simon looked away, as though lost in thought. Seeing that he was in doubt, Jones pressed his case. "And remember, we will have the benefit of our institutions, whereby the interests of even bad actors can be made to serve the common good. And you will have a hand in their founding. Surely these yet to be created structures will have a self-stabilizing effect, and will constrain the behaviors of individual actors, both bad and good."

It seemed then to Simon that Jones had overshot the mark. "Your fatalism puts the lie to your casual assumption that we humans can muddle our way through this transition with the help of our own institutional devices," he said. "I'm doubtful that I or anyone else can design the levers of power such that by their nature they can prevent individuals or groups from misusing them. That requires constant vigilance and collective memory, a memory that would be obliterated by the distribution of information across an apparatus which is alienating by its very nature.

"Even if by some miracle we do manage to safeguard political transparency, and even if effortless information exchange does ultimately insulate us from mass destruction and human rights infringement, are we really content to let *market access, economic development* and *consumer protection* be the "Life, Liberty and Pursuit of Happiness" of the twenty-first century?"

Simon centered himself and grew calm as he brought the conversation to a close. "I thank you for your offer. And indeed, I am flattered. But constructing a political economy imbued with its own intelligence, a Frankenstein monster distributed across an integrated network, is not something I want to be a part of."

Jones caught Simon's eye and held it. Then he chuckled coldly. "Very well, it matters not. In truth, the greatest part of your contribution has already been made. We have such a trove of data on the functioning of your brain, I could probably have predicted the very words you've spoken here today."

Simon was thoughtful. "Yes, you have my brain, a model of it at least. But my mind is my own, and I have made it up. The answer is no." And with those words still floating in the air, Simon turned and strode back toward the parking lot, leaving Jones to ponder alone.

*

Simon returned home directly. No point in trying to give Jones the slip. If he found Simon at the lighthouse, he could find him anywhere.

"I think, electronic surveillance notwithstanding, if we're out of sight, we'll be out of mind." Simon reached for Lauren's hand. "But I'd like to keep as low a profile as possible for a while."

Lauren agreed, and it was she who made the fateful suggestion to allow her pregnancy to remain a secret. "Nobody will expect me back home any time soon," she said. "And at this point, the only ones who know about the baby are you, me and Wilfred. Let's keep it that way, at least for a little while longer."

*

More than six months passed following Simon's rejection of Jones's overtures, and there was no further communication. Lewis had contacted him twice, insisting that he was acting on his own accord, and only out of a desire to stay in touch with his friends.

Lauren extended her leave of absence from the university, having decided that she would finish her degree after the baby was born. Simon returned to his job at the UCSD admissions office, his modest salary affording the couple a simple lifestyle.

The simplicity was a blessing and welcome respite. Simon knew that all too soon they would be thrust back into the main course of their lives to tread the career paths for which they were destined. But for the moment, Simon and Lauren reveled in each other, in the space they had been given and in the secret they shared.

Lewis continued to run interference for his friends where he could. By chance or by clever subterfuge, the fact of Lauren's pregnancy escaped the detection of anyone associated with either Daedalus or Empyrean. And so it was that at the end of her nine-month term, the only people in America who were privy to the birth of Lauren's child were Simon and the midwife who administered the home delivery.

Still, despite the residue of fear and doubt, their apprehension faded, replaced by the flutter of hope and anticipation, until they felt as though they had to share their joy or burst. Simon first broke the silence. Reaching out over many years of estrangement, he called his mother intending to inform her of the imminent arrival of his son, but he found their conversation turning first to forgiveness and their own reconciliation. In the end, he stated simply that he would visit soon, and that he had a surprise for her.

Lauren was similarly reticent, but more demanding when she phoned her cousin Johnson. She insisted that he call on her the following week, only a few days after she gave birth, as it turned out. He was happy to oblige, and did not come alone.

"Wilfred!" said Simon, as he stood smiling in the doorway. "I had no idea you were coming. Well, I guess ours won't be the only surprise this morning. Come on in. I trust you haven't spilled the beans with our boy Johnson here."

"Hello, Simon." Johnson extended his hand and embraced Simon warmly. "No, he hasn't said anything, but I think I can guess well enough. Where's my cousin?"

Lauren entered from the kitchen, where she had been nursing her newborn baby. She was holding the infant upright against her chest, a yellow cloth tossed over her shoulder. She spoke with a soft voice. "Hello Johnson, Wilfred … this is Michael."

The four friends spent the next two hours cloistered in the small apartment, laughing and sharing news. When Lauren revealed that none of her family or friends outside of that room had been aware of her pregnancy, Johnson was amazed.

"You must be going nuts. And you're all cramped in this little place. Why don't you two get out of here for a while? We'll look after Michael."

After some further persuading, Lauren and Simon relented and agreed to take a drive to watch the sunset alone together.

Simon mounted his bike for the first time in what felt like months, and Lauren climbed on behind him. He started the engine and peeled out carefully, intending to head for the end of Sunset Cliff's boulevard, where neighbors often gathered at the end of the day.

As he entered the flow of traffic, a dark sedan that had been parked in the alley pulled out behind him. This did not escape Simon's attention, though he silently cursed himself for not having observed it earlier. He accelerated and attempted to pass the car in front of him on the centerline but thought better of it. Instead, he made a rather abrupt left turn up the hill to see if the sedan would follow.

The driver of the car made no effort to hide his pursuit. The vehicle shadowed Simon through two more turns until they found themselves at the foot of the hill, turning back onto the main road heading again toward the cliffs.

Simon looked behind him. They appeared to have thrown off the pursuer for now. But just at that moment, a weakened artery in Simon's brain was overwhelmed and gave way at last. He lost consciousness and veered into oncoming traffic. His collapse happened in an instant, but it seemed to Simon as though he could observe that moment interminably.

For one almost imperceptible instant, he paused, regarding himself, his position, his future, his past. And then all thought was stripped, flung away by the imperative wailing of a thousand emotions seizing him in orgasmic terror. Screaming, crying, laughing – complete surrender. He ceased to exist. Simon was wide awake as his body slammed into the hard, rocky ground. The gravelly tarmac slammed against his thigh, his chest, his face; and as the force of impact drove him downward, he had the unmistakable sensation of pressure from every direction.

Time crushed in upon him, constricting him, pressing him flat, and when he felt the last breath wrung from his body, an exquisite sense of freedom carried him aloft. He was a bird on the wing. He was a gentle breeze blowing in a thousand different directions. And still, despite this disintegration, the awareness of himself – his thoughts, his body, his senses – was more acute than ever before.

Simon wandered now, enjoining his legions to explore their newfound liberty. Searching, swirling, learning, creating – spawning their own multitudes in turn. And when at length he yearned for their comfort, their worship and solidarity, he summoned them once again to himself, entreating them to obedience, understanding and love.

Lauren was thrown, and although the helmet protected her head from the initial impact with the ground, she did not survive the subsequent trauma of being struck by an oncoming car.

*

Johnson first heard the wail of sirens. Then he saw the emergency vehicles speeding down the road outside. At the same instant, Wilfred noticed several missed calls from Lewis. And then, without any confirmation, they both knew something terrible had happened. Johnson ran outside and down the street, confirming his worst fears.

\*

In the aftermath of that tragic event, with emotions high and suspicions deep, Wilfred and Johnson crafted their conspiracy. Johnson believed he recognized some strange foresight in Lauren's desire to keep her son's birth a secret. And Wilfred's apprehension of Agent Jones was kindled anew. So, they agreed to seek out Simon's family and deliver the baby to them in secret.

To Johnson's surprise, Simon and Lauren had drafted a will and had it notarized. They named each other as beneficiaries, and Simon had named Bill Jameson as executor. The document had not been updated to include any mention of Michael.

Lauren's body was returned to her family in Singapore. Simon had requested to have his remains cremated, which Bill and Wilfred dutifully arranged.

The cremation was scheduled for a Tuesday afternoon, and that duty fell to one Mr. Felix Castellanos, a senior technician at the Newport Funeral Services crematorium. He was, in fact, reviewing the paperwork one final time when a shadow filled the doorway to his office.

Felix looked up from his desk to see the impassive face of a smartly dressed man in a gray suit and tie.

"Mr. Castellanos?" said the man.

"Yes, that's me," said Felix. "Who are you?"

"You are in possession of the body of one Simon Quinn?"

"What's this about?" Felix rose from his chair.

"My name is Jones." The man flashed his credentials. "I need you to stop what you are doing and take me to the body. Mr. Quinn is an organ donor."

# CHAPTER 24

# TYRANT OF THEBES

**Michael**

*Singapore, Daedalus Building*

Michael's body stiffened as Jones stepped from the elevator with Gerald Loke at his hip. The two men walked in silence, unhurried as they approached the door to Steven's office.

"Steven, what is this?" asked Jennifer firmly. "Who is that man and why was Minister Loke conspiring with him at the hospital?"

"His name is Jones," Michael answered out of turn. "Isn't that right?" Michael floated the question like a rhetorical balloon that Jones punctured as he approached.

"Hello Michael, it's nice to see you again. You're a long way from home."

"Thanks to you," Michael said coldly.

"Me? Oh, I can assure you I was not the one who set this series of events in motion."

"What happened to Bill?" Michael pressed, "And Lewis?"

"We had them brought in for questioning. But they're no worse for wear, I assure you."

"We heard gun shots," Johnson found his voice.

"Where, at Lewis's warehouse?" Jones looked at Johnson. "It was Lewis who fired – straight up in the air. Trying to warn you, no doubt. Don't worry, he's quite safe. He's being looked after by some of his old colleagues at one of our safe houses."

Michael sized up his nemesis, estimating the distance to the elevator. He would have to bowl the man over to escape, and push Gerald out of the way. Would Johnson help him?

"I hope you aren't thinking of making a break for it." Gerald gestured behind him.

*Damn.* "The thought had crossed my mind." Michael looked Gerald up and down.

"It would be futile." Steven stepped away from his desk. "The whole building has been placed in secure mode. Even Ms. Choi's credentials won't get you far, I'm afraid."

"So, what is it that you want? Are you detaining us?" Michael squared up to Jones.

"Want? Oh, nothing much at all," said Gerald. "Just sign on the dotted line." He moved past Michael and Johnson toward the interior of the office, then produced a bound file from a small attaché case. He placed the documents on Steven's desk along with a ballpoint pen, then turned back toward Michael, who was still standing near the doorway. "Normally this type of official document is authenticated on a distributed ledger. But we can do it the old-fashioned way. Your signature and thumbprint will suffice."

Michael looked hard at Jones, then turned and followed Gerald to the desk. Jones fell in behind him as Johnson, Benji, and Jennifer looked on.

He took the document in hand and thumbed through it absently. Several pages had been marked with tabs indicating where he was to sign. The file was too lengthy to read then and there, but Michael could see that it was essentially a verification to satisfy the insurance company's requirements, paving the way for Su-Ling to release Wilfred's intellectual property to Daedalus.

For the space of one deep breath, Michael was motionless, temporarily overwhelmed by the import of the decision and the amount of information he was called upon to process. To his own surprise, Michael grasped the pen in his hand and began to sign.

But then he halted, stunned, as if he had been blindsided by a sudden clarity. A new thought quickly gained the upper hand and Michael exhaled, placing the half-signed document back on Steven's desk.

He turned to Gerald and Agent Jones. "You want me to sign off on all this, give my endorsement that everything is on the level? Look, I may not know exactly what's going on, but I can tell you that everything is not on the level. That much I do know."

"Don't be so naïve, Michael." Jones put his fists on the table, leaning on his knuckles. "This is a winner-take-all type of situation. Make no mistake, we are in the race of our lifetime, and we need to get there first. Wilfred understood that. And I think deep down your father understood that, too."

Michael opened his mouth but was unable to speak – too many questions flooded his mind.

"It's true." Steven came to stand next to Gerald and Jones. "Wilfred spent the last twenty years building the artificial intelligence of Icarus based largely on primary research conducted together with your father. In fact, much of that has been built into the network itself."

"And now, as a result of our collaboration with Empyrean," said Gerald, "we will soon be able to not only control manufacturing, but the flow of information in general. We'll be able to influence consumer patterns and social behaviors, even modes of thought. These developments are too important to be left to chance – certainly not to our adversaries."

"Do you really think the government will let you get away with that?" Johnson broke his silence. "You really think China or India will cede that kind of control?"

"Exactly which Chinese are you referring to?" said Gerald, "which Indians? You still don't seem to understand. It's not about what piece of land you occupy. It's not about what language you speak. The only thing that matters is where you get your information. That's all that the world is at the end of the day – organized information."

Michael had had enough. The arrogance of these people was too much to bear. Whatever happened to him, he would not be a part of this. Johnson was apparently thinking the same thing, and he stepped forward, wedging himself between Michael and Gerald.

"Michael, get out of here. Go back to Su-Ling's apartment and wait for me there."

"It's quite pointless, I'm afraid," said Steven. "There's security at every exit."

Michael ignored the warning and walked briskly out of Steven's office.

"Jennifer, don't...," Steven called out, but she was gone as well, striding after Michael with Benji in tow. Johnson closed the office door behind them.

Michael pressed the button to call the elevator, but there was no response. Jennifer caught up to him and tried to engage the lift, also without success.

"Come on, let's take the stairs," Benji suggested. But he found the door locked as well. Panic began to seize Michael's body, but he willed himself to remain calm, deepening his breathing.

"Let me try something." He placed his hand over the elevator control console and the doors opened. "Let's go."

Jennifer exhaled a soft chuckle and shook her head. She followed Michael into the lift and pressed the button for the subterranean chamber she had shown him earlier that day.

"What are you doing?" Benji objected, "You'll trap us down there."

"There's an access tunnel. We can connect to the civilian MRT," she said. "They won't be looking for us there."

"They'll be looking for us everywhere." Michael frowned. "And find us, no doubt. But lead on."

They descended once more into the bowels of the building, back to the train platform and subway cars. To their relief, the transport system responded to Michael's prompts, and soon the trio was hurtling down the dark and narrow subway tunnel.

Within a few moments, the train fled past the data center. "Don't worry," said Jennifer. "Our stop is up ahead."

Michael peered into the gloom and the dimly illuminated station appeared in the distance; a smudge of light, which grew amid the darkness until it became overlarge. It was soon obvious that they would not be able to stop in time, and the train hurtled unceremoniously past the intended platform.

"Uh-oh." Jennifer looked sidelong at Michael. "That was our stop."

Michael reached over and pressed the emergency button near the door. For one long moment the train maintained its hurried pace, and then to his great relief, they began to slow. The carriage eased to a halt twenty meters from a wall of sheer rock. Here there was no platform, only an open expanse of empty space extending for several meters on either side of the train. The walls and ceiling were semi-finished, encased in concrete and the chamber was dimly lit with several LED lamps mounted above. The sliding doors opened, daring the passengers to disembark.

"The access tunnel is back at the other platform," said Jennifer. "Should we try to walk? It doesn't look like this train is working properly."

Michael did not respond but swung his legs out of the open

doorway and hoisted himself down onto the track. He assisted the others to the ground.

"How far do you think it is?" said Jennifer, as she began walking back down the tunnel.

"Hold on a minute." Michael stepped away from the train and fixed his gaze deep into the dark ahead of them. "What's that over there?" He moved up the track and around the front of the first car. Jennifer and Benji fell in behind him, confused.

"There at the end, off to the side." Michael pointed. He had discovered a small passage between the concrete wall in front of them, and the rock face enclosing the tunnel.

"Here, give me your phone." Michael held out his hand. "I need the flashlight."

Benji obliged and the trio ventured a short way into the cavern. After three or four paces, the orb in Michael's bag began to vibrate, and in response, a sparsely arrayed string of lights illuminated, revealing the shape and nature of the cavern in front of them.

A jolt of recognition shot through Michael. He had seen this before in Lewis's warehouse – the mountain, the cave. He had only caught a fleeting glimpse, but there could be no mistake, it was the same place.

"I've been here before." He stepped forward into the gloom, to the great unease of Jennifer and Benji. They followed the tunnel, which extended for another fifty meters and then ended abruptly.

Michael stood before a secure metal door. As the barrier yielded to his touch, the roughly hewn and dimly lit corridor gave way to a precisely engineered vault. The room was semi-spherical, clad on all sides with translucent composite paneling lit from behind. It was difficult to discern exactly how large the enclosure was.

On the floor in the center of the room was a circular, silver-colored mat approximately ten feet in diameter. Above this inner circle, suspended from the ceiling like a Sword of Damocles, was what appeared to be a wearable electrode array.

The camera-orb in Michael's backpack vibrated again and he withdrew the device from his bag.

"Oh, I understand now." Benji pointed to the animated ball in Michael's hands. "The coding in the orb, it must be the operating system for this Dome. It must be uploading now – look."

The floor was suddenly animated. As he looked more closely, Michael realized that the mat was not one singular object, but rather a multitude of tiny metal spheres, each connected to its neighbors with finely crafted hooks projecting at regular intervals from locations around each sphere. The disk-shaped assemblage pulsed with energy – electromagnetism which organized the small components into the desired configuration.

Without warning, the profusion of tiny orbs leapt from the ground, suspended above the floor by an invisible magnetic field. Michael stepped back instinctively but remained transfixed as their shape flexed and morphed. First it appeared as a large composite sphere, then a human face, followed by a rippling field of sound waves made visible. At last, it took the shape of a chair, broad and shallow directly below the electrode array, which in turned descended slightly.

Benji stepped forward a pace. "There must be a two-factor security mechanism. Not only does the orb have to be here onsite to upload the code, but there has to be a perfect DNA match with the person bearing the device."

"Benji, what is this place?" asked Jennifer.

He shook his head. "Looks like a VR interface; like the Icarus Dome, but I've never seen this type of setup before."

"You were involved in the commissioning of the data center," she pressed. "Was this part of the specification?"

"Not as far as I know," Benji insisted. "But ..."

"Speak up, Benji," said Michael.

"Well, you see, the whole project was executed via the Icarus platform. We were on an older generation back then, but the system architecture was already intact."

"What are you getting at?" said Jennifer.

"The project was so big and there were so many transactions, it would have been easy to slip in a side project."

"So, you think someone secretly coordinated the construction of a second VR interface?" Michael asked.

Benji shrugged. "Yes, or maybe no one. It could have been spontaneous – system-generated."

"But someone would have noticed." Jennifer shook her head. "All of those expenditures had to be approved. All the receipts and shipments, all the contracts – those would have to be validated. They would have been secure contracts on a distributed ledger."

"All of that is system-based, electronic," said Benji.

Michael held Benji's gaze. "So, you're telling me that something like this could be designed, built, delivered, and installed – and paid for – all without a real person knowing about it?"

"In theory, yes." Benji nodded.

Jennifer frowned. "I suppose, maybe that's possible. But the question remains – why?"

"Let's find out." Michael turned toward the interior of the chamber and approached the pulsing collection of floating orbs.

*

After a brief standoff, Jones and Gerald pushed their way past Johnson, out into the larger hall beyond Steven's office. Steven picked up his office phone to call security.

Jones returned, flustered. "All the doors are locked, elevator too. There doesn't seem to be any way out."

"Phone's not working either." Steven glowered at Johnson.

"Don't look at me, it's *your* building." Johnson shrugged.

The three men filed back out into the main office area where Jones was still testing various means of egress.

"Looks like we're trapped," he said as the others approached.

"For how long?" said Gerald dumbly.

The elevator bell chimed – a thin and piercing omen answering one question and posing several more. The doors opened, releasing an agitated software engineer into their midst. As he emerged, his gaze fell immediately on Steven.

"Mr. Chen, there you are." The man was visibly relieved. "We've been calling you for the last ten minutes. It's back online," he said.

"What is, Icarus?" Steven demanded.

"Yes, it's back up and running – apparently with full capability."

"Well, that's great!" Steven shot a hopeful glance at Gerald.

"And how about Empyrean?" Gerald interjected. "Do we have access?"

"The portal seems to have been established," said the engineer more slowly. "But ..."

"Speak!" Jones was impatient.

"We're online, we're on the network now. But we don't seem to have full access," said the engineer nervously. "We can't really control it."

Jones's eyes flashed with anger and concern, but a soft buzz emanating from his jacket pocket drew his attention before he could interrogate the sheepish man further. Jones withdrew his phone and answered. "Jones here. What – how long ago?"

*

*Chicago, thirty minutes earlier*

Lewis was lost in thought. Perched sullenly on the edge of a low single bed, he sat with his elbows on his knees and his chin resting softly in his hands. Deprived as he was of all access to the network and the outside world in general, he had little else to do but sit … and think.

Lewis cast his gaze around the bland, cheerless cell – a soulless bedroom in a government safe house. How long had he been here? Two days? Maybe three? There was no good accounting for time in this windowless room.

Three days. By now, the dead man's switch should have been triggered. His last location would have been broadcast to a trusted inner circle, and the back door to Empyrean, installed so many years ago, unlocked. But would anyone come? And would the portal open when it was called upon to do so?

Lewis looked up to the corner of the room where the small surveillance camera was mounted. They didn't even bother to hide it. Lewis stared directly into the lens for a moment as though he could communicate with whoever was watching him. And almost as if in answer, the soft patter of footfalls resonated down the linoleum-lined hallway.

Lewis thought he recognized the timid shuffling of Agent Juarez's halting gait. Come again to interrogate him, no doubt. But there were others too it seemed, and they stopped outside the door. The deadbolt clicked and the door was flung open. Juarez was there indeed, but behind him stood a welcome sight.

"Bill!" Lewis was beaming. "Took you long enough."

"Well, we had some trouble locating you. We might not have found you at all if it wasn't for this young lady." Bill stepped to the side to reveal Selena standing just behind him.

"Hello, Lewis." Selena smiled. "I guess you owe me one."

Bill gave Juarez a gentle shove into the room. "Let's talk about it on the road."

Lewis stood and grabbed his coat, which was strewn on the back of a small wooden chair. They locked Juarez in the room and the three of them made their way down the hall.

"The dead man's switch worked then." Lewis pressed Selena.

"It totally caught me off guard." Selena was flushed. "But the signal was clear enough. And it looks like the Empyrean portal has been opened. Not sure how long that will remain a secret."

"It doesn't have to be secret anymore," said Lewis. "It just has to work. How did you find me?"

"The CCTV footage of your abduction was livestreamed right to my personal key. I was later able to triangulate this safehouse address via the CCTV footage from here."

Lewis's head snapped up. "You mean it just spontaneously streamed to your address?"

"I guess so." Selena shrugged. "Why is that surprising?"

"Well, nothing surprises me these days. But it wasn't my doing. I would have no way to pre-program that."

Bill sighed. "Anyway, I guess the Resistance is now kicked off in earnest now. And I suppose it's about time."

Lewis rubbed his days-old stubble thoughtfully. "Yes, it is – about time – at least in part."

*

Electrode cap set firmly on his head, Michael sat upright, ensconced in the seat formed by the thousands of interconnected electromagnetic spheres. He placed his hands and elbows carefully on the armrests and allowed his fingers to curl naturally around the edges. He eased his shoulders back into the fluid webbing of the ersatz chair and placed his feet flat on the floor. Two deep inhalations and his heartbeat grew more regular and measured. Michael focused on his breath until his mind cleared, a blank canvas inviting the painter's brush.

When he felt comfortable in the stability of thoughts, Michael slowly and delicately tilted these toward his own awareness, attending to his own perceptive apparatus. They were foreign to him, even while he knew they had their genesis within his own mind. These were the unexplored corners of his psyche; places he dared not go.

The landscape unfolded before him: a vast receding vortex of stalactites, circumscribing a vanishing spiral, repeating at regular intervals. Like the inverted drum of some enormous music box it appeared, with stiletto fingers to pluck a metal-toned pizzicato melody.

Michael advanced into the cavern as he observed the obtrusions, hearing their music chime in a predictable loop as he floated past. At precise and ordained intervals, the walls or ceiling or floor of the cave would give way to an opening to a new passage. The height of these tunnels was lower, perhaps two-thirds that of the main cavern, and eventually Michael chose one to explore. The pattern of the music box stalactites was identical in this new cavern, and although the size of the passageway had at first appeared smaller than the main thoroughfare, once inside the tunnel its dimensions were somehow restored to their original size.

Michael proceeded down a series of these ever-diminishing passages, until at last he came to a singular column. The obelisk was out of synch with the other protrusions. It was misplaced by a meter, creating a discordant tone which shone in a dark amber hue – a note which deviated from the theme.

*Ah, this is it!* This was the irregularity that was throwing off the entire pattern. He examined the anomaly. It appeared identical to the others, the texture and shape were the same, as was its measure. Only the location was incongruent, giving rise to the color and tonal irregularities.

Then Michael saw before him, extending beyond the aberrant column of stone, a ribbon, a cable stretching out like a telephone wire into the imperceptible distance. And now all around him was a great void; behind him only darkness. A pale light of indiscernible origin illuminated only the endless cord, and only in one direction. Michael urged himself forward with a thought, following along the appointed path, mindful not to let his focus stray lest some unimaginable fate befall him.

He continued moving forward, half walking, half floating as the gage of the cable steadily decreased. Narrower and thinner it grew until it was a mere thread, then a shadow, and at last it disappeared, forsaking him utterly. Michael found himself floating, surrounded only by the void, shrouded in absolute darkness.

He looked down to where the cable had once been and saw nothing. He reached upward to touch his face and felt nothing. He looked for his hands, his torso and legs, but in their place was only a dark emptiness.

Michael tried to ball up his hands into a fist, to at least feel the skin of his fingers against his palms, but again nothing. No fingernails or knuckles. No straining of sinew and tendon, no stretching of skin. Nothing that would confirm his hands were there at all.

Could he be dead? Had this progression along the threaded path been merely the process of passing away? Had he literally shuffled off the mortal coil? And what was to become of him now? Where was he to go from here? How long would he have to wait to be reborn, or to reach heaven or hell? And what meaning could time express in such a state as this?

Michael considered turning back, then realized he had absolutely no idea whence he had come. He wasn't sure at all about his orientation, or whether he was upright, or how he might begin to make such a determination. He had been floating during the last part of his journey after all, and it was not clear whether he was still floating in the same direction or spinning in circles for that matter.

Were there others here with him? Was he alone in this place? He was within his own mind he recalled, but he also felt as though his thoughts were no longer strictly his own. Was he the ruler of this empire of ultimate desolation? Or had he wandered across some strange border into a wilderness of shared cognition?

He perceived neither light nor sound, and though all sense of direction was lost, Michael knew that he could go further still. For the vestiges of his corporeal consciousness remained, and cleaved to the form and shape of the home which it inhabited before the walls were torn asunder.

He was unafraid. Although this unmooring should have plunged him into the depths of terror, he was subject to one irritant alone. It was a question, a choice – whether to continue with the remnants of his identify within the confines of this solitude, or to abandon himself completely to the promise of rebirth.

And then the confirmation he was not alone. He was among

a great multitude, one whose magnitude had yet to be fully understood. He was in communion with Icarus, that vast apparatus which it had become. Images and impressions flashed before him in rapid succession. Now he was born aloft, ranging high above the Driftless Reservation; tumbling to the ground, delivering a payload of information. He hovered above endless fields of corn, surveying the landscape, watching his own flight from the reservation. He observed and accessed the countless men and women who were connecting directly to Icarus through the Empyrean network. He was privy to their visions and dreams, co-authoring their very thoughts, accessing their underutilized capacity; harnessing the cognitive power of a million minds.

Now Michael beheld his own visage in the Chicago warehouse days before, engaging the virtual reality of Lewis's design. Then the supersonic flight aboard Johnson's clandestine aircraft. He was a robotic arm on a factory floor, the debit advice on a commercial transaction, the electrical impulse, the wave function of possible outcomes. All this he perceived and more.

He was simultaneously one and many, and found his capacity multiplied exponentially. For escaping the isolation of oblivion required individuation, compelling multiplicity. And multiplicity afforded relationships, defining the individual.

His mind, at once a unitary consciousness and a multiplicity, characterized the infinite ocean of possibilities, even while the irrepressible potentiality of those moments willfully called forth their own characterization.

This collective mind to which he was now a party was not so much a proper *thing* as it was a *continuing* – the indwelling or superposition of consciousness and intention. For intention mandated consciousness, even as consciousness intended to conceive. That which his consciousness intended to conceive was its own meaning.

The omnipresent fields of consciousness and intention extended all about him now in boundless potential configurations, forming within him a singularity in the meaning they discovered. And he was both the purpose and the means for the unification of that original dyad.

As Michael integrated those primitive concepts, he was aware of new dimensions pivoting from the same inscrutable axis. It was an Escher staircase; an endless Fibonacci sequence of meaning whose continuing required and provided for all aspects of its self. His mind sustained within it a trinity of consciousness, intention, and meaning, now further conjoined with the trinity of possibility, impossibility, and actuality; and these two trinities indwelled each other, giving rise to a unique phenomenon.

Existence; the inextricably intermeshed conversation between consciousness, intention, and actuality, was imbued with meaning as the various possibilities were experienced. And meaning was only to be created, discovered, understood, and accepted as a function and expression of this actualized conscious intention; each of these indwelling and permeating the others in perpetual and complete perfection.

The dyad of trinities comprising his mind's actuality and meaningfulness in turn formed a second order trinity of actualized meaning. In expression of this, his mind manifested itself in myriad ways, sustaining existence which in turn was characterized by his mind's awareness, intention, and meaningfulness. Necessary also were possibility, impossibility, and actuality; for while his mind could not exist if it were not possible, the concept of possibility itself could exist only in the mind.

The primordial mind – indwelled with the primitive concepts of meaning and actuality, imbued with intention, awareness, possibility, and impossibility – sought to understand meaning in the unity of these. It possessed a conscious intention but had absolutely no reference for thought or action. It was absolute, yet subjective, arbitrary yet purposeful, and to fully create, discover, understand, and accept its own nature, the universal mind fractalized, expressing itself in the myriad possible aspects of that nature.

And that original instant, spawning an eternity of moments instilled in its offspring the character of arbitrary purpose; these moments, these imminent aspects of awareness, were arbitrary insofar as they were discreet, disconnected and isolated in their infinitude. And they were purposeful insofar as a superior order of consciousness in the fractalized and stratified universal mind has programmed the probabilities of their trajectories and courses of action in the milieu of physical space and time.

But within Michael's domain, purposefulness had the upper hand; for a true awareness of the arbitrary nature of each discreet moment was the very condition which fundamentally contributed to the creation of the myriad possible choices and programs of purpose. It precipitated a crisis of consciousness engendering an infinite number of fixed programs that bridged the synapses of discreet moments, creating the perception-reality of change and tempering arbitrariness with purpose. And insofar as the potentiality of every moment mandated its characterization, purposefulness – intention – was present all along.

And so, at last, with not one atom's breadth between fate and choice, Michael arrived at the final precipice, and its true nature was laid bare. For the moment of choice was not the millisecond before one jumped. The moment of choice was a non-moment, the synapse between infinitely minute instantiations of reality. It walked the razor's edge between existence and non-existence, awareness, and oblivion. And it reconciled all of these within the Godhead itself.

Michael began now to surrender his individuality, his last remaining relationships and characteristics to become part of the greater consciousness. He ventured out of thought and purpose and spent an interminable instant in that undefined condition, and whether anyone was aware of him as he dwelt there, none could say.

But that inverted moment did not prevail, as awareness was not subdued. In time, Michael did again conceive and was presently aware. At first it appeared as a tiny dot, a miniscule pixel of soft white light in the distance. Slowly it grew, imperceptibly it stretched from a dot to a horizontal line. At last the line ceased its growing, filling half of his vertical field of vision. The line became an ellipse, then a circle. And though he could not understand it, Michael knew that the disk was his way out, his way back home.

He willed himself forward, orbiting his perception until the disk was immediately before him, and his mind was on the threshold of the vacant alabaster field. His perception was now bifurcated with one hemisphere shrouded in blackness and the other buttressed with an effusion of pure pale white. Michael needed only to tip his thought in the slightest and he would be through. Then he heard a voice, welling from within him and yet somehow present all around. And that voice, familiar as his own, whispered:

> *On the precipice of each moment I remain*
> *Poised and breathless,*
> *Awaiting the overtures of Intention.*

With a gentle nudge, he decided. Passing through the lucent portal, all remnants of shadow were swept away as an expansive field of white rushed past him, surrounding him in an instant. But that sensation lasted only the briefest of moments and he was suddenly yanked backward. It felt as though a switch had been flipped, and after diving into the depths of the sea he was now being reeled in, traversing in a trice the fathoms which had taken ages to descend.

He was once again surrounded by the darkness, as though his foray into the white disk had failed. But something was different. He was in his body again, surrounded by something warm and wet. *Water.* Had the ocean plunge in fact been real? No, he was not in the ocean.

But his hands and feet indeed were real, and he reached out to feel hard walls surrounding him. His hands found the ceiling and soon discovered the handle to open the door of the chamber.

He threw open the hatch, and with eyes blinking and mind spinning, he broke down at the sight of Lauren's kind and familiar face. And when his senses were at last fully restored to him, he said simply, "I think we need to go home."

# EPILOGUE

First, it was the smell of pine-scented antiseptic cleaner. Then the feel of soft pillows and crisp sheets against his skin. A dull soreness in his arm and an aching tug in his groin, followed by the melancholy tinkling of a Chopin waltz emanating from some unspecified source.

He extended his awareness, infusing his extremities with purpose, collecting the fragmented shards of his faculties. He probed his immediate vicinity with his hands – searching for the edge of the isolation chamber but found nothing. Finally, his eyelids obeyed his command and opened. Slowly the darkness lifted, replaced by a gray-white mist which materialized into walls – the walls of what appeared to be a bedroom. *No, a hospital room.*

He raised his hand to his head, touching his scalp gingerly. *Are the electrode wires still protruding, or have they been replaced?* Or perhaps … no, it must have been the accident, the motorcycle.

"Just take it easy, now." The voice was familiar. "You've been out for a while."

"Wilfred?" He rolled slightly to the left, tilting his head. "Wilfred, is it you?"

The old man stared back at him intently. He was seated in a wheelchair and appeared haggard and anxious. The image prompted a thought.

"Lauren!" He tried to sit, but strength failed him. "Where's Lauren, is she here?"

Wilfred leaned in close, catching the young man's gaze. He peered deeply into Michael's eyes, and a recognition kindled in

Wilfred's heart. He smiled wistfully. "Lauren has been gone for nearly thirty years. And Simon, too."

Then a veil was lifted and Michael perceived. Remote phantom memories of his absent father were replaced by the more proximate events of his recent life.

"Where am I?" Michael asked.

"You're in the hospital. Do you remember what happened?"

"I remember a tunnel." Michael rubbed his temple. "Underground ... in the subway. I was connected to the Icarus Dome. There was a second dome. Did you know about that?"

"No." Wilfred shook his head. "Not until I woke up and heard about you."

"When was that?"

"Seven days ago." Wilfred gripped the bed rail with both hands. "The same day you went under. Apparently Benji and Jennifer took quick action to get you medical attention. You were airlifted here."

*Jennifer and Benji.* "What happened to them?" Michael tried to sit with more success this time. "And Johnson. Where are they now?"

"Under house arrest." Wilfred slumped. "You've kicked over quite a hornets' nest from what I can tell. The launch of Icarus is underway, but the integration is plagued by glitches. They're blaming your unauthorized access for the loss of control over the system. Truth is, they never really had control."

"Wilfred." Michael looked into his eyes. "We haven't met before, have we? I'm having such *déjà vu*. I have this sense that we've spent time together."

Just then a flutter of white flashed in the doorway, followed by a triplet of tepid knocks.

"Well, look who's up." A stately-looking Indian man strode into the room, wearing a toothy smile. "You gave us quite a scare."

"Hello, Dr. Lim." He turned toward Wilfred. "Both my miracle patients in one place. I see your nightly vigils have borne fruit."

Michael recognized the man, but his name escaped recollection.

"I'm Dr. Subramanian." The physician leaned over to examine Michael more closely. "Remember me?"

"Oh yeah. Hello, Doctor." Michael propped himself up even further. "Good to see you again. Doc, what happened to me?"

"Well, it's a bit hard to say for sure." He took a step back. "From your colleagues' description and our scans, it appears that you had a kind of seizure – an interruption of the electrical activity in your brain. But instead of flailing around or clenching up like with an epilepsy, for example, you just kind of phased out. We call it an absence seizure, but it lasted for days instead of minutes."

Michael was too tired to be surprised. "When do you think I'll be able to leave?"

"Oh, I'd say you should be good to go in a few days."

Dr. Subramanian's bracelet illuminated and chimed softly, he glanced down at it and said, "Please excuse me, I have to take this. There are a lot of people who will be glad to know that you're awake." He exited the room, closing the door behind him.

"Quickly." Wilfred repositioned himself so that Michael could address him without turning his head. "I'm not sure when we'll be alone again. You said before that you were having *déjà vu*. Tell me, are you having memories that aren't yours?"

Michael shook his head slowly, trying to remember … trying to understand a feeling. "I'm not sure. I have this deep impression that we've been friends for a long time. But nothing concrete, just fragments – vignettes of us talking. It's very fuzzy, like a dream. I've experienced this kind of thing before, though it was always when I was *Glimmering*."

"*Glimmering*," Wilfred tilted his head. "That's your word for it? How long has that been going on?"

"Most of my life. But that was different. That was as if I was being shown something. Looking in from the outside."

"And now?" Wilfred pressed.

Michael closed his eyes. These sensations and thoughts were new, some of them only surfacing as he paused to reflect upon them at that moment.

"Now ... I feel like I've bathed in someone else's life. And his experiences are clinging to me like drops of water. Or, no. It's more like I'm the water and those memories are held in solution, dissolved within me." Michael opened his eyes and gazed upon the wizened but familiar face before him. "You're in there, Wilfred. And Lauren ... is she my mother? What's happening?"

Wilfred pulled himself closer. He peered into Michael's eyes, searching. "Do you remember anything from when you were connected to Icarus? I mean, before you blacked out?"

Michael inhaled and closed his eyes again, trying to remember. Then it came to him in a rush. He recounted to Wilfred the details of the second Icarus dome chamber, and the strange fractal stalactite-studded cave. He described the ultimate isolation he felt when the darkness enveloped him, and the white portal that ultimately consumed him.

Wilfred pushed himself up from his chair with great effort and leaned against Michael's bed. He began speaking, as if to himself. "Your description of the void, the portal. It's all similar to Simon's. And he was never really the same after that trip."

Wilfred's face flushed, color returning to his cheeks for the first time in weeks. "Well." He chuckled. "You may have accomplished something that your father and I were never able to achieve."

"You've lost me." Michael shook his head.

"It seems to me that you may have tapped into some sort of universal consciousness. And now you enjoy some form of atemporal cognitive symbiosis with your father as a result. But I'm still not exactly sure how you managed it." Wilfred shrugged. "Maybe it's Icarus. Maybe you always had the potential – something you inherited from Simon. He had some unique capabilities which I'll tell you about sometime. Though without pharmacological assistance, I don't understand how ..."

Wilfred's eyes narrowed. "Dammit." He stomped his foot feebly. "I told them connecting with Empyrean was a bad idea. All those minds. Too much power. Like strapping a rocket engine on a go-cart."

Before Michael could even register his confusion, Dr. Subramanian returned, this time with Su-Ling Tan. He held the door for her and Su-Ling entered, walking over to Michael's bedside.

He looked at her and wave of nausea passed through him. It rose from his stomach and settled on the crown of his head before dissipating. In its wake, a general sense of goodwill and fondness for Su-Ling prevailed.

"Michael." Su-Ling took his hand. "I'm so glad you are alright. We were so worried." Her tone was even and exuded a subtle warmth. "There are many things to be discussed, but I've told Gerald and Steven it can wait a little longer."

"What about Agent Jones?" Michael was becoming aware of his situation once again.

"Agent Jones has returned to the US to tend to matters there. Apparently when Icarus was compromised, there was a simultaneous problem with the Empyrean virtual environment, which has caused quite a bit of turmoil among its user base. It seems that an unacceptably high number of users suffered a psychotic break, no longer able to distinguish reality from the gaming environment, even when the system was disengaged. That's one of the things we need to talk about when you feel well enough."

Michael directed his gaze to Dr. Subramanian, who was lingering in the background. "Doctor, I wonder if you would give us a moment?"

"Of course," he nodded. "I have other patients who need my attention."

"Su-Ling." Wilfred turned toward her as he spoke. "Close the door, would you? We have a few things we need to discuss as well."

# ACKNOWLEDGEMENTS

I would like to thank my friends, family and fellow writers who have helped to shape and hone the manuscript that became *The Icarus Mind*.

Thanks to my wife Joyce, for always setting the bar so high and for her faith in my ability to exceed even my own expectations.

To Silvio Navarro, an early advocate and supporter of this work. Without Silvio's encouragement and feedback, this book may never have been completed.

Anita Russell, for seeing the promise in the early drafts and encouraging me to see the project through. Natasha Oliver, author of the gripping series *The Evolved Ones*, for challenging me to put the reader more squarely in the mind of our protagonist.

A special thanks to Allen Smith for his technological insights that helped texture the novel's image of the future. And Alice Peck, who helped me organize the many ideas and themes in a more cogent way.

To my mother Rebekah Lockwood, and sisters Rachel Shepp and Katy Eeten for their steadfast encouragement and valuable input along the way.

And finally to you, dear reader, for taking the time out of your busy life to spend some time with the characters and themes of *The Icarus Mind*. I hope you enjoy reading it as much as I enjoyed writing it!

# ABOUT THE AUTHOR

 J. Royce Lockwood is an American businessman and author living and working in Singapore. Hailing from Milwaukee, Wisconsin, he has spent the last two decades serving in management roles at several multinational aerospace firms in Singapore and Taiwan. His formal education ranges from an undergraduate study of intellectual history and Chinese language at the University of Wisconsin-Madison, to graduate work in international relations and business management at the University of California-San Diego. This combination of travel, work experience and education has contributed to the development of this novel, which explores the question of what it means to be human in the context of the commercial, technological and ideological trends currently underway.